UNTAMABLE LOVER

A *Warriors of Lemuria* Novel #2

by

ROSALIE REDD

Rosalie Redd

Cover Design: Melody Simmons
ISBN: 9781944419073
United States of America

UNTAMABLE LOVER

A *Warriors of Lemuria* Novel #2

Chapter One

Deep in the Cascade Mountains of the Pacific Northwest

Present day

Demir was a hostage in his own body. Immovable, invisible bonds bound him tight. Unable to open his eyes, constant darkness engulfed him, an eerie reminder of how much he relied on his vision. His sense of hearing and smell sharpened, heightened, compensated for his lack of sight and only increased the knot of frustration in his gut. He concentrated on his fingers, willing them to move, but they remained motionless. The smooth, cool satin sheets caused goosebumps to form on his skin, sending a mental shiver along his nerves. His supine body didn't flinch.

He'd been this way for several weeks, ever since the enemy's dart had penetrated his hide, poisoning him with some kind of mysterious liquid. How much longer could he stay like this and survive? The muscles in his arms and legs screamed to move, to flex, to exert the strength his body once contained.

The familiar scent of his leather jacket hanging on a hook near his bed stirred his senses. Heated sunstones lined the cave ceiling and walls, yet even the warmth couldn't bring him any solace.

Tick, tick, tick.

The clock on his bedside table magnified into the tolling of a bell. He wanted to grab the thing and smash it against the rock walls. The vision of the shattered timepiece and its bits scattered across the stone floor made him smile inside.

In his current state, he couldn't even mark his territory. How wrong was that? As a shape-shifting Lemurian Panthera, that was torture.

The underground Keep was as much a prison to him as his own body. He longed to be free, to search out Ram and his Gossum minions, to rid the earth of the foul beasts. The battle between the Lemurians and the Gossum had gone on for millennia. His Goddess, Alora, had placed the Panthera and the other Lemurians here to win the war to ensure Earth remained a free planet. If they failed, Earth would be enslaved, and the humans would be forced to give up their most precious resource—water.

The echo of footsteps eased through the crack under his door. He had visitors. As the door opened, a cool breeze wafted into the room, caressing the skin on his arms. A squeaking wheel in need of some oil pierced his sensitive eardrums, grating across his nerves. Fresh and clean, the scent of soap could only mean one thing—a bath.

Quick footsteps entered. The door clicked shut.

"Good evening, Demir." Bet's cheerful voice reverberated around the chamber. "I brought Til with me. It's time for your bath."

Demir mentally stiffened, although his body remained still. The last thing he wanted was another bath. *Grrrrrr.* The growl echoed in his mind, but no further.

A thin film of sweat broke over his skin. The Keep's Jixies were back and despite their best intentions, a bath would be another lesson in humiliation. He didn't need to go through that again. Helplessness was the worst kind of torture.

"Til, thank you for coming with me today. I can't move him on my own." Bet's melodic voice only increased Demir's anxiety, and a bead of perspiration raced over his brow, pooling along the edge of his ear.

"No problem." Til's words were clipped.

The table rolled closer to Demir. The wheel squeaked and water sloshed as if over the lip of a bucket. Demir strained against the bonds, and he tried to open his eyes.

"Are you sure you're up for this?" Bet asked.

Silence stretched out for several seconds. "Yeah, I'm fine. I…I don't know." Til sighed.

"What is it?" Bet's soothing, encouraging response rolled over him.

"It's just—do you think he can hear us? Does he know what's going on?"

Of course he did, he heard every damn word, felt every touch. His anger boiled beneath his skin, hot and fevered. His need to break free threatened to drive him mad.

Bet shuffled across the floor, away from Demir, the sound of her soft leather shoes imprinted on his brain. "I don't know. Gaetan told me that he hasn't responded to any form of treatment. It's as if he's—"

"No, don't say it."

"Oh, sweetie, if you aren't up for this, I can get someone else."

"You're King Noeh's chambermaid. Why do you do this?"

"Demir saved Noeh's life. It's the least I can do for this honorable male."

He winced. Honorable was the last thing he was. He'd had a lot of time to think about why he'd taken that dart for Noeh. During a battle in the middle of a small clearing, Ram had aimed the dart straight at the Stiyaha king. Noeh hadn't appeared to hear the click as their enemy fired the gun. In his Panthera form, Demir had jumped in front of the projectile's path. His impulsive choice had changed everything. If he could raise a sarcastic eyebrow, he would.

Instead of getting rid of his rival, and taking his place as king of the Stiyaha and the Jixies, he'd saved Noeh's miserable life and ended up in a coma. That had worked out great, hadn't it? The only good to come from the deed was some clarity. Whatever was in that dart had paralyzed his body, but purified his mind. *I have much to atone for.*

"All right, Bet. If you can do this, so can I."

Blankets lifted off his body, and the cool air swirled over his exposed skin. The only garment he wore was a pair of loose briefs tied at his hips, courtesy of the Jixie tailors.

"Oh, my," Til purred.

"Your cheeks are red," Bet said.

"I can't help it. Look at those muscles. I didn't realize Panthera were so…firm. I guess I expected a thinner build."

"Okay, enough ogling, let's do this before the water gets cold."

Gentle hands lifted his head and placed a towel on his pillow. Water dripped into the bucket, as if someone wrung out a rag. A warm, wet cloth started at his brow and circled around his face and ears. The sensation should've felt good, but instead, a scream built in his throat. He didn't like others touching him.

Tepid water from another rag dripped over his feet. They tag-teamed him, and he dreaded where they would meet.

"What does Gaetan think will happen to him?"

Bet didn't respond right away, and a chill ran over Demir's arms. He ached to know, yet, part of him didn't want to hear her answer.

"He's been like this for almost a month. If he doesn't come out of it soon, Gaetan thinks he'll get weaker and—" Bet stopped washing Demir's chest and a stream of water trickled down his side.

"Bet, I'm sorry, I shouldn't have asked. Please don't cry."

Bet's crying? Over me? He'd been nothing but rude to her. A wave of guilt raced along his spine.

Bet sniffled. "I'm ok, thank you. I can't imagine what would've happened to Noeh if… The Gossum are brutal creatures. I despise their evil, hairless hides."

"Uh, Bet? What now?" Til's voice wavered.

A lukewarm washrag lay draped over the top of Demir's thigh. He pushed against his invisible shackles, desperation making him want to turn into his panther form and lash out. As much as he tried, his body remained still, lifeless.

"Let's turn him over and untie the string. We'll wash his backside first."

The rags disappeared from his thighs and abdomen. Footsteps converged on his right and small, strong hands pushed under his back and legs. Against his will, he rolled onto his left side.

Soft fingers tugged at his shorts. The string holding the two sides together fell away, revealing his buttocks to the two female Jixies. He tensed, waiting for the reaction he knew would come.

A quick intake of breath.

Skin slapping, as if a hand had covered a mouth.

Silence.

"C'mon. Let's be quick. Don't keep this warrior waiting," Bet said.

"The...scars. There's so many."

"Til. Help me wash him." Bet's tone turned harsh.

Demir's face burned. The disfigurement was a constant reminder of his failure. Bet and the females who washed him were among the few who had ever seen the tracks. Not even his once-beloved Eleanor knew of the lines that marred his body and soul. The female Jixies' reactions brought back the embarrassment and pain as if he'd earned those scars yesterday.

Lukewarm water rubbed against his rough and mottled skin. The rag's torture made him scream inside. His mind fogged. The pet frog he'd had as a child surfaced in his thoughts. He'd captured the small creature by the bank of a stream one night. The frog had lived for several days, until his constant touching killed it as surely as the lack of water. A new appreciation for what he'd put his little pet through raced across his mind.

When they were done, they rolled him onto his back. As if he needed any more humiliation, they washed his groin. He endured the cleaning as best he could. What choice did he have? Soft hands retied the string at his hip, covering his maleness and giving him a modicum of privacy.

"He looks so peaceful. I wonder how he got those scars," Til asked.

"I doubt we'll ever know," Bet replied.

"Should we trim his beard?"

"Aramie likes to shave his face and clip his goatee. We'll leave that for her."

A pleasant warmth spread through his body. Aramie, his second in command, had spent quite a bit of time by his side, taking care of him. Her constant chatter had helped ease the loneliness.

When Til spoke, her words were soft, quiet. "Really? Isn't that interesting."

Silence filled the room.

Bet cleared her throat.

"What? I was just admiring. He's a handsome male in a rugged sort of way."

"That's enough. Time to go. *Now*. We'll come back later and change his sheets."

"Okay—"

Smooth fingers pulled the sheet up and tucked the soft material around his shoulders. The towel was removed from beneath his head. Now that the bath was done, his racing heart slowed back to its normal pace.

Water sloshed and a squeaky wheel crossed near the foot of his bed. Clothing rustled and soft footsteps padded toward the exit. As the door opened, a cool breeze blew across his face. He relished how it tingled his skin. A desire to go with them rose to the forefront of his mind, but he couldn't and that burned deep in his gut. The door closed behind them, and he was left alone with only his tortured thoughts to keep him company.

Chapter Two

Aramie scanned the training facility, searching for her next opponent. Several Panthera males and a few females worked out either alone or in groups. The room stank of sweat, assailing Aramie's sensitive nose. Her jaw flexed. It was only a matter of time before one of the males challenged her, again.

As Demir's second in command, she'd assumed the tenuous role of interim Pride leader. Even though she and her sister had been with the Pride less than a year, she'd risen in the ranks through sparring match wins and her impressive number of Gossum kills. She refused to relinquish her authority, and she'd had to fight a few males to remind them why she'd earned her position.

Although she had the ability to lead this ragtag group, she ached to find a cure for Demir. Her chest tightened. Demir continued to deteriorate. Her Pride leader still looked healthy, but his organs were slowly shutting down.

Gaetan, the Keep's *Haelen*, had analyzed the empty dart casing. He'd found nothing but untainted, ancient water. The old healer had exhausted all of his options trying to find out how that had put Demir in a coma, but so far nothing had worked. He continued to give Demir fluids on a regular basis, but Demir wouldn't last much longer.

Tension tightened Aramie's insides, clenching her stomach into a ball. Aramie wouldn't give up—she couldn't imagine life without her Pride leader. Biting the inside of her cheek, she headed for the closest rack of weights and grabbed a twenty pound dumbbell in each hand. She lifted the load, silently counting the number of hammer curls.

Sidea walked into the room. Aramie relaxed, the tension leaving her chest.

"Hey, sis!" Sidea approached, her wide smile brightening Aramie's mood. "Got your message you wanted to talk. What's up?"

Aramie placed the weights back on the rack and glanced around the room. No one seemed to notice them. Adrenaline surged through her bloodstream as her excitement got the better of her. She stepped closer to her younger sister and lowered her voice. "I ran into Ginnia in the Hall of Scriptures. She showed me an ancient text describing a place called Blue Pool. The scripture spoke of a sacred blue sunstone, one that might heal Demir."

Sidea gripped Aramie's arm. "That's fabulous. Where is this place?"

"That's the problem, no one knows."

Her sister's shoulders slumped, but she gave Aramie a slight smile. "You want to look, anyway, don't you?"

Aramie couldn't stop her own smile as it tugged at her lip. "You know me so well. The description leading to Blue Pool sounds familiar—we have to try."

"When are we leaving?"

"I wish we could go immediately, but the sun's still out. We'd burn to a crisp if we left now." Aramie exhaled. "It irritates me that we're forced to be night creatures. We leave at nightfall."

Sidea wrapped her arm around Aramie's shoulder and leaned in. Her breath tickled the back of Aramie's neck, sending a chill over her shoulders. "Perfect. Until then, we should burn off some energy. Kitani and Jonue look like they need a good spar. You interested?"

Aramie scanned the small crowd of warriors in the training center. In the far corner, Kitani and Jonue seemed focused on their tasks. Jonue was in the midst of a push-up, her hands and toes pressed firmly against the mat.

Kitani held a large weight in each hand. She raised them to her shoulders and pushed the heavy metal over her head. When she moved, the thin shoulder strap on her shirt revealed the scarred puncture wounds at the base of her throat—the sign of a mated female.

She caught Aramie's gaze. Her eyes brightened and a smile crossed her face. She lowered the weights, patted Jonue on the shoulder, and pointed at Aramie. Both females jogged over.

"Sidea, check out these muscles." Jonue flexed her bicep and winked.

Sidea squeezed Jonue's arm and nodded. "Nice, very impressive."

"Aramie, I beat one of the males in a sparring match today." Kitani's breaths came hard and fast, evidence of her recent workout.

Aramie's chest expanded at her friend's enthusiasm. "Good. You're ready to go on patrol."

"You've both come a long way." Sidea beamed at Jonue and Kitani. "Watch out Gossum, here they come!"

Kitani's laugh reverberated off the stone walls. As she calmed, her focus riveted to the entryway. Her laughter ceased, her smile faltered.

A couple of males stood at the entrance to the training center, Leon and Hallan—Kitani's and Jonue's mates. Hallan had deep-set brown eyes partially hidden behind his furrowed brow, disapproval in his stark stare.

Leon was slender with well-defined muscles in his chest and arms. Long braided hair fell over his shoulder. His gaze narrowed, and his eyes turned into slits. He stalked toward his mate.

Kitani stiffened.

Leon clenched her arm, yanking Kitani to him with a swift pull. "I told you not to train. How dare you disobey me."

Aramie squared her shoulders and took a step toward him. "Stop! Let her go."

Hallan stood next to Jonue and placed his hand on her shoulder to show his possession of her. The sunstones lining the walls brightened, heating the room as the Keep reacted to the tension emanating from the group.

Leon's fingers dug into Kitani's skin. She inhaled through gritted teeth, but didn't cry out.

He sized up Aramie, his gaze raking over her body. A pointed tooth glinted from his curled lip.

Indignation coiled in Aramie's stomach. How dare he bare his fang to her.

He loosened his grip on his mate. With a slow, predatory gait, he approached Aramie. "Mated females shouldn't spar. Your decree goes against Demir's will and our tradition." He spat on the ground at her feet. "I won't abide by your decision. Kitani won't train."

Hallan nodded. "Neither will Jonue."

The hair on the back of her neck rose. She put her hands on her hips and leaned forward. "Females should have the right to choose whether they fight or not. As leader of this Pride, I make the rules. You have no choice but to follow."

The other males stopped their training to watch the scene unfold. With hushed whispers and pointed fingers, they stepped out of the way.

Leon stared her down. "I challenge you for the right to lead this Pride."

At almost twice her size he outweighed her, but she was the alpha. After her mother had abandoned her and Sidea, she'd honed her battle skills defending herself from males like him. If he wanted to take her on, let him try. The release of pent-up energy would be good for her.

She smiled, showing her fangs in a display of dominance. "I'm all yours."

Leon backed up, the muscles in his arms taut with tension. He pounced, shifting into his panther form. His sleek, black coat glinted in the light, and his eyes were slits of amber. She followed suit, the dark pants and shirt she'd worn absorbed beneath her fur. They collided in mid-air, claws and teeth glinting in the light.

He ripped into her skin with his razor-sharp claws. Pain radiated up her arm and into her shoulder, but she ignored it. She bit him on the ear, her teeth sinking into the soft tissue. His eerie howl echoed around the chamber, and the scent of blood mixed with the stale odor of sweat. As they landed on their feet, they broke apart.

He circled her, his predatory gaze focused, determined.

Aramie waited. This male favored his right side.

Just as she expected, his body tensed, and he attacked from the right. She slipped under him, scratching his belly, leaving a trail of four lacerations from her knife-like claws. He snarled a feral cry of rage and bit her on the flank, his teeth sinking into her tender flesh.

The sharp sting caused her to flinch, but she wouldn't let that affect her. Cold and calculating, she contained her anger, using the added energy to track her prey. She stalked him this time, staring him down.

He bared his teeth.

A soft chuckle bubbled up from one of the males to her left.

In the fraction of a second Leon turned to look, she attacked. Barreling into him, she knocked him over. With her preternatural speed, she straddled him and closed her teeth around his throat.

He stilled.

She didn't move, but maintained her position of dominance over him. Fast breaths heaved in and out of her nostrils. Her heart pounded from the exertion. She closed her jaw another inch, tightening her hold on Leon's throat. He mewled and changed into his human form, his clothes fitting back to his body.

She released him and transformed as well. Still straddling the humiliated male, she leaned in and stared into his eyes. "I am Pride leader until Demir regains consciousness."

In a sign of submission, he lowered his eyes and placed the bridge of his nose under her chin. Now that she'd secured another victory, the males would think twice before challenging her anytime soon.

She fisted his shirt and dragged him to a standing position.

Leon's shoulders slumped forward, and he backed up, out of her way. He made eye contact, and hatred, hot and deep reflected in their depths. "When Demir wakes, you'll be lucky if he doesn't kick you out of the Pride."

A tendril of fear snaked its way into her heart. *He might be right.* If that happened, she and her sister would be on their own once more. She raised her chin, unwilling to let him know his words had hit a soft spot. "Do you wish to challenge me, again?"

His eyes narrowed, and he held her gaze. A small smile curved at the corner of his mouth. "I have better things to do."

He turned his attention to Kitani and pointed his finger at his mate. "This isn't over between us." He visibly clenched his jaw then headed out the door.

Hallan raced after Leon, but the look he gave Jonue could've melted stone.

A chill ran over Aramie's arms. By training the mated females to fight, she'd done what she thought was right, even if it went against Demir's rule. Although part of the mating ritual, she'd never believed in the practice of females submitting to their mates and it was one of the reasons why she'd stayed single for so long. Submitting was so old-fashioned, left over from the days before the great scourge, when the females could still bear children. In Aramie's eyes, mated Panthera should be equal.

Kitani pursed her lips and glanced at Aramie. "Thanks for standing up for me."

Aramie gave her a brief nod.

"He'll be a bear to deal with later, but I know how to handle him." Kitani winked at her then raced after her mate.

Aramie's chest constricted. Challenging Leon's dominance would strain Leon and Kitani's relationship. Hopefully, the mated pair could work through their issues.

Jonue hugged Aramie. "I better go, too. Hallan's a bit more understanding, but even he's having a hard time with this. Thank you for helping us break through the old ways."

Her friend patted Sidea on the shoulder before heading toward the exit.

Leon's threat rang in Aramie's ears. What would happen if Demir regained consciousness? Would he kick her out of the Pride? She didn't know, but she'd rather find out than lose him forever. After watching her mother submit to male after male then run away, Aramie had vowed never to follow in her footsteps. *I will never become a mated female.*

Now that the spectacle was over, the other males returned to their workouts. The tense atmosphere dissipated and loud, male banter filled the room.

Sidea ran her fingers along Aramie's arm. "Hey, you did great. Only a few scratches, pretty impressive."

"Leon has been itching to challenge me ever since Demir—" She couldn't finish her sentence. Her throat was too tight.

"Sis, it's ok. We'll be out of here in a few hours. We'll find Blue Pool and that sacred stone." Sidea's eyes gleamed with pride and respect. She glanced around the room. "Besides, these males need a good kick in the pants once in a while. I love to watch you do it."

Aramie couldn't help smiling. Sidea had a way of bringing out the best in others. Maturing while on the run without the protection of a Pride had turned them into formidable warriors and close siblings. What would she do without her sister at her side? A cool breeze raised goosebumps on her arm. She suppressed an unsettling shiver.

Chapter Three

Strong fingers massaged Demir's scalp, pushing shampoo through his shoulder-length hair. The soapy water, mixed with Aramie's unique strawberry fragrance, relaxed him to the point of bliss. He didn't like being touched by others, but something about Aramie's fingers made him give in and unwind. Not that he could move, but he could still feel, and her touch lit a fire under his skin.

"I read something interesting in the ancient text today." Aramie had found that book a few weeks ago and he'd been surprised at how entranced she'd become with the strange Stiyaha tome. With each visit, she'd told him more about their shared Lemurian past. "Did you know our Lemurian ancestors lived in the islands of the South Pacific during the last ice age?"

Unable to answer her, he concentrated on her tender care. Cool water cascaded over his head and down the back of his neck where the familiar sound of liquid dripped into a bucket. Fingernails scraped the skin at the base of his scalp, wringing out the water from his hair. A warm towel caressed the skin on his cheeks.

"The book says after a flood caused by melting ice, various races of shape-shifters migrated to the continents. The need to hide from humans forced many into seclusion. We had to battle our enemy in remote locations. I guess that explains why the Keep is underground."

A comb ran through his wet untamed hair, catching on a knot only once. Gentle hands lifted his head and shoulders from the edge of the bed and back onto the pillow. He didn't deserve her devoted attention.

Her hand rested against his shoulder, the sensation tickling his skin. "I've always known we fought this war for our goddess, Alora, but I never knew we had brethren until she sent us here to join forces with the Stiyaha. I wonder when the others will arrive. In any case, it will be good to have other Lemurian species at the Keep to help fight the Gossum."

The door creaked and soft, feminine footsteps approached. Demir recognized Sidea's familiar gait. "Hey, sis. Need any help?"

"I'm almost done. Just need to trim his beard." Aramie's smooth fingers ran across his cheek and around his goatee leaving little lightning bolts everywhere she touched.

"It's almost time to leave." Sidea spoke in a rush.

The bedspread near Demir's hip bunched as if Aramie had clenched the material in her hands. Her chair squeaked against the stone floor. She moved away, her unique scent trailing in her wake.

"Not so loud, just in case." Aramie's voice was a tight whisper. "We'll leave after the evening repast. If anyone asks, we're going for a run."

Demir strained to hear her words. What was in that dart that kept him down? How much more could he take?

"I can't wait to go. My body aches to transform." Sidea's words carried across the room, despite her hushed tone. "Once we find the blue sunstone, Gaetan can heal Demir."

Demir tensed. A healing stone? Was it possible? A tiny drop of hope weaseled its way into his chest.

Sidea inhaled and let out a slow breath. "With Demir back, you won't have to fight the males anymore. Even though our species heals fast, I hate to see you get injured defending your role as interim leader."

He fought against the invisible bonds, straining, kicking in his mind. In his condition, he couldn't lead, and because he still lived, Aramie wasn't officially Pride leader. His gut twisted into a tight knot. He'd put her in an awkward position, and he hated himself for it.

"I need to finish." Aramie's voice returned to a normal volume.

The chair creaked as she settled in her spot next to his bed. Tools clinked together. Cool metal caressed the skin on his cheeks.

Snip-snip.

Small tendrils of hair fell onto his cheek, tickling his skin. He relaxed again under her care. His mind reeled through a storm of confusion, but he couldn't pinpoint its source. All he knew was a welcoming peace at her touch.

"I'll see you in the Grand Hall." Sidea's words hung in the air.

Her soft footsteps retreated across the floor. The door clicked shut.

"I wish you would talk to me, tell me what I should do." Aramie caressed the hair around his mouth, wiping away the stray strands she'd clipped. Her finger circled his diamond stud above the hairline of his lip.

He wanted to grab her wrists, make her stop, and part of him was glad he couldn't. All his adult life he'd avoided physical contact. Even with Eleanor, his deceased mate, he'd controlled when and how she touched him. To have Aramie touch him now, in such a personal way, beat against his spirit, reinforcing his weakness.

"The males only follow my command in deference to you." Her voice contained a small hitch.

The flat end of the scissors rubbed against his skin. With gentle care her fingers glided over his upper lip, and he wanted to lick her, taste her skin on his tongue. Her attention to him teased his nerves, increasing his yearning. He'd gone from relaxed to being enticed in a matter of moments. In his mind, his cat howled in frustration.

"Sidea and I will find Blue Pool, find the healing stone. I won't stop until we do."

A drop of wetness splashed on his chin, and she wiped it away. Why did the females cry over him? Had she gone soft? If he could, he'd tell her to suck it up. He'd chosen her as his second in command for a reason.

Metal clinked against metal. She must've put the scissors back on the tray. That meant she would leave him soon. His stomach clenched. Why did he care? The only females he'd ever cared about were Eleanor and Melissa.

Eleanor had been timid and submissive—a perfect mated female. She'd always done as he'd asked, and never once challenged his authority. Her beautiful smile and deep green eyes were as clear to him as the last time he'd seen her, over five hundred years ago when the great scourge had claimed her life. Bile rose in his throat. It seemed like only yesterday.

Even though his lifespan was over two thousand years, he still had more time than not…or so he used to think. At this point, he wasn't sure he had more than a few days left.

The memory of his mate reminded him of Melissa, who'd looked so like his Eleanor he'd obsessed over her. What a fool he'd been, pining for a female who didn't want him. When she became pregnant with the king's child, he'd lost his lucidity and threatened her. Aramie had interfered, commanding him to stop. He'd slapped his own warrior across the face for her insolence, but he'd let Melissa go.

After all he'd done, Aramie was here now, attending to his needs. *I'm such a shit.*

"I'll be back as soon as I can." She rose from her chair and padded to the door, lingering there for a moment. Her soft breaths sounded loud in the quiet room.

"Please come back to me," she whispered.

She really doesn't want to be Pride leader…

The door closed behind her, but the enchanting scent of strawberries lingered.

Chapter Four

Ram grimaced as the stairs groaned under his new, red high-tops. It was as if the steps were aware evil invaded the old farmhouse. The squeak of his soles was a reminder of Noeh, their battle, and Ram's little tumble into the river.

"That bastard king just won't die," he muttered.

Shaking himself, he focused on the old wooden door. He peered through the glass panes, the edges coated with the remnants of too many bad paint jobs. The white house was *so* not like his dark personality and that would do fine to camouflage their new lair.

He twisted the knob and opened the door. The smell of bacon and stale cigarettes infiltrated his sensitive nose. He gagged and placed a hand over his mouth. "Open a window."

Inside, a Formica table stood in the middle of the neglected kitchen. Steel-framed chairs with cheap plastic cushions surrounded the small eating place. Over the large sink, pink floral print curtains covered the window. Decoupage pictures of peppers, cucumbers, and melons lined the walls, adding to the country flair. The faint scent of grass and manure from the nearby pasture completed the sense of happy, happy, home, home.

Ram glared at Jakar, his first lieutenant. The male stood still at the bottom of the stairs, his hands clasped in front of him. Jakar had secured this place while Ram had been out of it, healing from his battle wounds. Ram touched the scar that ran along the center of his chest and flinched. The disfigurement would remain a constant reminder of his failure to defeat Noeh, the Stiyaha king.

Ram raised a hairless eyebrow. "A farmhouse—not my first choice, but this could work."

"You need to see the basement." Sunglasses covered Jakar's eyes, but the slight lift to his mouth gave away his eagerness.

"Are there fluffy kittens and baby chicks down there?" Surely, this country comfort couldn't get much worse.

Jakar walked up the stairs, his hand extended in an invitation. "Please, take a look around, then I'll show you the prize jewel—the basement."

Ram walked into the kitchen, past the large living room, and evaluated each of the three bedrooms. A stack of boxes labeled "Smirnoff's" sat in the far corner of the last room. Alcohol was all his body or any of the Gossum needed to survive. His favorite—the hard stuff, vodka in particular. He smiled. Despite the feminine touches, this place was functional, nothing like the decrepit cabin they'd used as a safe house.

About a hundred miles from Portland, Oregon, the farmhouse was on the eastern edge of Mt. Hood, near the small community of Tygh Valley. Human neighbors lived a few miles away, but he could deal with that, as long as they didn't interfere. Overall, Jakar had done a good job. He'd used the funds they'd racked up from the stolen credit cards to rent the place. The owner hadn't asked any questions, which was a good move on his part. They could stay here, at least for a while.

Members of his brood sat on the overstuffed couch and the wing-backed chairs that lined the perimeter of the living room. A newer inductee still had a few wisps of hair hanging from his almost-bald head. He appeared to survive the change from human to Gossum without any ill effects. They always did. Humans were such easy prey. Easy to catch, easy to convert. Most of the new members came from the seedy side of Portland where it was simpler to hide their disappearance from their normal, human lives.

Ram cast a look at his first lieutenant. "Well, where's the basement?"

"This way." Jakar headed into the kitchen. He pointed to a door, the edges rough with age. "Down there."

"By all means, lead the way," Ram said.

Jakar bowed. "As you wish, my lord."

With a loud squeak, the door opened on rusty hinges. The sound was like rock grinding against rock, reminding him of his fall into the river at the hand of his nemesis. His claws extended from his fingers. He wanted to lash out at someone, anything to ease his mounting frustration. In the last battle, he'd lost to Noeh, and he didn't know how much time he'd have before Zedron paid him a visit. If he didn't have something to offer the finicky god, he'd die a painful death and never get the chance to prove to his ex-wife, Sheri, that he wasn't a failure. He shivered.

Jakar climbed down the long flight of stairs. A bare bulb in the middle of the ceiling provided a small measure of light, but Ram didn't need it. The temperature decreased with each step, and the smell of damp earth and rotting vegetables grew as he descended. If he'd had any hair on his bald head, it would've stood on end. He missed having hair—his cap didn't quite fit the same way anymore.

When he reached the bottom of the stairs, he stopped. A jolt of excitement raced along his spine, and he held his breath. Before him, the room spread out in a large arc. Bottles, beakers, lab equipment, and assorted sundries lay on the large workbench. His heart beat in a fast rhythm. He had a lab again, and that was a wonderful thing.

When they captured another Lemurian, he had all he needed to extract the blood and create another serum. This time, Ram wouldn't fail. Once he had their preternatural powers, he and his brood would bring down the Keep and all its inhabitants. Then, they could enslave the humans and start transporting water back to Lemuria.

He scanned the room. Scattered among the glass beakers and metal bowls lay an assortment of tools—screwdrivers, hammers, pliers—probably left over from the prior tenant.

Ram glanced at his first lieutenant. His loyalty was unusual among the Gossum. Must've been Ram's good timing. He'd saved Jakar from an ass-fuck by two guys in an alley. Ram had killed the attackers and bit Jakar, transforming him into a Gossum. His first lieutenant's loyalty had paid off, big time. "You outdid yourself."

Jakar shrugged. "It is to your liking then, excellent. While you were…indisposed, I had the brood work on expanding this room. As you can see, the back corner was excavated with plenty of space for prisoners. You shall have all that you require."

Ram laughed so hard his body shook. His fingers tingled, and he was eager to begin the search. Maybe he still had a chance to please his god, Zedron, and win this war. Now, all they needed was some Lemurian blood. "Let's break out the vodka. We need to fuel up before the hunt."

Chapter Five

Aramie peered through the branches of a young fir tree. The wet needles still held on to the recent rain, and a drop of water landed on her arm. Even in the dark, her night vision picked out small details, like the mouse quivering next to a fallen log. Somewhere in the vast forest was a sacred pool, one with a gem that might heal Demir. Could she find it? A nugget of doubt crept into her mind.

She'd searched with her sister Sidea for the past three nights, but the hallowed lake had eluded them. When she'd asked Gaetan about the mythical place, his eyes had brightened, and he'd chuckled. His words echoed in her mind. *Blue Pool doesn't exist. It's a legend.*

Aramie wouldn't believe that, she couldn't. In the Panthera culture, myths were always based on truth, so Blue Pool had to exist, somewhere. She had to find the crystal. Her encounter with Ginnia in the Hall of Scriptures emerged in her mind. The Stiyaha seer had walked through the many stacks of ancient books until she'd found a small volume with a red cover. Her eyes had twinkled and she'd flipped through the pages, stopping on a sheet with a picture of a blue crystal.

Aramie's hands shook as she'd accepted the tome from the strange female. Her heart had pounded, the text swimming before her eyes. The ancient cuneiform writing held the answer to her prayer—a way to help Demir. She'd memorized the archaic story, word for word.

Tenida raised the blue crystal into the night air. Its brilliance outshone the moon. The stone had healed Grian, the greatest of warriors, the one who'd sacrificed himself for another. Standing at the base of a large waterfall, the old haelen threw the crystal into the pool to hide it from the enemy. A brilliant flash of light erupted from the water, turning the color to a deep blue and stopping the waterfall's flow. The healer spoke, his voice booming through the trees. "The stone shall rest here until needed once again."

Maybe Blue Pool was a myth as the Stiyaha healer presumed. She bit her lip. No, she wouldn't give in to her skepticism. She needed to believe the place existed—for Demir's sake, as well as her own.

Sidea crept next to her. "What is it? Why did you stop?"

Jonue and Kitani flanked them on either side. When she'd asked them to join her tonight to look for the sacred crystal, they hadn't hesitated. Leon had balked at the idea of Kitani leaving the Keep on this trek, and Jonue's mate, Hallan, hadn't reacted much better. As leader, Aramie had insisted. Another wedge between her and the males wasn't what she needed, but she didn't trust them to help her at this point.

The frigid wind whipped through Aramie's hair, stinging her cheeks. Carried along on the breeze—the bitter tang of her ageless enemy, the Gossum. Aramie's claws extended from her closed fist, piercing the soft flesh of her palm.

Sidea placed a hand on Aramie's shoulder. "We're in Gossum territory."

Aramie grasped her sister's fingers, the close contact like a salve on a wound. "Yes, but we're close. We must continue." Aramie glanced at Jonue and Kitani. "Are you ready?"

Kitani's eyes lit up when she smiled. "I've longed to return to battle ever since I mated to Leon."

"I can't wait. Bring it on." Jonue stared straight ahead, her hand clutched over her throwing stars. Her smooth, dark hair reflected the small bit of light from the waxing moon.

Aramie smiled. Should they encounter any Gossum, her females would make her proud.

"Let's go." Aramie headed deeper into the forest, following the river. Even in the depths of winter, the remains of overgrown blackberry bushes, rhododendrons, and azaleas impeded their path, making their journey difficult. Forced to the edge of the small ravine, they followed the river, away from the protection of the forest.

Sidea stopped. "The scent of Gossum is stronger."

Sidea's hair hung around her cheeks and dark circles rimmed her eyes. Aramie worried about her sister, always had, ever since their mother had walked out on them when they were children. The bitter sting of her mother's last words still echoed in Aramie's mind. *"Aramie, I'm heading out—to find more food. Take care of your sister while I'm gone, you hear?"* Her mother had left with a small knapsack over her shoulder. That was the last time Aramie had ever seen her.

Aramie shook her head to clear her mind. The last thing she needed was the distraction of the female who'd taught her how to build walls around her heart. She steeled herself for the task at hand.

Sidea's soft touch on her arm brought Aramie back to the present. "Did you hear me? We've been out here for hours and this is our fourth river. With the Gossum around…I think we should call for a portal. We can come back again tomorrow."

Aramie glanced at her two warriors. Jonue had a rip in the sleeve of her shirt, most likely from a stray tree branch. Kitani's pants were covered in mud and sweat stains marred her shirt.

Her sister was right. Aramie didn't want to stop searching, but she'd put them in danger by bringing them so far into Gossum territory. If they stayed much longer, they'd risk seeing the sunrise and face exposure to the sun's killing rays. Ever since their goddess, Alora, had interfered directly in the war, breaking the most sacred rule of the game, all of Alora's characters were relegated to the night. A knot formed in Aramie's stomach. They needed to return to the Keep.

Chapter Six

Noeh unsheathed his sword. The blade vibrated, sending a shiver up his arm. He stroked the handle, the sunstones embedded in the gold heating from his touch. "We're practicing, my friend. No killing this evening." He leaned his favorite weapon against the stone wall and picked up a wooden sparring sword.

Saar slid the chain into place, locking the antechamber's door. Noeh had asked his Commander of Arms to join him in the private room, away from the main training facility and the other warriors with their unwanted, curious eyes.

Saar leaned against the heavy wooden door. A toothpick dangled from his lip, twisting the scar that ran across his face into a strange grimace. "You ready?"

Ever since Melissa had the baby, Noeh had been preoccupied with ensuring his queen and their son, Anlon, had everything they needed. He'd never realized taking care of a newborn could be so much work. After nearly losing them both, he hadn't left their side. Not until Melissa had had enough of his hovering and shooed him out of the royal chamber.

Adrenaline raced along his nerves. A spar was exactly what he needed. "Yes, my body craves a good workout."

The skin around Saar's eyes wrinkled, and his lips moved as if he'd spoken.

Noeh couldn't quite make out the words, but by the smirk on Saar's face, he'd given Noeh a verbal jab. Noeh shook his free hand, eager to expel the extra energy coursing through his veins. He raised his sword and crouched into a fighting stance. The combat would relieve some of his tension and get his head back into the war with the Gossum. "What's taking you so long?"

Saar stepped away from the door and grabbed his own sparring sword. Raising his weapon, he circled Noeh, his eyes focused, narrowed.

Leaning against the wall, Noeh's sword visibly quivered, emitting a cry, but the sound seemed muted, as if far off in the distance. The noise should've pierced his ear, ricocheting around the antechamber.

Craya. I'm almost deaf.

As they circled each other, Noeh relied on his other senses to track his opponent. He focused on Saar's movements, his small tells, like how his eye twitched before he struck. And…there it was.

Saar's sword crashed down, connecting with Noeh's blade. The two warriors strained and pressed blade against blade. Noeh twisted his body, throwing Saar off balance. The tip of his sword came dangerously close to his friend's nose.

Before Noeh could pull back for another strike, Saar clipped him on the shoulder. A drop of blood bloomed on his white shirt. The wooden swords were sharp enough to mark, but not strong enough to do serious damage. Noeh clenched his teeth. The sting was a reminder he wasn't invincible. "Nice shot."

Saar circled Noeh and winked. "Would…y…ike another?"

Only pieces of the words filtered into Noeh's brain. He gripped his sword tighter. His fingers turned white with strain. A growl erupted from his throat as his beast woke. He came at Saar, unleashing all his pent-up frustration on his friend.

Swords clashed together in a blur. Blood welled from a nick on Noeh's forearm and another on his thigh. Noeh pressed forward, forcing Saar to parry.

A sharp sting bit into Noeh's forehead. Wetness dripped in front of his eye. The room turned red with each drop. A nick on his forearm, another on his thigh, yet a third on his cheek. He listened for the sound of Saar's blade—

In a swift, surprising move, Saar undercut him with the back of his sword. Pain blossomed in Noeh's leg. He landed on the mat, his breath escaping in a whoosh.

The tip of Saar's blade dimpled the skin under Noeh's chin. He glanced at his Commander of Arms. Saar's brow furrowed, his face tightening. "Another round?"

A bead of frustration wriggled its way into Noeh's gut. He gritted his teeth. "Again."

On his feet, he focused on his opponent, watching, waiting. Saar attacked, and their blades met in mid-air. Noeh's muscles shook, but he didn't relent. He'd defeated Saar many times in previous sparring matches, he'd do so again.

Saar released the pressure. Noeh swung at him from below. Before he knew what happened, Noeh found himself on the floor.

The second round ended the same as the first, only this time he was on his stomach, the tip of Saar's sword digging into his back. A sudden coldness filled Noeh's veins. How could this happen?

The pressure in his back eased, and Noeh clambered to his feet. He stared at his Commander of Arms. Saar lowered the blade in deference to his king, but his gaze met Noeh's. The two evaluated each other, neither giving way.

Saar's brow creased. "....going on?"

Noeh looked away, the first time he'd ever broken eye contact with an opponent, even if it was only a sparring match. He ran his hand through his hair, his body trembling as the truth crashed down on him. His hearing loss, his one weakness that wouldn't heal, would be lethal on the battlefield.

Hadn't he learned that from Demir? The Panthera leader had taken a dart intended for him because Noeh hadn't heard it coming. Demir had ended up in a coma as a result. Noeh hadn't trusted the arrogant Panthera leader, but after his unselfish sacrifice, he'd earned Noeh's faith. Noeh prayed Demir would wake from his darkness soon. He could use the extra support from Demir and his Panthera Pride.

Saar's palm landed on Noeh's shoulder and his friend gave him a firm squeeze. Noeh peered at his toughest warrior and good friend. "T...me."

Tell me. Noeh read his lips more than he actually heard the words.

A great weight descended on his shoulders. He wanted to rant at the Gods, scream at them for creating this war, but then a vision of Melissa, and their son, Anlon, crept into his mind. Without Alora's help, they wouldn't be in his life. They'd be dead...at the hands of that traitor—Mauree. He exhaled and rubbed his eyes.

Saar stepped back, and the movement brought Noeh out of his reverie. His friend frowned and shook his head. "How....help?"

Noeh picked up his sparring sword from the floor and put it back in the rack. Retrieving his favorite weapon, he placed the blade back in his scabbard. He tapped the handle with his ring, the movement comforting despite the fact that he could no longer hear the familiar ting of metal on metal. "There's nothing you can do for me, but thank you for the offer, my friend."

He walked over to one of the tables lining the wall. A pitcher filled with water and several cups were displayed on an elegant tablecloth, along with an assortment of fruit, all thanks to the Jixies, the Stiyaha's helpers. He poured a drink and handed the cup to Saar, then filled his own.

Saar took a sip, and placed the mug back on the table. "Let...try."

Noeh laughed, the only response he could deal with given the circumstances. "If you can fix my ears..." He shrugged.

His friend leaned forward, his brows creasing. "Are...deaf?"

Noeh nodded. "Almost, and soon will be." He glanced at his Commander of Arms.

Saar's mouth fell open, his eyes wide.

"I can't go out on the battlefield. I'm a danger to others." Noeh's chest tightened. The words were like a blade thrust into his gut. He was king, not only of the Stiyaha, but of all the Lemurian races. How could he lead his warriors if he couldn't fight?

He held Saar's gaze. His friend's eyes shifted back and forth as he evaluated him. At last, Saar dropped to his knees, his fist wrapped around the hilt of his own sword. "…You…forever…my king."

Noeh's heart rate spiked, sending a rush of endorphins into his bloodstream. His friend's devotion was more than he could handle. He placed his palm on Saar's shoulder. "Rise, my friend."

"Who knows?" Saar's words were but a whisper to Noeh's ears.

"Melissa, Gactan, and now, you. I'd like to keep it that way, at least for now."

"As…wish…Majesty."

Noeh closed his eyes and let his friend's loyalty fill him. As king, he'd do what was necessary to win this war, even if it meant leading from the throne.

Chapter Seven

The quiet in the room and his rhythmic breathing left Demir on the edge of sleep. He'd fought against his invisible bonds for so long, his tired mind couldn't resist the lull of slumber. In and out of consciousness, he finally succumbed to the dream.

Demir walked into the forest, eager to escape the spring ritual and all the Panthera that had gathered in the clearing. Some came from far off Prides to exchange knowledge and information about their enemy. Others came to find a mate. Demir wasn't interested in either, but since his father died, he'd become Pride leader and had to attend. Demir clenched his fist. The last thing he wanted was a mate.

The woods swallowed him, surrounding him with ever deepening brush and trees. Even the glow from the moon struggled to reach the ground. Far enough from the celebration, the sounds of the forest permeated his senses—frogs croaking, crickets singing.

He inhaled, soaking in the night air. A scent, like spiced apples, made him still. I'm not alone. *With silent stealth, he crouched behind a large boulder and surveyed the forest. Shadows stretched into grotesque shapes amid the underbrush. He bided his time, out-waiting the intruder.*

Movement to his right caught his attention. The muscles in his thighs tensed. Ready to attack, he sprung from his hideout. The interloper ran. Demir followed in hot pursuit.

The figure eluded him only for a moment then stopped. The unexpected reaction caused him to plow into the intruder, and he reflexively wrapped his arms around the person. Soft, tender flesh teased the skin on his arms. Even in the dark, vibrant red hair reflected the moon's meager light.
A female.

He relaxed his grip and turned her to face him. Still wrapped in his embrace, he stared upon her features for the first time—vibrant green eyes, a pert nose, and full, inviting lips. Her spiced apple scent intoxicated him, sending a shot of adrenaline through his body, lighting up his nerves.

Her panted breaths caressed his cheek, and an overwhelming desire to kiss her lips washed over him. He held himself in check and curiosity got the better of him. "Who are you and what are you doing out here?"

"My...my name is Eleanor." She trembled in his arms and licked her lips, inviting him in. "Please...I saw you leave. I couldn't help but follow."

He furrowed his brow. "Why?"

She blushed, her cheeks reddening, endearing her to him. "Because...you are a powerful male. Forgive me for tracking you. I couldn't stay away."

He studied her, taking in her soft features and her warm, curvaceous body. Against his will, his fangs erupted from his mouth. "You play with fire."

She met his gaze then lowered her eyes to his mouth. "Please..." With delicate care, she trailed her fingertip over his chin to his lips. "Kiss me."

His panther roared with the need to claim this female. Even though they'd just met, he couldn't deny the intensity of the mating call. Rough and possessive, he kissed her, taking her with a ferocity he didn't fully understand. She mewled softly, stoking his desire all the more. Coming up for air, their combined pants echoed among the trees.

She nudged her nose under his chin. "If I were to be yours, I would submit to you, fully."

His cock strained against his pants, showing his eagerness for what she offered. His need rose to a fevered pitch, and he bit her on the shoulder, marking her, claiming her as his mated female. Even as his panther relished in the claiming, a morsel of doubt crept into his mind. What have I done?

Demir woke in a cold sweat, his eyes still shut. Remnants of strange dreams with Eleanor flitted through his mind, but as he grasped at the memories, they eluded him—and were forgotten. All he was left with was a strange feeling he couldn't identify, but one thing he clearly understood, no one could ever replace his Eleanor.

He lay sprawled on his bed, the satin sheet tucked under his chin. The material moved up and down with his breaths, scraping against his goatee. He couldn't help but focus on the irritating sensation and that only intensified his annoyance. A low growl built in his mind. He fought against his lifeless body, pushing, screaming, until the frenzy nearly broke him. A single bead of sweat ran down the side of his face.

He needed to concentrate on something else, anything to distract him from his misery. His first thought—Aramie. Her strawberry scent, her soft voice, and the way her fingers had trailed over the sensitive hairs of his mustache were memories he couldn't forget. The skin around his mouth tickled, as if she still touched him. Instead of a sense of peace, the strong need to be near her washed over him. His inner cat howled, but no sound escaped his lips.

Over the past few days, Aramie had only stopped by for brief visits. She hadn't told him what she'd done, but from her prior conversation with Sidea, he knew they searched for the blue sunstone. From the strain in her voice, she seemed exhausted. When he'd originally heard of the possibility of a crystal with magical healing power, hope had sprouted inside him. With each new visit and no news, his belief in the sacred stone waned. Without it, he'd waste away, die trapped in his body.

Another round of anger built within, and he lashed out once again. The silence in the empty room welcomed him into its embrace, and a cold shot of fear lanced through his chest. When he died, Aramie would take over the Pride. The males wouldn't like it, and sooner or later, she'd lose to one of them. What would become of her? A protectiveness he hadn't felt since before Eleanor died skittered along his nerves. His reaction to Aramie was unexpected—and unnerving. She needed to be second in command, nothing more.

The sheet rubbed against his chin once again. He fought to ignore the irritation, but couldn't seem to focus on anything else. His pulse rose. How could such a small movement bring such torment? He didn't know, but his helplessness left him cold.

Chapter Eight

Aramie and her warriors headed to a nearby clearing to call for a portal. She peered at her little sister. Tied in a short ponytail, Sidea's light brown hair accentuated her pale skin and full mouth. With soft brown eyes and high cheekbones, she'd inherited her beauty from their mother. Aramie didn't begrudge her sister's good fortune.

In sharp contrast, Aramie had thin lips and a dark complexion. Their differences in physical appearance were due to their separate fathers, which neither had ever met. A dull pain radiated from Aramie's chest. The hurtful truth was that after six hundred and twenty years of life on this planet, she would never know him. Often, she envisioned what he looked like and imagined he carried himself with an air of authority.

After their mother had walked out on them, Sidea had cried every night for several months. Without a father, Aramie had grown up fast, becoming the provider and the protector. She'd taught Sidea how to fight, and they'd learned to survive on their own.

The sounds of the forest called to Aramie. A chill ran along her arms. Something was different. The flow from the stream was off, changed somehow, less intense.

Aramie didn't want to keep her sister out here any longer than necessary, but she couldn't stop, not now. "Do you hear the stream? It's different. One more bend. We'll return if we don't find anything. I promise."

Sidea studied her face for a moment. Soft brown eyes filled with trust penetrated into Aramie's heart. She bit her lip. "Let's hurry."

Jonue and Kitani nodded in agreement.

Aramie pushed through the underbrush with a new intensity. The racing water calmed as they approached the edge of the ravine. A small outcropping of rocks appeared through the trees. She clambered past the stones and peered over the edge. Her breath caught in her throat.

There it was—Blue Pool.

Her Panthera vision cut through the dark. The water was a deep, rich blue. Rocks and downed tree branches lined the bottom of the small lake. The source of the stream appeared to come from the pool itself, evidence of an underground spring. In a lip of rock overhanging the water, smooth stones and the lack of vegetation were evidence of a once grand waterfall, now dry.

"It's beautiful," Sidea whispered.

"Yes, it is." Kitani approached and looked over the edge. She shuddered. "I hope we find the stone fast, I don't relish the idea of getting wet."

Aramie empathized with her warriors. Feline in nature, most Panthera avoided immersion in water and didn't like to swim. For some strange reason, she rather enjoyed the feel of the cool water surrounding her body. "I'll go. I used to swim for fun when I was a youth."

Sidea glanced at Kitani. "She's weird, I know. What Panthera does that, right?"

Kitani shivered in mock disgust. "I enjoy a nice shower, but to immerse myself in water... Ugh, it sends a chill down my spine."

"All right, knock it off." Aramie pursed her lips in feigned irritation.

"I'll go with you." Jonue stepped forward and raised her chin.

The small Panthera's strength and determination made Aramie smile. "Great. Let's go." She peered at Sidea and Kitani. "You two—spread out and keep watch. We'll return as soon as we can."

Aramie stared at the beauty of the pool, the moon reflecting off the surface. A mixture of excitement and trepidation ran along her nerves. They were close. The stone had to be here, somewhere.

Using her natural feline grace, she climbed over the boulders and stopped at the edge. A tinge of energy rippled through the air, causing the hair on the back of her neck to stand on end. Adrenaline surged through her veins. The stone was here, somewhere under the water.

"Where should we start?" Jonue asked.

"Good question." Aramie crouched along the bank. Upon closer inspection, the pool wasn't as still as she'd imagined. Pushed along by the underwater current, a dried leaf from a nearby birch tree floated past. She followed the crinkled boat's path across the pool and into the beginning of the river. It picked up pace and dived below the surface, swallowed by the raging waters.

She pointed to the water. "We track the current back from that leaf."

"Perfect. The source of the spring is as good as any place to start." Jonue crouched on one knee and unbuckled her boot.

Aramie did the same and tossed her favorite pair of shoes behind a bush. Dressed in her combat pants and long-sleeved shirt, she unclipped the red barrette from her hair and shoved it into her pocket. The hair clip, a gift from her Gran'ma, was her most precious item and one she wouldn't risk losing. As much as she longed to search for the crystal in her panther form, her human hands were needed to grasp the stone.

She peered at Jonue. "Ready?"

If not for the slight tick in her friend's jaw, Aramie wouldn't have noticed her comrade's uncertainty. She touched Jonue on the arm. "You don't have to do this."

Jonue blinked. Her brow furrowed. "You are my Pride leader. Where you go, I go."

Aramie's chest expanded, touched by her sincerity. She grasped her friend on the arm. "Let's find the sunstone."

She looked at the top of the rise where she'd last seen her sister and Kitani. They were gone, hidden in the underbrush, and would keep watch until she and Jonue returned.

Aramie pivoted and stepped into the pool. Small goosebumps formed along her arms.

Jonue gasped. "Damn. The water is freezing cold."

Aramie smirked.

Jonue sighed. "This is torture. You know that, right?"

"You're doing great." Aramie waved her friend onward.

They waded deeper into the pool taking careful, measured steps.

Aramie's feet skidded on the slick rocks, and she almost lost her balance. Standing waist deep in the cold water, the current pulled on her, trying to push her downstream, away from the dry waterfall. She fought with all her might, her legs straining to make headway, but the current was too strong.

Jonue pulled on the back of her shirt to get her attention. "Come back. If we go any farther, the current will pull us under."

Aramie clenched her fists. She couldn't give up, not when they were so close.

Per the legend, the old haelen had thrown the crystal into the waterfall, creating Blue Pool. Aramie looked at the spot where the water would have landed had the waterfall still existed. Her gaze rose to the top of the rocks. A lump formed in her stomach. She knew what she had to do.

Aramie peered into her friend's eyes. "You don't have to go with me."

Jonue's throat bobbed as she swallowed. "Yes, I do. Let's do this."

Aramie nodded. "You're a fine warrior."

They crawled to the boulders at the top of the ancient, dry waterfall. Aramie's nerves rattled under her skin. She inched her way to the edge. A sense of vertigo made her sway. Could she really do this? An image of Demir lying motionless on his bed steeled her resolve. Her hands curled into fists. She'd do it for him. Before she could lose her nerve, she took a few steps back and raced full speed toward the cliff and Blue Pool below. She jumped and prayed she'd survive.

Chapter Nine

A drop of water fell on Zedron's shoulder, the first sign the silver clouds above were about to release a torrent onto the Lemurian landscape. Standing on one of the pathways in the trees, the leaves would provide some protection, but not enough. He increased his pace, scrambling up the stairs and over the top of a riser. His pulse pounded in his temple, bringing on the beginning of one of his headaches. He clenched his jaw—that was not what he needed right now.

A few stray strands of hair blew against his cheek. Water splashed on his nose and caused him to blink. The drops came faster, hitting him on the back, the shoulders, and the top of his head. He hunched over to protect his shirt as best he could and prayed the droplets wouldn't leave circular stains on his brand new jacket.

Janala's Place was visible between the branches of the Etila trees. Lights bordered the doorway, welcoming patrons in for the evening meal. The restaurant was the place where anyone who was anyone went for an evening out. He loved this place and the opportunity it gave him to mingle with others from his class.

An elderly lady took up more than her fair share of space as she walked down the stairs. He pressed past her, knocking her against the bark of the tree. She cried out, but he ignored her. Water dripped onto his shirt, causing a streak to form. He ground his teeth. "Watch where you're going."

Free at last, he crossed the wooden slats connecting the last two trees and arrived at his destination. The scent of baked bread and Monton stew emanated from the eatery. He inhaled and the rich aroma calmed his jittery nerves and battered psyche. A glass of muldoberry wine was exactly what he needed—the best they had.

"How many tonight, sir?" The waiter clasped his hands behind his back, a practiced, formal smile on his face.

Zedron raised his chin. "One."

The male gave a slight bow and extended his hand. "Follow me, please."

The restaurant was nearly full, many of the tables occupied with the elite members of the Lemurian society—council members, enforcers, and colonizers. He always wore his best attire to dinner—leather shoes, a soft down shirt that accentuated his sleek torso, and the finest woven coat. To be disheveled in any way was an affront to his stylist nature. He buttoned his jacket and ran his hand through his hair. That was the best he could do under the circumstances—damn the rain.

The waiter pulled out a chair at a small table near the entrance to the kitchen. "Here, sir. This table is perfect for you."

Zedron furrowed his brow. "Surely, you must have something better."

With a quick intake of breath, the attendant blinked. "If this isn't to your liking, we have another. Of course."

Zedron glanced around the room. A flash of long blond hair from one of the booths in the far corner grabbed his attention. *Alora.* He'd know his ex-lover anywhere. Her curvaceous body and soft, silky tresses were forever ingrained in his mind. She was with one of her girlfriends, Bellamy. The headache he courted on the way here roared to life behind his eyes.

"Sir? Did you hear me? This way, please."

A lone booth, one big enough for a party of six, was open not far from Alora and her friend.

"That one." Zedron pointed at the booth. "That one will be sufficient."

The male's brow pinched together ever so slightly. "I'm sorry, sir. That booth is for a large party."

"Not anymore. That booth is for me."

"Sir—"

Zedron raised his hand. "You do know who I am, don't you?"

"Ah…" Confusion lined the waiter's forehead.

He glared at the male. "Zedron. Colonizer. Son of council member Alcion."

The attendant's head jerked back, his eye widening. "Oh, Colonizer Zedron. Of course…you may sit anywhere you wish."

Zedron headed for the table, his gaze homed in on Alora. *Glance at me. Glance at me.* If will alone were a strong enough force, she'd have looked his way, but she didn't. Her attention was focused solely on her friend.

As he pulled into the booth, Zedron scooted to the back, into the shadows. He had a perfect view of Alora. Her pale blue eyes gleamed with determination, her plump mouth pulled into a pout. His lips throbbed with the sudden urge to kiss her. He clenched his fist, hating how he still reacted to her, still wanted her, despite she'd chosen his one-time best friend, Veromé, as her mate.

The waiter bowed and circled his hand over the table. A small hum emanated from the center and a hologram appeared with different options for the evening's meal. "Your server will be with you shortly."

Zedron ignored the waiter and studied Alora. Even from this distance, she teased him—her smile, the way she wrapped a few strands of her hair between her fingers, her plunging neckline. Once she'd willingly given him that gorgeous smile, but not anymore—not after the mistake he'd made.

A young server blocked his vision, forcing Zedron to look at the male. "What would you like tonight?"

Zedron waved his hand in the air, dissolving the menu, scattering the images until they disappeared. "Bring me a bowl of Monton stew and a glass of muldoberry wine."

"Right away, sir."

Alone again, Zedron stared at his ex-lover. Visions of Veromé trailing his fingers over Alora's soft skin, kissing her tender lips, and loving her until she cried out his name made Zedron's pulse pound in his temple. His jaw ached from the tension, and he curled his hand into a fist. Zedron had money, power, and influence. Veromé had none of those things and yet, Alora had chosen Veromé over him. He still couldn't accept the defeat.

In a bid for revenge, during a council meeting he'd challenged her for the right to colonize Earth. Radnor, the council leader had honored the challenge, and the competition was on. The battle was fought with characters, like pieces in an elaborate game. His minions called him a god, but he was a colonizer just like Alora—a planet searcher—and one of the many residents that lived on Lemuria. The victor of the game won the right to control Earth's water.

Alora wanted to barter with the humans for the water with gifts of knowledge and technology. For Zedron, if, no…when he won, he'd enslave the humans and force them to load the resource onto the transport ships that would bring the much-needed water back to Lemuria.

During that ill-fated council meeting, Alora's pursed lips and furrowed brow had made his heart pound. He'd gotten a reaction from her, and if anger and resentment was all he could get, so be it. She'd once cared for him, and he vowed she would again, someday.

Zedron couldn't hear Alora and Bellamy's conversation, not above the din of other voices in the eatery. That was fine. He had a tool that would do the job. He pulled a long, thin rod from his coat's breast pocket. The trinket was something he'd found at a shady antique store and he wasn't able to resist the antiquated listening device. Since he didn't want to get caught eavesdropping, he shoved the rod up his sleeve, hiding it from any curious eyes.

A smirk pulled at his lip. He hadn't realized he'd get the opportunity to use the mechanism so quickly. Heat radiated from his chest and down his arms, causing his fingers to tingle. With care, he angled the tip toward Alora and placed the receiver in his ear.

Alora took a sip from her cup and winked at her friend. "Thank you for coming with me tonight."

Bellamy gripped Alora's arm. "Please don't make me wait any…me. What did Veromé…you?"

Zedron adjusted the wand, angling the tip a bit more toward Bellamy.

Alora peered around the room, as if searching for someone. *Perhaps me?* Zedron could only hope.

She rummaged in her bag and extended her closed fist to Bellamy. She released her grip, and a short chain dangled from her fingers. The bauble sparkled in the light. "This! He gave me this bracelet for our anniversary."

"Ooh, it's beautiful. Why aren't you wearing it?"

"I want him to put the bracelet on for me. We…didn't have time. As you know, we only have the few minutes at sunrise and sunset to be together."

"The sanction. Yes, I remember. You have to be careful. Zedron would like nothing better than to have you sanctioned again."

"I wouldn't change what I did. My characters, they needed to be saved from the great scourge. I must win the war on Earth." Determination lined the creases around her eyes.

His throat thickened. He admired Alora's courage and tenacity, even though he planned to bring her down. There was something between them, something neither could ignore, and he wanted her to admit it. The fingers on his free hand gripped the edge of the table. The wood creaked under the pressure.

He'd almost won the last round, coming close to toppling her king, Noeh. If that honor-driven cat, Demir, hadn't gotten in the way, Noeh would be dead. The Stiyaha warriors would've fallen without their leader, and the Gossum would've secured an important victory. Zedron's pulse pounded at his temple, his headache expanding with each beat. Somehow, he'd make Demir pay for his virtuous choice.

Bellamy patted Alora's forearm. "Hey, you'll win. I know you will."

"Thank you. Your support means so much to me." Alora squeezed her friend's hand.

The crackle of Monton stew distracted Zedron, and the waiter appeared with a steaming bowl. "Your food, sir."

Zedron's stomach growled at the warm scent.

The server placed the bowl on the table, along with a knife, fork, and a napkin. He glanced at Zedron then bowed his head. "Is there anything else I can get for you?"

"My wine?"

The male blinked, as if realizing he'd forgotten the drink. "Oh, yes, indeed. I'll return momentarily."

When the waiter left, Alora's table was empty. Zedron exhaled a loud sigh and sat back, leaving his food untouched. His hunger went with her.

Chapter Ten

Cool water enveloped Aramie in its embrace. Prepared to fight the current, her body tensed, and she was ready to move, to swim with all her might. As she broke through the surface, she gulped in clean, fresh air. To her surprise, the pool near the base of the dry waterfall was calm. Only a small trickle brushed over her arms as she treaded in place. Her mouth went dry, relief pouring through her veins like a drug.

She'd jumped off that cliff before she could change her mind. Demir would've laughed had he known she'd done such a thing. A soothing warmth radiated through her chest.

"Oh, damn! You—are crazy!" Jonue sputtered nearby. She splashed in the frigid water, trying to stay afloat.

Aramie hid the smile that broke across her face. "You followed me."

Jonue pursed her lips as she dog-paddled. "I guess that makes me crazier than you."

Aramie treaded on the surface, looking for the source of the spring. The blue sunstone was here—somewhere. "No time like the present. If you find the stone or anything unusual, let me know."

She held her breath and dove below the wide expanse. Stranded tree branches and rocks of all sizes lined the lakebed. A thin green slime covered the smooth stones, making them slick to the touch. She pushed aside pebbles and larger rocks looking for anything that could pass as a crystal. Her lungs ached with the need for oxygen, forcing her to resurface.

Jonue appeared by her side. "Anything?"

"Not yet." She peered at the sky. The crispness of the night had faded, giving the sky the presence of pre-dawn. Nearby, a Western scrub-yay sent out an early morning call. If they didn't find the stone… A soft cry broke from her throat, and her heart clenched. *No. I won't leave without it.*

She swam as close to the dry waterfall as possible. The hard stones were smooth to her touch. If only they could share their secrets with her. She glanced at Jonue. "We have, at most, a half-hour to do this. Let's check the base of the waterfall."

"If we don't find it, we'll come back." Jonue's encouragement made her feel better, but Aramie sensed if they left without the crystal, they'd never find this magical place again. She couldn't keep her search party out here much longer and risk losing their lives to the sun. With a quick nod to her friend, she decided. "Ok, let's make it a good one."

She inhaled a large breath and dove again. Her fingers moving with swift proficiency, she pawed among the rocks. Panic welled in her mind. *The stone must be here, it has to be.* Warm water passed under her hand. With care, she traced her fingers back over the spot.

She followed the warmth to a small opening, hidden behind a large boulder. Soft blue light emanated from the hole. A tendril of hope raced along her skin. Her lungs ached, but if she went back to the top now, she wasn't sure she'd find this spot again. All the rocks and boulders looked so similar.

Jonue brushed her fingers over Aramie's arm to gain her attention and then pointed at the hole. Without a second thought, Aramie pushed her way through the opening.

A large, underwater corridor stretched beneath the rocks. Blue light glowed softly in the distance, and she swam toward the source. The need for oxygen made her lungs ache. White spots appeared in her vision, mixing with the blue light. When she couldn't go a moment longer, she resurfaced into a hidden chamber.

Sputtering, she breathed oxygen into her lungs to fuel her starving brain. Jonue joined her in the chamber. Their combined breaths reverberated off the walls of the small cave.

As her heart calmed, Aramie glanced around. The chamber was no bigger than her room back at the Keep. Mud lined the small shore and smelled of dampness and age.

"What is this place?" Awe and wonder were clear in Jonue's tone.

A strange sense of peace wrapped around Aramie. She seemed safe here, protected. Pulling herself out of the water, she rested on the wet soil. Wetness dripped from her hair, her blouse clung to her arms, and her pants weighed heavy on her hips. Blue light cast an eerie glow on the rocks.

"Look." Jonue pointed to the far edge of the cave.

The light began to pulse.

A shot of adrenaline brought Aramie to her feet. "The stone!" She raced to the light's source. Her breath bottled up in her lungs as hope welled inside.

Behind a small boulder, the blue glare strengthened, pulsing as if in rhythm with her pounding heart. She placed her hand on the smooth lip of a rock and peered over the edge. The intensity of the light pierced her brain. She shielded her sensitive eyes from the radiance. Blood pounded in her ears.

"You found it." Jonue whispered.

Aramie couldn't believe they'd actually discovered the sacred sunstone. She reached for the crystal. As she grazed the tip of her finger over the stone, the light went out.

Darkness surrounded them.

Chapter Eleven

"Did you burp him?" Noeh searched through the extra blankets at the bottom of the crib. His blood pressure spiked along with his frustration. He ran a hand through his hair. "Craya! I can't find the pacifier."

Melissa walked across their bedchamber, Anlon cradled against her chest. She patted his back, and as she turned, his son's scrunched face and open mouth were an indication all was not right in the world. Even with his weakened ears, a hint of the babe's shrill cry rang in Noeh's head.

There's a new pacifier still in the package in the second drawer of my dresser. Melissa's words echoed in Noeh's mind thanks to their special connection. During Anlon's birth, Melissa had almost died. Noeh's chest clenched at the memory. He'd been unwilling to accept her death and had used the power of his beast to forge a connection to her spirit, sharing his energy, and giving her the life-force she needed. In return, they were permanently connected at the soul and could communicate telepathically.

"Dresser…dresser." He opened the drawer and sifted through diapers, wipes, creams, and an assortment of other baby paraphernalia until he found the unopened pacifier. Gripping the package, he ripped the plastic from the paper wrapper. The pacifier flew through the air. Noeh caught it before the weaselly thing landed on the stone floor.

With shaking fingers, he handed the rubber soother to Melissa. She nestled the knob over Anlon's open mouth. At the contact, his wail ceased, and he accepted the pacifier without further complaint.

Noeh released the tension in his shoulders and breathed a sigh of relief. "I never thought I'd say this, but thank the gods for human markets."

Melissa pursed her lips. *It's called a grocery store. And, yes, I'm glad the Jixies go there once in a while for supplies we don't have in the Keep.*

Since Anlon was the first babe in over five hundred years, the Stiyaha had had no use for such items. The great scourge had rendered the surviving females infertile. No one understood why, but Melissa was a rare exception. Noeh rubbed the back of his neck and studied his queen.

She was his world. Her spirited green eyes and red hair had captured his attention from the moment he'd found her. She'd fallen in love with him, changing him for the better. Their road to be together hadn't been easy, but he couldn't imagine life without her now. The marking under his eye for compassion burned as the line thickened.

Tell me what happened. You've been pent up ever since your sparring match with Saar. He peered at her. She was right. He'd been a beast all evening—figuratively, not literally. Now that they were connected, his innermost thoughts and fears were on display. He couldn't hide them from her even if he'd tried.

He ran his hand through his hair and exhaled. "Saar..." *He defeated me, twice...*

She ran her fingers over his arm, the gentle caress tickling the fine hairs. *I'm not sure I understand why that's a problem. You've sparred on many occasions, each winning your fair share.*

He glanced at her soft features, her gaze penetrating into his heart. "True, but I've never lost so easily." Not wanting to admit how much this bothered him, he headed over to his desk. He leaned on the ancient wood and tried to calm his racing heart.

Melissa didn't send him a message, so he turned to look at her. She was bent over the crib, placing Anlon down for a nap. Noeh caught a glimpse of his son's face—closed eyes, cute button nose, ruby lips sucking on the pacifier. He held his breath, and a new wave of contentment warred with his frustration.

Melissa straightened and looked at him. Her lips scrunched into a frown. *That's not all there is to it. Tell me the rest.*

"It won't be long before I'm completely deaf..." He raised his clenched fist. "I won't...I can't go out on the battlefield again. I'm a danger to others."

Her brow pinched together and her own pain for him filtered along their connection. His heart ached.

He tapped his ring against the hilt of his sword. With great care, he unbuckled his belt and removed his scabbard. The blade shook, causing a tremor to ripple up his arm.

He placed his sheathed sword on a hook on the wall. Emptiness filled him, and he seemed naked without his most valued weapon.

Melissa didn't speak, she didn't need to. Her acceptance was confirmation she, too, knew he could no longer fight. She closed the distance between them, running her hands over his forearms. He encircled her in his embrace and studied her features.

There's a reason Alora and Veromé picked you as king of all the Lemurians. Although you can't fight in the traditional sense, you now have the opportunity to strategize and plan. I will interpret for you, at least until you've mastered lip reading.

A heavy weight settled into his stomach. The other races would arrive at the Keep sooner or later. How they react to his weakness? Would they follow a deaf king? Shaking his head, he ran his hand through his hair.

She lightly touched his chin, and her smile buoyed his confidence. *Hey, I believe in you. We'll get through this…together.* Her eyes glowed with her determination.

Her support made him love her even more, something he thought impossible.

He forced a smile and kissed the top of her nose. "With you by my side, we shall conquer the Gossum and win this war for Alora."

Of that, I have no doubt. We shall see this war end, you and I.

A thought crossed his mind, and he glanced at the door. "Do you think Tanen has had any success with getting the Gossum's new location out of Mauree?"

Melissa pulled away from his embrace and went to check on Anlon. *Not as of the last time we spoke with him. She's been difficult, to say the least.*

He leaned against the bed's giant carved footboard and crossed his arms. "Now that Ram is dead, we need to find Jakar and eliminate the remaining Gossum. I should've insisted on more drastic measures."

No. Please. You promised you wouldn't hurt her.

He pushed away from the bed and wrapped his arms around her from behind. "After everything she did to you, I'm still amazed at how you protect her."

Despite her attempt to kill me, I can't help it. Deep inside, I think she loved you to the best of her ability. Can't you see the pain and torment in her eyes?

"I see a traitor, plain and simple. Tanen has searched the scriptures for the past few weeks to find any details on the required sentence for treason and has spent countless hours trying to pry information out of Mauree. I won't wait much longer. If he's not successful, then I will have no choice but to seek alternate means." Noeh let out a sigh. He prayed to the gods it wouldn't come to that.

She turned in his embrace to face him. *You're a good king. I know you will do what's right.* Her mouth curved into a sexy grin. *By the way, Anlon is asleep.*

Arousal spread through his body, and he became hyper-aware of her scent and how her warm, soft body molded against his. *Indeed, let's not waste this precious alone time.* He pulled her closer, and wrapped his hand in her long hair, capturing her in his grasp. With gentle nips, he kissed his way from her neck to the sensitive spot behind her ear. He let loose a low growl, knowing the vibration would tickle and make her squirm against him.

She responded to the vibration just as he'd expected, squirming and rubbing against his already firm shaft. He growled his appreciation and picked her up. She wrapped her legs around his waist, squeezing his torso with her taut muscles.

He carried her to their bed, their passionate kisses driving him mad. His knee bumped into the mattress and they fell onto the comforter. He wrapped his arms around her, caging her where they landed. A smile pulled at his lips. *Little kitten, you're going to mewl my name before we're done.*

The rhythmic nature of her laugh vibrated into his chest. *Promise?*

Oh yes, I promise.

Chapter Twelve

A chill ran over Aramie's arms. Panthera could see in the slightest bit of light, but here in the cave total darkness reigned.

"Aramie?" Jonue tensed up beside her.

Aramie clutched the stone in her fist. She wouldn't let go and risk losing it. "I've got the stone. You ok?"

"Yes, fine. This is eerie. I've never been unable to see before."

"Head back into the water. Maybe there's some light coming from the outside—from the hole we came through."

Aramie placed the stone into a side pocket in her pants and zipped it closed. The weight against her leg made her heart still. If the ancient legend was true, the crystal would heal Demir. A niggle of hope lodged itself in her chest. With a new sense of urgency, she headed back over the rocks, using her fingers to guide her.

A small splash came from somewhere in front of her. Jonue was back in the water.

Aramie traced her fingertips over the edge of a boulder. Something soft and wet coated her hand. When she moved her fingers, a thin film stuck to her skin. *Spider web!* The creepy, crawly critter skittered over the back of her hand.

She screamed.

Skidding on the slick rocks, she scurried to get away. Even with her Panthera grace, she wasn't able to maintain her balance. Her back hit the jagged edge of a rock, sending a spark of pain into her leg.

"Aramie!" Jonue's shout echoed off the walls, making Aramie's ears ring.

Time slowed. Aramie's heart pounded. Without her cat-like vision, the world closed in on her. Imaginary spiders crawled all over her body. She kicked out, flailing around on the rocks, causing further injury to her back and legs. Her hands scraped against the rocks as she tried to regain her balance. The anxiety attack had her in its grasp.

"Aramie!" Jonue's hands landed on her shoulder and thigh. "I'm here. What's wrong? Are you injured?"

Her friend's words broke through the fog in Aramie's brain. Fast, hard pants wracked her lungs and her body ached from the brutal rocks. "Sp-sp-spider."

"Can you stand? We need to get out of here."

"Yeah. I...I think so." Aramie's parched throat made it difficult to speak. Her face heated. She'd been afraid of spiders ever since she was a kid. She'd woken up one night to find one on her pillow, inches from her face. The creature had jumped on her arm, and she'd screamed. She'd killed it, but not before the spider had bitten her. Ever since then, she'd feared the hairy, multi-legged, multi-eyed creatures with a passion.

Jonue pulled Aramie to her feet. "This way."

The cool water eased Aramie's battered nerves and sore muscles, but she couldn't get out of this cave fast enough.

"Do you see any light? Anything at all?" Jonue asked.

"No…wait. I see a faint glow." Aramie grasped Jonue's arm. "This way."

Together, they dove. The light grew brighter, and they swam through the hole.

Aramie broke through the surface. As she inhaled, the bitter tang of astringent raced into her lungs. *Gossum.*

Rushing water roared in her ears. Wetness splashed in her face, making her blink. She glanced up. The large, majestic waterfall flowed once again, as if freeing the stone had released the water. The brightness of impending dawn cast an orange glow on the clouds. She treaded in place, trying to stay afloat in the bubbling wake.

A shrill cry rang through the air and was cut short.

"Kitani!" Jonue shrieked.

A Gossum's gleeful chortle rang through the air. Above the waterfall's roar, the muffled sound of grunts and bones breaking cascaded into the ravine.

"Oh, no." Jonue's voice echoed Aramie's own thoughts.

A kernel of dread formed in Aramie's gut. If the overwhelming smell was any indication, the Gossum outnumbered Kitani and Sidea.

About thirty yards away, a Gossum grunted near the rocks where she'd last seen her sister. Small pebbles rained from above. They plopped into the water and left concentric circles in their path. A growl erupted into the air.

The hair on Aramie's neck stood on end. Her anger built within, sending adrenaline into her bloodstream. She headed for shore, swimming against the current.

Her sister, in panther form, appeared among the rock outcropping high above Blue Pool. Three Gossum stood right behind her, one wore a cap over his head. *Ram.* She clenched her hands into fists. Noeh had killed him, or so she'd thought, but she couldn't deny the truth seen through her own eyes.

One of the Gossum lashed out his long tongue, hitting Sidea in the haunch. The Gossum's stinger would numb her leg in a matter of moments.

Aramie stilled in the cold water. Time slowed. Her pulse pounded in her ears.

"No," Aramie whispered. She reached into her belt, palming one of her throwing stars. While treading in the water, she attempted a throw, but the star missed its mark.

Sidea lashed out at a Gossum with her front paw, gouging one through his blue jeans. Blood oozed from the injury. Her back leg trembled and gave way. The second Gossum landed on her back, and the scales running over the base of his neck flared. His serrated teeth glinted as he closed his jaw around her throat.

"Sidea!" This time the scream that erupted from Aramie's throat echoed up the walls of the ravine. Vengeance, deep and powerful, rushed through her veins.

Ram turned toward her. His black eyes gleamed in the eerie pre-dawn light. The sinister smile on his face would be forever etched into her brain.

Sidea squirmed below her captors. Ram pulled a syringe out of his pocket. The sharp tip pierced her shoulder. A fine red liquid oozed into the vial.

Aramie bobbed in the water's current. She aimed as best she could and launched another throwing star. This one lodged itself in Ram's bicep. He didn't even flinch, and then casually pulled the metal from his skin.

He glanced at Aramie, pocketed the syringe filled with Sidea's blood, then slit her throat with his long, pointy claw. Blood gushed from the wound, her vital fluid seeping from her body. Sidea slumped to the ground, her fingers already disintegrating, turning to sand.

Heat raced up Aramie's neck and into her face. Her pulse pounded in her temple. A red haze covered her vision. An overwhelming urge to split open Ram's skull made her clench her hands into fists. Fueled by her need for retribution, she swam for shore, Jonue at her side.

The current caught Jonue in its grasp and pulled her under. Aramie couldn't help her sister or Kitani, but she'd be damned if she'd let Jonue die, too.

With a new purpose, adrenaline surged through Aramie's veins. She swam after her warrior and helped Jonue grab a tree branch near the river's edge. As Aramie reached for a nearby shoot, the current caught her in its torrent, yanking her under the water. She sputtered, fighting to break free. The turbulence tossed her around and she rolled, hitting her head against a rock. Pain splintered through her brain.

Fighting consciousness, she surfaced long enough to get half a breath of air—and some more water. Aramie choked and spun as she floated down the river. *So this is what it's like to drown.* Darkness closed in and she passed out.

*****

Aramie woke to gentle hands pressing against her cheeks, forcing her mouth open.

"Breathe." Someone spoke, but she couldn't identify the source.

She inhaled, and a wracking cough made her double over on the ground. Water spewed from her lungs. The damp scent of moss wafted into her senses. On the sodden bank a few feet from the river, mud covered her arms and legs. Strands of wet hair hung in her face.

"I think you'll live." Jonue's stern voice broke into her brain.

"Kitani! Sidea!" Aramie stood, but couldn't get her bearing. She swayed and strong hands grasped her arm to steady her.

"We couldn't save them. There were too many Gossum. I'm sorry," Jonue told her softly.

Aramie couldn't process the information. Her mind was in a fog of denial.

Jonue pulled her close. "You helped me get to the river's edge. I followed the shore, keeping you in sight. When you hit a tree snag, I pulled you out." She placed her hand against Aramie's cheek. "Hey, stay with me."

Aramie pulled her gaze up to meet Jonue's. The other female's mouth was pursed and worry lines creased her brow.

"We have to get farther downstream, away from the Gossum. The sun will break soon."

The truth in Jonue's words was evident all around them. The sky's brightness hurt her sensitive eyes. Daylight, like she'd only seen a few times in her life, cascaded strange shadows along the ground.

"Can you walk? We need to hurry."

Aramie wavered on unsteady legs, but she took a few steps. She peered at the awakening sky. A part of her wanted to stay here, let the sun take her. She couldn't imagine life without Sidea. A great weight descended. *My sister is dead.* A soft wail escaped her lips. Tears blurred her vision, and she swiped her hand across her face to wipe them away.

She fisted her hand and punched her thigh. Her fingers crashed against a hard bulge. Intense pain radiated through her leg. The ache was but a drop compared to the agony in her heart.

The pain cleared her mind. *The stone!* A shiver ran over her shoulders and down her spine. She had the blue sunstone of legend, but the cost was great—her sister's and Kitani's lives.

Aramie glanced at her friend, thankful she'd survived. "Let's go. Call for a portal."

There was always a balance in life. Aramie wouldn't let the death of her sister and Kitani stand for nothing. She'd get this stone to Demir, heal him. Then, she'd search out Ram and slice his throat with her own claw.

Chapter Thirteen

Zedron jogged up the stairs two at a time, eager to arrive at the market. Although he was in decent shape, his ragged breaths heaved in and out of his lungs. He'd spent too much time deciding which sandals complemented his tailored pants and fine woven shirt, making him late to the auction. Straightening his jacket, he smiled. With his clean-shaven face and slicked back hair, he was as handsome as ever.

Up in the trees, the Lemurian landscape was a sea of branches and leaves, interspersed with the pathways, platforms, and stairs that wove their community together. A warm breeze blew, flapping the leaves to and fro, creating a soft hum. The Etila and Rolmdew trees were the lifeblood of Lemuria and the safest place for its inhabitants.

With one hand to steady himself against the smooth bark of the nearest tree, he glanced over the edge of the fence. Branches and vines snaked between the trees obscuring the dense Lemurian forest, and the dangers that lay on the surface—rhondo beasts. The large black animals with their oily skin, sharp teeth, and scissor-like claws were a danger to anyone who dared to roam the surface of the planet. The idea of being ravaged by one of those beasts caused goosebumps. He shook himself, and continued on his way.

A giant platform with wooden slats stretched between four tall Etila trees. The small limbs and leaves at the top entwined as if holding hands. They provided a nice canopy, keeping the heat to a bearable level and would adjust as the sun moved across the sky.

A few dozen Lemurians stood in small groups. Their loud voices and laughter carried along on the breeze. Merchants and buyers alike, they smelled of money and too much drappervine. An older male stood nearby. He had the round paunch and red nose that went along with overindulgence.

Zedron curled his lip. He disdained others without control.

The overweight male made him feel dirty. Reflexively, he brushed his sleeves, as if whisking away some imagined dirt. Along the far edge of the platform, a small group of Arotaars stood close together. The shackles around their wrists and ankles identified them as the auctioneer's trade. A female with short blue hair stood out from the rest. The orange spots on her light skin signified her origin.

A sense of giddiness sent Zedron's pulse racing. There were only a few Arotaars from the planet Arotin on Lemuria. Not all survived the transport, but those who did were excellent slaves.

An image surfaced in his mind. Alora with her hands clenched into fists, a few strands of blond hair escaping her tight bun, her brow furrowed over blue eyes. Anger was all he saw from her anymore. Although Alora had grown up in a slave faction family, she hated slavery. She'd rebelled and switched to the free faction

not long after leaving her family home. For him to purchase an Arotaar would

ignite her temper like nothing else. When she found out what he'd done she'd

chastise him, but he'd get to see her again.

He smiled. *Absolute perfection.*

"Time for the auction. Gather round!" The robust fellow he'd spotted earlier

motioned with his giant paw of a hand for everyone to come to the center of the

platform.

The wood creaked and groaned as the trees swayed in the breeze. The draft

caressed the back of Zedron's neck, cooling the sweat he'd emitted despite the

tree's canopy. The perspiration would stain his collar and ruin his perfect, styled

image. He clenched his jaw.

The crowd swarmed around the merchant. Zedron pushed himself to the

front, garnering a few scowls and shoves along the way. In the middle of the

platform, a small dais stood ready for the first slave.

A petite, yellow-skinned female from the Drakin colony hopped onto the raised

floor. Her fingers trembled as she gripped the edges of her shirt. With her eyes

downcast, long white hair covered her features. One of the bidders would become

her new master, but not Zedron. He'd already selected his next servant.

"Bidding starts at twenty livins." The slave trader strutted back and forth in

front of his merchandise, his large gut straining against the buttons of his shirt.

Zedron smirked. Surely, one would pop soon.

"Twenty-five livins."

"Thirty livins."

Zedron tuned out the bidding and focused on the Arotaar female. She studied her surroundings, as if looking for a way to escape. With her head held high, her eyes glowed with intelligence and determination. She would challenge him, and he'd punish her for it. *Perfect.*

A newb no more than seven years old approached, and he focused on Zedron's lapel pin—the one that identified him as a Colonizer. He stopped mere inches away and gripped Zedron's pant leg. "Sir, are you a Colonizer?"

Zedron bent down on one knee, bringing himself eye level with the young Lemurian. "Why, yes. Would you like to touch my pin?"

The young male's eyes widened. "Could I?"

Zedron nodded. The youth grazed the finely etched gold, reverence forming in his eyes.

Zedron clasped his hand on the young male's shoulder and stood. "Study hard, and you, too, can become a Colonizer."

"Utaun! Utuan!" A female's voice rose above the din of the crowd. The boy bowed, and then ran off toward her call.

Zedron smiled, his chest filling with pride. The merchant's litany brought him out of his reverie, and he refocused on his task. After the sale of a few males and another female, his prize stepped onto the platform. A visible tic formed in her clenched jaw. She pulled against the manacles binding her wrists. The chains rattled above the din of the crowd.

"Ooh, we have an Arotaar here. She's lean, strong, able to handle much hard work." The trader's sweat reeked of his addiction. He released the top button of his shirt and wiped his brow with the back of his hand. "She will command a much higher price. Bidding starts at one hundred livins."

A low murmur rippled through the crowd. The minimum bid was high, but the cunning trader knew his job. He was right to request such a sum. Zedron had anticipated as much.

He stepped forward to have a better look at the female. Her tattered pants and ripped shirt hung on her frame. She seemed to have lost weight on her journey here, but strength showed in her taut legs and developed biceps.

He nodded in appreciation. "One hundred fifty livins."

She caught him looking at her and held his gaze. Her nostrils flared. She had spirit and that brought a smile to his face.

"Two hundred livins," another bidder shouted above the noisy crowd.

Zedron clenched his jaw. He wouldn't participate in a bidding war for this female. When he spoke, his voice was low, but commanding. "One thousand livins."

The female flinched at his words. Her eyes narrowed.

The crowd quieted.

When no one else bid, the trader pointed his finger at Zedron. "Sold…to this fine male."

Zedron's fingers tingled as a sense of giddiness raced along his nerves. He couldn't wait to bring his new servant home and begin the domestication process.

Chapter Fourteen

The heat from the upcoming day settled over Aramie's skin. Her heartbeat raced. Fear crept into her gut, twisting it tight. She had the cure for Demir in her pocket. Could she and Jonue make it back to the Keep before the sun killed them?

A vision of her imaginary father formed in her head, as he often did during times of stress. She longed to ask him what to do, but even in her mind, the words wouldn't come. He placed his dream-like hand on her shoulder. *Fight, Aramie, live!*

"The portal." Jonue's words held a tinge of hope, pulling Aramie out of her daydream.

Aramie stared into the mist. Through the fog, the outline of rocks formed, solidifying into the Portal Navigation Center. In the middle of the chamber, Rin stood over the *Porte Stanen*. As he moved his hands over the crystals, the ring of concentric sunstones burned bright beneath his fingers.

He waved his hand. "Hurry!"

Aramie raced through the hole and into the Keep, Jonue right behind her. Having left their boots at the edge of Blue Pool, their bare feet slapped against the stone floor.

"What did you do? You said you were goin' hunting? The smell of Gossum clings to you like dirt." The little man put his hands on his hips. His pinched eyebrows and downturned lips would've made Sidea laugh. A spike of pain burrowed into Aramie's chest.

"Weren't ya a party of four?" His mouth remained open and his gaze slid between them.

Jonue lowered her chin. "We lost two to the Gossum."

"Ah, *craya*!" His shook his head. "Are ya injured? I called for medical when I got yer message."

"Just a few scrapes and bruises. Nothing to worry about." Aramie wiped her mouth with the back of her hand.

The sound of several pairs of running feet echoed from the hallway. Saar, Noeh's Commander of Arms, entered the room followed by three of his fellow fighters. Saar seemed ready for battle with his gold armbands and a short sword that dangled from his waist. His comrades wore similar attire.

Saar evaluated Aramie and Jonue. "Rin called for medical. Do you need help?"

"I need to see Gaetan. I…have something to show him, something he won't believe." Aramie stared into his eyes.

Saar chuckled. "Gaetan is older than the hills. I doubt anything would surprise him at this point, but be my guest. I believe he's in the infirmary."

Even though she shivered with the pain of losing her sister, Aramie clamped down on the tears that threatened. Instead, she turned to Jonue and forced an encouraging smile. "You did well tonight."

Jonue's features softened for the briefest moment, and she placed her hand on Aramie's arm. "I'll catch up with you later."

The skittering of claws on stone caught Aramie's attention. Leon and Hallan entered the room in panther form. Leon searched the group, and his eyes flashed yellow, displaying his displeasure. Both males changed into human form. Hallan approached his mate and wrapped Jonue in his embrace.

Leon puffed out his chest, blocking the doorway. "Where's Kitani?"

Aramie swallowed, and the hair on the back of her neck stood on end. She raised her chin and held his gaze. "I...I'm sorry, Leon. We were attacked...Kitani...she fought against the Gossum and died a warrior's death—"

"No! I told her not to go." He breathed through clenched teeth, his shoulders visibly heaving from the exertion.

Aramie's heart ached for this male's loss. "Leon—I wish—"

The angry male lunged at her, but before he could get close, Saar wrapped him in a bear hug. "There'll be no fighting in the Keep, unless it's in the training center."

Aramie raised her hand. "It's ok, Saar. He's hurting...that's understandable." She focused on Leon. "I'm truly sorry for your loss."

Leon thrust his arms into the air, pushing Saar away. He turned his attention to Aramie. "It's your fault she's gone. You'll pay for this." Spittle flew from his mouth.

"I'm sure I will, but right now, I have to see Gaetan." With her head held high, she walked past the distraught male and raced down the hallway. Her heart filled with conviction, causing her chest to ache. She'd make sure Ram paid for killing her sister and Kitani. The bulge in her pocket pressed against her thigh, and the need to get the sacred stone to Gaetan burned in her raw throat.

*****

"Gaetan."

"Aramie, it's good to see you again." Gaetan gripped her hand between his warm palms. His scrutinizing gaze roamed her face. "Come, sit down."

Releasing her hand, he grabbed his cane that leaned against the edge of the counter. He sat on his stool, the wood groaning under his weight. With tender care he rubbed his misshapen leg, and the dark marking that ran down his arm and into his hand moved eerily in the light.

The scent of cleaning fluid masked the smell of blood and sweat. Scalpels, scissors, tape, and gauze were scattered across the countertop, some partially covered by a towel.

"I don't have time. I…We…" Her voice wavered, and she pursed her lips.

"I can tell you have something important to say. It will be easier if you relax." He motioned to one of the examinations tables.

She sat on the nearest one, her feet dangling over the edge. Adrenaline raced along her nerves, and a wall of pain threatened near her heart. She kicked her legs back and forth, anything to burn off some of her energy—and stave off her grief.

A sad smile crept across his face. "What brings you to visit me?"

"I found the blue sunstone." With shaky hands, she pulled the sacred crystal from the pocket of her damp pants. The room lit up with an eerie glow.

Gaetan gasped and stood faster than she imagined possible. His stool crashed against the stone floor. "How? Where?"

"Blue Pool is real. The crystal was in a small cave underneath the dry waterfall. We found it—" She choked on the words. Her sister had sacrificed her life for this stone. Tears welled in Aramie's eyes, and she glanced at the floor.

Sidea would never take another breath, would never laugh, would never shed another tear. There wasn't anything Aramie could do to bring her back. A sob broke through Aramie's control, wracking her body.

Gaetan squeezed her shoulder, his hand warm and soothing. "Tell me."

She peered into his eyes. Like an old sage, comfort and experience with loss were evident in the wrinkles in his brow and around his eyes.

"Sidea—" She bit her lip to stop the quiver.

Gaetan pulled her into an embrace and rubbed her back with his strong hand. "I'm sorry for your loss."

He released her, yet the warmth he'd provided still lingered. Her mind fogged with grief, her chest so tight, she wanted to scream. She slid off the exam table and walked over to the cabinet. A myriad of bottles lined the shelves, some with elixirs, some with herbs, others with different colors of sunstones from opaque to orange to deep red. She studied her nails, the edges ragged from her attempts to grab hold of the rocks as she'd tossed and turned in the current before she'd lost consciousness.

"Do you want to talk about it?" Gaetan's encouraging words brought her back to the present.

She nodded. "While I retrieved the sunstone, Gossum attacked our party. Ram—" Her breath caught in her throat. She turned to face Gaetan. "He's still alive."

"That's…not possible. Noch killed him."

"There's no doubt in my mind. Ram lives."

"He killed your sister." Gaetan whispered.

"And Kitani. I can't believe they're gone." A storm brewed inside, her grief fueling her need for vengeance.

"We have to tell Noch." Gaetan's words hit home.

Of course, the king should know his nemesis lived.

Her heart still heavy with the death of her sister, Aramie offered the crystal to the old healer. "Gaetan, the stone—Demir."

He glanced from her eyes to the stone and back again. "To touch the blue sunstone is a great honor. To use it, a great opportunity. With any opportunity, there is risk. If I use this on Demir, it may not work. Even if he revives, he may not be the same male you once knew. Will you accept the consequences?"

"I will, I must. He is our leader." Aramie's jaw ached from tension, and the muscles in her arms and legs were rigid. Demir needed to live, no matter the cost. Sidea would expect nothing less, and Aramie couldn't let her sister's death stand for nothing. Besides, once healed, Demir would rule the pride once again, and she'd be free to seek her revenge.

Chapter Fifteen

Mauree crossed her legs, but she couldn't get comfortable on the rickety old chair. It squeaked when she moved, the solitary sound loud in her single cell. The Strong room was far under the main levels of the Keep and she was its only inhabitant...ever. They'd built the cell long ago, just in case, but the Stiyaha were an ever-loyal bunch. *Gah!* Giving up on the chair, she walked the three steps to the iron bars that graced the entrance to her humble abode.

She placed her forehead against the barrier, straining to see down the hallway. Light emitted from the sunstones lining the corridor, the soft illumination stretching off in either direction. A knot built in her stomach, hardening until her blood pressure spiked, sending a wave of adrenaline through her veins.

Wrapping her hand around the bars, she tried to force the iron to bend to her will, but to no avail. She was stuck in here until someone decided to let her out...that someone being King Noeh. At the thought of him, all her anger dissipated. Instead, a great weight settled onto her chest.

"I was supposed to be queen." She choked on the words, and they sounded pathetic even to her own ears.

A single tear ran over her cheek, and she caught it with the back of her finger. She carefully studied the droplet. *I won't cry over him, not anymore.* Yet, even as she told herself this, another tear escaped. After she'd kidnapped and turned the future queen over to the enemy, she'd earned her status as a traitor, and *that* she couldn't ignore.

The scent of fresh pineapple wafted along the slight breeze. Mauree's pulse increased and she stepped to the bars once again. "Ginnia, is that you?"

"No." Ginnia's youthful voice echoed off the stone walls.

"C'mon dear, you must be here to visit me. Right?"

"I suppose, but I don't want to. You're Meanie Maureenie."

Ugh. Of all the ones in the Keep to come here, it had to be her…the scatterbrained seer. They'd never gotten along. Ginnia had always been a bother, someone to avoid. For her to visit now meant something was up. A shiver of hope raced into Mauree's heart.

Ginnia came into view, her brown hair sticking out in all directions. She wore a yellow dress with bright pink polka dots. Even though she was an adult female, she looked and acted like a young child. Ever since her accident as a newb, her body had grown, but not her mind. Mauree couldn't stand the female, but she had to put on a front to find out why she was here.

Mauree pasted on her best smile. "Hello, Ginnia. Good to see you."

"You no like me. I know."

Mauree rolled her eyes. "Aw, dear, can we forget about that?"

The strange female kicked at some imaginary dirt, her gaze directed at the stone floor. Her hands were behind her back, a book in her grasp, the edges visible as she moved back and forth.

Goosebumps formed along Mauree's arms. "What do you have there?"

Ginnia stomped her foot. "You weren't supposed to see this yet."

"See what? I don't see anything." Mauree held out her hands in mock surrender.

"You're a liar. No wonder Noeh doesn't like you." Ginnia's eyes flecked with gold.

Mauree huffed. "Tell me why you're here, or don't bother me."

"See, I knew you'd be that way, but I had to come. You need to tell Tanen where Jakar is."

Mauree slapped her palm to her forehead. "You, too?" *Craya*. She had no idea that bit of information would be so valuable. Tanen has been relentless with the same questions. Mauree jutted out her chin—let them try to get it out of her.

Returning her focus to Ginnia, she leaned against the bars, a slow, sly smile tugging at her lips. "Let me out, and I'll tell you Jakar's location."

Ginnia's gaze darted down the hallway then returned to Mauree. She ran one hand up her arm and when she spoke, her voice was a mere whisper. "You have to tell Tanen."

"What happens if I don't?"

"I can't tell you that, not now. Why do you have to be so frustrating?" Ginnia gripped the book in her hands, her nails digging into the soft leather. She glanced into the hallway once again. "I have to go. Here, read this."

The strange female shoved the book through the bars and let go. The old tome tumbled from her grasp. Mauree caught it before the ancient text hit the hard stone floor. Ginnia fled down the corridor, her soft footsteps receding until silence regained its foothold.

Mauree flipped the tome over and read the cover. Her heart skipped a beat. Why had the strange seer given her this book? She touched the gilded lettering as she reread the title. *Basic Self-Defense.*

A twinge of hope grew inside. Ginnia giving her this book was an omen. Whether the harbinger was good or bad, she wasn't quite sure, but it didn't matter. She'd fight for her freedom if she got the opportunity. Without further delay, she cracked open the text and read.

Chapter Sixteen

Demir's body rattled and shook as the medical cart raced down the corridor. Two large Stiyaha warriors held on to his legs and arms as the cart careened over the rough floor. The cart tilted twice as they rounded a bend, sending Demir sliding dangerously close to the edge.

A door groaned on its hinges. Air blew across Demir's face, causing his hair to tickle his cheeks. Cleaning fluid and dried blood filtered into his senses. The edge of the cart bumped against something. Demir jostled against the gurney's hard surface. Gentle they were not. He expected nothing more from these warriors. They had a job to do, and taking care of the infirm was not on their normal to-do list.

Wood creaked nearby. Someone huffed and groaned, as if they'd risen from a chair or a stool. Footsteps approached.

"Lay him on the exam table." Gaetan's steady voice gave no clue as to why Demir was here.

Demir was placed onto a cold surface. Goosebumps rose on his arms and legs. The thin shorts still covered him. Thank the gods the string hadn't come untied. He didn't need the humiliation of baring his male parts to these fierce warriors.

Anger built inside, festering, until bile rose in his throat. Great, he'd given himself an ulcer. He growled in his mind, his caged cat eager to break free.

"If you need anything else, let us know." The two warriors departed. The door's latch clicked shut behind them.

"Good morning, Demir. I'm going to check your vitals and get some readings. Ok?" Gaetan placed his warm hand on Demir's shoulder. His fingers moved to Demir's wrist and held on for a few seconds.

Demir felt like a child and that burned inside. He was a grown male, leader of the Panthera Pride. To be stuck in his body unable to move was a torture far worse than death.

Gaetan's fingers tugged on Demir's eyelids and a bright light flashed over his lenses. Pain lit up in his brain, and he caught a glimpse of Gaetan's pursed lips before his eyelid shut once again.

Demir's catlike hearing caught the sound of running feet sifting under the edges of the doorway.

A soft knock on the door beckoned.

"Enter." Gaetan's calm voice echoed around the infirmary.

The door creaked. The scent of strawberries wafted into the room. Aramie—he'd know her perfume anywhere.

"I stopped to change out of my damp clothes. He…looks—"

Gaetan's brisk words cut her off. "Fine. He looks fine."

Silence. Soft footsteps approached. Her warm fragrance seeped into his senses and ran along his nerves, calming him and exciting him at the same time. She grazed her fingers over his arm, leaving a trace of electricity in her wake. Her fingernails dug into the skin on his forearm.

"Gaetan—"

"Did you bring the stone?"

"Yes. Since you insisted I hold on to it, the crystal hasn't left my possession."

She released her grip on his arm. The emptiness left him cold.

Clothes rustled next to him. An eerie blue glow replaced the soft orange light that filtered through his eyelids. Straining against the bonds that imprisoned him, he tried to open his eyes, but he was helpless. He squirmed inside his skin.

Gaetan gasped. "It's…glowing. The blue sunstone was dark earlier."

"Do you think the crystal senses its purpose?" Aramie whispered.

"Perhaps. If I remember the legend correctly, the blue sunstone healed a warrior who sacrificed himself for another." Gaetan shuffled toward his cabinet filled with herbs and concoctions.

"Maybe the sunstone knows that Demir saved Noeh's life. Is that possible?"

"As you well know, anything in our world is possible. Here, let me hold it."

Aramie left Demir's side and her absence made his chest ache. *What is happening to me?* Ever since she'd joined the Pride, he'd seen her as a warrior and had treated her like one of the males. His stomach hardened with his frustration.

The cadence of uneven footsteps headed his way. Gaetan pulled the sheet to his waist. Demir cringed inside. He didn't want Aramie to see his weakened body. He was her alpha, she his second in command. Weakness was something he could never show her. A twinge in his brain told him there was another, deeper reason, but he refused to acknowledge it.

A soft gasp escaped her lips.

A cool, hard object rested on his abdomen. A flicker of hope grew in his chest. The object warmed, and heat radiated from his center, penetrating under his skin.

"The crystal…hurts my eyes." Aramie's words were strained.

Energy built from the stone and traveled along his nerves. Every fiber vibrated to the cadence of his increasing heartbeat.

Medical utensils clattered to the ground. Footsteps retreated. Glass shattered. A cacophony of sounds blended in with the blood rushing through his ears. The room heated, and the Keep rumbled.

"Cover your eyes!" Gaetan shouted.

Demir's body shook. Power filtered through his veins. Bones rattled along with the energy pulsing from the sunstone. His head hit the exam table, sending white sparks to blend in with the blue light. Against his will, his body bounced on the table. The clatter banged against the stone walls and reverberated around the room.

Pain filtered into his brain as muscles and tendons expanded, grew to encompass the strength his body once possessed. The blue light brightened, sounds seemed louder, his body moved faster. He had no control. Maybe the stone would kill him.

Noooo. He wanted to live.

The blue light blinked out. He stilled.

Heavy breathing was the only sound in the room.

"Demir." Aramie's soft voice grounded him. She gripped his hand, her fingers tight around his.

Wood creaked as the old healer settled his weight on his stool. "That was quite a show. Is he conscious?"

Demir tried to open his eyes, but his muscles wouldn't respond to his command. Frustration built inside.

Aramie's hand was soft against his, and the skin-on-skin contact lit up his nerves. He pushed against the invisible barrier, concentrating on Aramie and her hold on him. His finger twitched.

She gasped, and released his hand only to put her warm palms on his chest. Her fingers pressed into his skin as she gave him a small shake. "Demir. Wake up."

Lightning bolts of sensation radiated from the contact. He inhaled and sat upright. Instinct drove him, and he pulled Aramie close, chest to chest. The smell of her recent shower blended with her unique scent. He had the sudden urge to bite her on the shoulder, to claim her as his mate. A growl of pure masculine possession and need broke from his lips.

She stilled next to him. In the spur of the moment, her hands had landed on his biceps. He wanted her to run her fingers all over his body and light up more than his nerves. Her beautiful brown eyes danced with a liquid fire he wanted to devour.

She pulled back, and he released her.

Confusion blurred his mind. Where did these thoughts come from? He'd never noticed Aramie before. She was one of his warriors, nothing more, yet he couldn't deny his attraction to her.

"Aramie." After weeks of non-use, his vocal cords made her name sound rough and sensual.

"Demir." She bowed her head.

Her allegiance floored him.

Gaetan cleared his throat. "How do you feel?"

Demir pulled his focus away from his second in command. A part of him didn't want to, and a sense of unease rippled through his gut. The reason for his primal reaction to her was something he didn't want to contemplate.

He peered at the Keep's haelen. The old Stiyaha leaned on his cane. Amber reflected from the stick's tip where a large sunstone glinted under his palm.

Demir rubbed the stubble of his goatee and ran his hand through his hair. The strands fell around his shoulders, almost to his biceps. No one had cut it while he'd been in his coma. That was fine. He liked the feel of his hair on his skin. As a Panthera, physical sensations were heightened, especially touch.

"I'm fine. Seems the blue crystal works."

Gaetan gave a quick nod in response.

Demir stretched his arms over his head, enjoying how his muscles responded to his command. The sensation was so freeing, so powerful. As he relaxed, his need for information burned in his chest. He frowned and focused on Gaetan. "Tell me. What happened?"

A slow smile pulled at Gaetan's mouth, and he pointed at Aramie.

Demir glanced at her. Memories of their conversations in his room invaded his mind. "You took over the Pride."

She focused on him and raised her chin. "*You* are Pride leader."

He studied her. The red barrette in her hair caught his attention. It was the only bit of color he'd ever seen her wear. He'd never paid much attention to the bauble before, but its brightness brought out the redness in her lips. For a brief instant, he wanted to ravish them.

She dropped her gaze and bit her lip.

In the short time he'd known her, he'd learned enough to know she hid something. She'd looked devastated for a moment, but it wasn't fatigue in her eyes, it was something much worse. He placed his finger under her chin and forced her to look at him. "Who died?"

Chapter Seventeen

Zedron took a sip of muldoberry wine from his favorite glass. He traced his finger over the long stem, enjoying its smooth elegance. With a quick swirl, the sweet bouquet wafted into the air, comforting and relaxing him. He placed the edge of the glass against his lips and downed the last swallow. *Now, this is the true nectar of the gods.* He chuckled to himself.

The afternoon sun beat down on the trees, heating his home to a stifling level. The muggy air caused him to break out in a sweat. He pursed his lips. There was no relief from the relentless heat except at night. Until then, he'd have to tough it out. His shirt clung to his back, the wetness cooling him off, but this was one of his better shirts, and he refused to ruin it with sweat stains. Time to change.

After placing the empty glass on the table next to his beloved armchair, he headed upstairs. The wooden stairway creaked under his feet. In his bedroom, he ripped off his dirty shirt and tossed it into the hamper. Carine would wash his clothes later. A smile tugged at his lips. The more work he made for her, the better. A bowl of water sat on his dresser, along with a rag. She'd anticipated his needs. Maybe she'd work out after all.

He placed the small towel in the water, wrung it out, and wiped his torso. The precious, cool water was not to be taken lightly. Lemuria had a diminishing supply of the valuable liquid, and the rainy season became shorter every year. This was the reason Earth was so coveted. To win the war for the blue planet's water would be an important victory. He inhaled, a new determination forming in his gut. After pulling a fresh shirt from his drawer, he redressed.

The smell of smoke wafted through the window. Even through the Elita tree branches, a soft glow burned in the distance. *Fire.* Adrenaline shot through him. This was his chance to pad his generous coffers. Others would need a loan to rebuild, and he had the funds to help out those poor souls. Their loss was his gain.

"Carine!" He ran back the way he'd come, his feet pounding the stairs with the force of his urgency. "Carine!"

"What is it?" She appeared from the bathroom, a cleaning rag in her hand.

"There's a fire. I need to go…assess the damages…help the underserved."

Despite all the technology his race possessed, they hadn't figured out a way to tackle the fires that plagued the planet with anything better than water and a bit of talmet powder. The water reserves dwindled more each time a fire erupted. There was still enough for several more years, but eventually they'd run out, and Lemuria would become a desert, forcing the Lemurians to seek shelter on other planets. The need to secure Earth's water spurned him on.

He gripped Carine's arm. "Don't worry. I'll return shortly."

The lines around her eyes tightened as she studied him. Her defiance radiated from her body in waves. "Of course, *master*."

He raced out the door and ran along the platform connecting his treehouse home to the network of other homes in the area, crossing pathways and stairways along the way. The smoke thickened, and the horrible stench of burning leaves and wood eased into his lungs with every breath. A wracking cough burst from his lips, but he didn't stop. His need to see the flames, and the damage it would do, drove him forward.

As he approached, Lemurians fleeing the scene raced by, making it difficult for him to proceed. He pushed his way past a young mother, her hand gripped tightly around her daughter's hand. The young girl squealed in pain as he stepped on her foot. He didn't stop to apologize, his need to arrive spurning him onward.

Arriving at the scene, he slowed. Flames engulfed several trees, the hungry blaze reaching and trying to devour unscathed leaves in nearby branches. Standing on a large platform, several Lemurians held a long hose and worked together to put out the flames. Precious water spewed from the tube's end, dampening the fire, preventing it from spreading. In the middle of the group—Veromé.

He wore a black, insulating suit and a pair of protective eyewear, but his brown hair hung loose around his shoulders. His body shook from the force of the water pouring through the hose. Of course Veromé would help, that was his style, at least in public. Zedron's jaw popped, as it did sometimes when he clenched his teeth. He seethed inside, his breaths ragged.

Males and females alike worked in teams to battle the flames. A male he didn't know shoved a large bag of talmet powder into his hands. "Here, throw this into the fire. Anything it touches will become non-flammable."

Zedron gripped the heavy bag, his arms straining from the weight. He pursed his lips. "I'm not here to fight the fire. I'm here to assess the damages."

The male raked his gaze over Zedron's body, appraising him. His lip pulled up at the corner. "Put out the flames. Assess the loss later."

Zedron's face heated. For him to help in this mundane way was beneath him. He raised his chin. "I'll help with the hose." He dropped the bag, and before the other man could respond, he headed for the platform—the one with Veromé.

He grabbed a protective coat and glasses from a nearby pile and put them on. His heart pounded. He'd never fought in a fire before, and a mixture of excitement and fear flooded his system.

He slipped unnoticed behind Veromé and gripped the hose. The moment his hands connected with the line, the water's power vibrated up his arms. His biceps strained from the force.

Standing behind his one-time best friend, he observed how the male moved. Veromé's physical strength and determination radiated from his feat. Zedron's stomach hardened. He wanted to throttle his rival, bring him down, and make him pay for stealing Alora. His grip on the hose tightened.

Despite the intensity of the flames, the group's efforts against the fire brought success. The contained fire would burn itself out in a matter of minutes. Cheers from the crowd of civilian firefighters rose into the air.

A young woman approached, her mouth pursed, eyes determined. "Turning off the hose in five, four, three, two, one," she ordered.

The line slackened, the power of the water reduced to a trickle.

Veromé's shoulders visibly relaxed and a loud whoop burst from his lips. The male in front of him slapped Veromé on the shoulder in a good-natured jab. Veromé turned to face Zedron. His smile faltered, his laugh subsided.

Zedron's lip curled at the corner, and his heart rate picked up. "My, my, aren't you glad to see me." He raised an eyebrow. "The feeling is mutual."

"What are you doing here?" Veromé's face was a mask, his rage only evident in the tic in his jaw.

"Helping out. Why else would I come here?"

"To find a way to take advantage of someone else's loss and misery, no doubt."

Zedron compressed his lips. "You have such a high opinion of me, how charming."

"This is ridiculous. I have better things to do." Veromé turned his back on Zedron and helped another male gather the hose.

Zedron's face reddened at the blatant dismissal. He clenched his fist, the desire to strike out almost more than he could bear. "Your taste in fine jewelry is, shall we say, a bit suspect. No wonder Alora won't wear the bracelet you gave her."

Veromé visibly tensed under his jacket. With a slow turn, he faced Zedron. "What did you say?"

"I think you heard me just fine." Zedron studied his fingernails and let his grin spread.

"How do you know about the bracelet?" Veromé gripped Zedron's coat at the neckline.

Zedron lifted his gaze and placed his hand around Veromé's wrist. "Let go, or I will have you placed into custody for assault."

Veromé released him with a shove. "Stay away from Alora. She's my female, not yours."

Zedron narrowed his attention on his rival. "Do you know what your mate does at night when you're not around? Hmmm? Maybe you should find out."

Zedron didn't see the punch coming until his head whipped to the side. His jaw ached and the taste of blood filled his mouth.

"Stop."

"That's enough."

Two males, one on each side of Veromé, had their arms wrapped around Veromé's biceps, holding him back.

Zedron wiped his lip. Blood coated his fingers. The pressure in his veins rose along with his temper. He curled his lip. "Better watch yourself, Veromé. This game we play...I *always* win and when I do, Alora will be mine."

Chapter Eighteen

"Who died?" Demir's words pierced Aramie's heart. His coarse hand still held her chin, and his gaze bore into her. Deep pools of brown, his eyes reminded her of rich, dark chocolate. She melted under his scrutiny and couldn't maintain eye contact any longer. As she pulled away, his fingers trailed along her chin in the process.

"Sidea and Kitani." Her throat constricted and she couldn't say another word.

"Tell me." His voice was as coaxing as it was commanding.

"I'll give you two some time alone." Gaetan rose from his stool and hobbled to the door. "Come to the King's Chamber when you're done. Noeh will want know about the stone and that you've recovered. I'll let him know you're on your way."

Demir's eyebrows creased. "We'll get there when we're ready."

Now that was the leader Aramie remembered. The command in the timbre of his voice sent a chill over her arm. He wasn't the kind of male who took orders from anyone. He'd ruled his Pride long before she and Sidea had joined them, and long before they'd come to the Keep.

"Take all the time you need." Gaetan's eyes sparkled with amusement. He pocketed the blue sunstone in his pants, its brilliance snuffed out like a fire.

The door closed behind him with a soft click, leaving Aramie alone with her Pride leader.

A memory of when she'd first met him surfaced in her mind. She tried to push the image aside but failed.

"Stop struggling. Who are you?" A large male pinned Aramie down on the ground. Dirt rubbed against her cheek and a blackberry bramble scraped her arm. His warm scent of musk and incense filled her senses.

She struggled anew, unwilling to give an inch to this male that had jumped her in panther form. She and Sidea had tracked the Pride from afar for several days. They were the lone survivors from their own Pride which had been attacked a few weeks ago.

This wasn't the first time they'd been on their own. They'd lived for many years by themselves after their mother had abandoned them.

"Let me go." She kicked out, planting the heel of her boot into his thigh.

He grunted and tightened his grip around her body. His legs closed over hers. She strained against his hold, but couldn't move.

Sidea's cry filled the air.

"I've got the other one." The deep timbre of a male's voice echoed between the fir trees.

"Release her." Aramie said through gritted teeth.

Demir laughed. "You trespass on my territory and then threaten me while I hold you down. You are a unique one." His chuckle reverberated through her back and into her chest setting off all kinds of strange, pleasant sensations. He bent his head close to her ear, and the short hairs on his chin tickled her skin.

"What's your name?" he purred.

Her muscles strained against him. She didn't want to give in to this male, but she couldn't break his hold on her. Bastard. Fine. *She'd play along. "Aramie. Now let me go."*

Instead of releasing her, he pulled her further under his body, his control complete. "Aramie. Such a fine name. Now, what are you doing in my territory?"

Although he'd pinned her in place, he hadn't hurt her. The truth was he'd been extra careful with her, protecting her with his own body from the sharp rocks that littered the path.

Her muscles ached from the strain of fighting against his hold, so she exhaled and relaxed. "My sister and I are on the run. Our pride was attacked by Gossum. We are the only ones left."

Demir released her and stood. Strong hands lifted her from the ground, and she faced him for the first time. His deep brown eyes and full lips made her still. He was handsome in a rugged sort of way.

As he studied her, his gaze roamed from her eyes to her shoes, taking in her tattered shirt and mud-stained pants. His focus returned to hers, and his features softened. "I am Demir, and my Pride lives in this territory. Where was your Pride?"

"On the Eastern border of the Rockies. We're passing through."

"Take your hands off me." Sidea's voice was like a melody to Aramie's ears.

A large male crashed through the trees, his hand wrapped around Sidea's arm. Aramie's nerves calmed at the sight of her sister.

"Where were you headed?" Demir asked.

Aramie didn't have any idea. Away from the Gossum was the only answer that came to mind, but she wasn't going to tell him.

"By your silence, I assume nowhere." He raised an eyebrow. "We recently merged with a Pride who suffered a similar fate. We could use a couple more females. You shall join our Pride."

His arrogance flared the flames of her anger. She narrowed her eyes at him. "We are warriors. What makes you think we want to join you and your Pride?"

He laughed. Despite her anger, she enjoyed the deep resonance of his voice and how it sent a tickle down her spine. Aramie didn't want to be in a Pride, but something about Demir called to her.

"Because you have nowhere else to go."

She held his gaze. He was right, and that galled her. "We'll stay, but as warriors, not as some male's mated female."

"Aramie? What are you doing?" Sidea's voice wavered.

Aramie didn't look at her sister, but held up two fingers, their sign for "trust me."

"If you can best the warriors who try to make you their mate, then I agree. Are you up for the challenge?" Demir smirked. The diamond stud above his lip glinted in the light.

"Accepted." A drop of trepidation raced along her spine, but she and Sidea couldn't run forever. They needed the protection of a Pride. It might as well be this one.

"Aramie, did you hear me?"

The sound of Demir's voice pulled her out of her reverie, and she wiped her face with the back of her hand. "Say again?"

Demir stroked his goatee, his gaze tracking her. "I think I've pieced together what's happened over the past few weeks—from your visits."

Aramie's breath caught in her throat. "Um. Y-you heard me?"

He studied her. Close enough for her to see her own reflection in his eyes. She swallowed, afraid of his response.

"I did. You led the Pride in my absence. I couldn't have asked for a better second in command."

Her cheeks heated as a mixture of delight and disappointment coursed along her nerves. She glanced at the ground to hide her reaction. What did she expect him to say? He'd pined after Melissa for so long he'd never noticed her standing by his side. Not that anything would ever happen between them. She was a warrior and would stay that way.

Demir's unique scent of musk and incense crept into her system. She trembled, unable to suppress the shiver. Memories of her mother, controlled and dominated by an endless string of males, skipped through her mind. Chantre had escaped one bad relationship only to end up in another while towing Aramie and Sidea along for the ride. That was a path Aramie refused to walk.

She'd had one relationship with a male as a young adult, but he'd become possessive and tried to claim her against her will. Fear had driven her adrenaline to the point she'd bested him and escaped. After that, she'd fought off every male who had attempted to claim her. Demir had never tried. Thankful he hadn't, a part of her wondered what it would it be like to be his mate. She shook her head to clear her rambling thoughts.

He gripped her elbow, and when she looked into his eyes, a strange compassion burned in the brown depths, something she'd not seen from him before. "Tell my about your sister and Kitani. What happened?"

She swallowed, but her throat was dry. "They died…" An image of Ram slicing Sidea's throat filled her mind, cutting off her words.

Demir focused his attention on her. "Aramie, tell me."

Like a flood cresting over the river's boundaries, she couldn't stop the words as they tumbled from her mouth. "They went with me to search for the sacred crystal. Jonue and I found the stone hidden in a chamber underneath a dry waterfall. Sidea and Kitani kept watch—"

Demir's grip on her elbow tightened. "You chased after the blue sunstone to bring me back, but two of our Pride lost their lives to obtain this…crystal. You should never have taken such a risk." His voice became tight, strained.

Adrenaline fueled by her fear and anguish raced through her veins. She couldn't control the fluctuation in her voice when she spoke. "You are our leader. How could I not do whatever was necessary to bring you back?"

"Your desire to revive me is admirable, but I have to live with the shadow of those females' deaths. Why were Kitani and Jonue—mated females—with you in the first place?"

What could she say? She'd broken his rule and let the mated females spar and fight. If he was mad before, wait until he realized what she'd done. She raised her chin and held his gaze. "I did what was necessary to lead this Pride while you were in a coma. I allowed the mated females to train for battle. Kitani and Jonue were ready to fight."

"You did what?" His face reddened and a tick pulsed in his jaw. "You trained the *mated* females and purposefully took two into the forest prepped for combat? Let me guess," he rubbed his goatee with his fingers, "the Gossum found you. Didn't they?"

Her own ire built in response, but the deaths hung heavy on her spirit. "Demir. It's my fault—"

"No. It. Is. Not." He closed his eyes and pinched the bridge of his nose. Although he'd regained his composure, the way his muscles bunched let her know his control was razor-thin. "As Pride leader, the responsibility lies on my shoulders."

His pressed lips and creased brow revealed his torment and pain. "Aramie, as you have broken my rules and lives were lost as a result, I have no choice but to strip you of your role. You are no longer my second in command."

She gaped at him. A deep pain built inside. Her vision swam. A soft whimper escaped her lips turning into a single word. "Nooooo."

She reached for the wall to steady herself. His powerful hands gripped her arms, and she fell against him. This male she'd respected and cared for had ripped her insides to shreds, tossing her pride and sense of self-worth on the ground like scrap, yet she couldn't help her need for *his* comfort.

"I'm sorry, Aramie. I had no choice but to mete out punishment." He massaged her scalp at the base of her neck with his strong fingers. She trembled in his embrace, her devastation and humiliation complete. When he spoke, his words were a harsh whisper. "You knew better, yet you took this chance—for me. Why?"

I care about you, more than I should. Unwilling to look at him, she pulled away and focused on the ground. He let her retreat only so far then lifted her chin. She expected to see pity, but instead raw desire burned in his eyes.

Heat flooded her core, the warmth a gentle surprise. He traced a finger down her jawline, and around to her bottom lip. His gaze riveted there. She licked her lips, and a shiver made her tremble in anticipation.

With a slow grace, he pulled her to him, nearly brushing his lips against hers. A slow moan eased from her parted mouth.

"If I kiss you…I may not stop." His smoky words stoked her desire.

She knew he was trouble, but she couldn't resist him.

"Kiss me," she whispered.

Chapter Nineteen

Demir held Aramie tight. The walls in the infirmary closed around him, pinpointing his vision on the female in his arms. The sunstones dimmed and illuminated her face in a soft radiance. Her sweet scent filtered into his senses. Although he didn't understand what drove his sudden desire to taste her plump lips, he couldn't resist the pull she had on him. He'd given her one last chance to deny him, but instead, she'd spurred him on.

Her panted breaths tickled his skin. The slight breeze of her exhalations tingled the hair on his goatee. Her mouth beckoned to him, and her tongue glided over her bottom lip, stirring a craving he'd never encountered. A strange need to claim her filtered into his mind. He didn't hesitate, capturing her lips with his own. Her wet, warm mouth greeted him, and she moaned under his onslaught.

He wasn't gentle with her, his kiss bruising in its intensity. His heart pounded, pumping blood through his veins. Her fingers trailed along his neck and into his untamed hair. With a tight squeeze, her nails bit into the skin on his scalp, marking him in her own way. A fire burned to life in his chest, fueled by her brazen attitude. Male Panthera were the aggressors, the females passive and submissive.

For her to be so bold was unheard of in their culture. Despite the traditions, or maybe in spite of them, he reacted to her with his own need to claim.

A low growl erupted from his throat, and he broke their kiss. He gazed into her eyes and bared his fangs in a sign of dominance, a traditional move before he bit her and marked her as his. Her eyes dilated in response, but she stiffened in his arms. The contradictory message confused him. He closed his mouth, shielding his fangs, and let her go.

Aramie stepped away. Her furrowed brow and clenched fists made him wince.

Beads of sweat broke out on his skin. His mind fogged. What was he doing? He'd almost bitten her and claimed her as his mate. The temperature in the room plummeted as the Keep reacted to the emotions in the room. A soft rumble shook the walls. The sweat on his arms and back sent a chill racing along his skin. Tension held his muscles taut, along with the realization he'd almost tied himself to a female without much thought. He swallowed the lump of ice-cold fear that had lodged itself in the back of his throat.

Aramie stood her ground and stared at him. "Why…did you…"

Up until now, she'd been a loyal warrior, and from the day they'd met, she'd made it clear she had no intention of becoming a mated female. Then, why had she begged for his kiss, and why did he kiss her? Better yet, why did he want to mark her as his? He shook his head, giving her the best answer he had.

Her cheeks reddened and her lips pursed, but she didn't break eye contact. Her will and determination sent bolts of desire through his body. He didn't want this.

She was nothing like Eleanor. Eleanor had been the best mate a male could ask for—contrite, willing, subservient, quiet—all excellent traits for a mated female. Aramie had none of those qualities and never would. Deep in the recesses of his mind a single word echoed—*good*.

Aramie held his gaze for a moment then closed her eyes. Her shoulders visibly tensed, as if shuttering herself from him. "Gaetan is waiting for us. We should see Noeh." She raised her chin, creases lining her forehead. Despite it all, she still had her pride.

He nodded. "Yes, the king. I'm sure he has many questions."

He didn't want to face Noeh, not after everything that had happened with Melissa. From Aramie's constant litany while he'd been comatose, he'd learned Melissa had bonded with Noeh and was now his queen. She'd born a son, the new prince. He cringed at how he'd treated her. Once the fluid in the dart had filtered into his bloodstream, his warped mind had cleared. His obsession over Melissa had gone too far. He needed to make amends to both the king and the queen.

"After you." He waved his hand toward the door.

His prior second in command passed in front of him. Her strawberry scent lingered and reminded him of their passionate embrace. A part of him longed to kiss her again. Frustration built in his veins, and he slammed the door on his way out.

Chapter Twenty

The bare bulb in the middle of the room cast an eerie glow around the cellar. Ram raised his arms and extended his claws. Against the bare wall, his shadow distorted his true size, making him appear bigger, his claws longer. Euphoria caused his skin to prickle.

The syringes filled with the female's blood leaned against the back of the rickety table like little soldiers ready for battle. Ram had perfected the dosage, duplicating the red blood cells until he'd created enough serum for his entire brood. Unwilling to share the first dose with anyone else, he'd taken the initial hit. A shiver ran down his arm. The new power he possessed would turn him into a creature like his menacing shadow.

Gods, the rush of energy that had coursed through his veins still made him weak with want and brought back memories of another drug, one not nearly as potent. He shook his head. Even after months of not using any heroin, he still craved the high. Too bad the drug no longer worked on his body.

Changed from human to freak almost a year ago, he'd been initiated into this band of Gossum by his prior boss, Ashton. Too bad the old chump hadn't pleased their touchy god, Zedron. Ashton had met an untimely end, one Ram intended to avoid. If the replication worked, he'd be fine.

The scent of stale earth mixed with the sulfur from the chemicals he'd used to create the serum. Beakers lined the tables, surrounded by paper cups and empty vodka bottles from last night's celebration. Obtaining the Panthera's blood before they killed her was crucial. Since the Lemurians disintegrated so quickly once dead, he had to steal the vital fluid before they died.

He chuckled at the memory of the Panthera struggling beneath one of his brood's grasp. The scent of fear had infiltrated into his brain, intensifying his desire for the kill. He'd obtained the blood before the lust broke free. Score one for his team.

"My lord?" Jakar peered through the open door at the top of the stairs. The light from the kitchen encircled his head like a halo, backlighting his face into a mask of shadows. Ram snickered. An angel his first lieutenant was not.

"Jakar, c'mon down. You're the next contestant on The Price of Your Life." Giddiness overwhelmed Ram's senses, and he clapped his hands together. The sound absorbed into the dirt walls in an uncanny fashion.

Jakar took a couple of tentative steps. "You seem…happy, my lord."

"Oh, yes." Ram accentuated the word and it came out in a long hiss. "As my first lieutenant, I'm giving you an…opportunity. Please, come." He waved his hand in the air.

"As you wish, my lord." Jakar descended the stairs. His thin build and short stature belied the strength and stamina he possessed. He fought with astonishing speed and agility. Ram couldn't ask for a better sidekick.

"This," Ram brushed his hand over the plastic containers filled with serum, "is the key to our success."

Jakar sucked in an audible breath. "Is this—" he glanced at Ram, "*all* serum?"

"I knew there was a reason I made you my first lieutenant." Ram chuckled and placed his arm over his comrade's shoulder.

"How did you make so much?"

"I copied the blood cells and—"

Jakar's eyebrows furrowed.

"...uh, never mind." Ram pinched the bridge of his nose and shook his head. Since Gossum were culled from the derelict portion of human society, he often forgot the average "Joe" hadn't had his medical training. Jakar would never understand all the jargon. "Suffice it to say, there is enough for the entire brood."

"Noeh and his kind don't stand a chance." Jakar looked at Ram. "Have you tried it yet?"

"What do you think?" Ram raised an eyebrow.

"Show me." Jakar's body trembled, his eyes brightened.

"I'd rather you experience the serum for yourself." Ram picked a syringe off the table. He flicked the needle's tip with his finger. Droplets of liquid flew through the air. "Here. Enjoy."

Without waiting for a response, Ram jabbed the needle into Jakar's shoulder and pressed the plunger.

Jakar didn't flinch. When the vial was empty, Ram tossed the syringe onto the table. The plastic container bounced a few times before coming to rest next to a pair of pliers.

Jakar's face reddened. His tongue snaked out of his mouth, snapping in the air like a whip. "It burns. My blood—what have you done?"

"Feels wonderful, doesn't it? Try to shift." Ram stepped back, giving his first lieutenant the maximum amount of space in the middle of the room.

Jakar keeled over, his hand covering his abdomen. His face contorted into a mask of pain. "You didn't say it would hurt."

A smile tugged at the corner of Ram's mouth. "I rather like it that way."

On his hands and knees, Jakar's body arched. Rapid breaths expended from his lungs. Saliva dripped from his mouth onto the dirt floor, the small drops darkening the surface.

His feet and hands transformed into paws. Serrated teeth enlarged into canines. His chest expanded and his waist shrunk. The khaki pants and dark polo shirt he wore disappeared under his skin.

A thrill ran along Ram's arms. "You're an ugly son of a bitch, you know that?"

Jakar snarled and circled Ram. Where the Panthera had dark black coats covering their skin, his first lieutenant was as hairless as a newborn babe.

"It seems we can change, but are still without hair. What a pity." Ram tsked.

On unsteady feet, Jakar took a tentative step forward. His front legs shook, and he stumbled. A soft gasp escaped his lips as his chin connected with the dirt floor. He shook his head and righted himself once again.

Jakar changed back, his clothes reforming on to his body as if he'd never removed them. He rolled his shoulders, as if shaking away the last of the pain. "This will take some time to get used to. How long will this skill last before it wears off?"

Ram raised an eyebrow. "If the shield power I stole from that female Dren, Melissa, is any indication, I'd guess a couple of weeks."

"Excellent. Shall I distribute the rest of the serum to the brood?"

Ram nodded. "Once you've completed the task, take them outside for a little run. They'll need time to practice with their new form."

"As you command, my lord." Jakar bowed. He scooped up the syringes and ran up the stairs.

Alone in the basement, Ram rubbed his chin, the old habit engrained in his memory even though the beard was long gone. "I shall win this war for you, Zedron."

Once he'd won, Earth would become a slave planet. Ram looked forward to shackling the humans, forcing them to bend to his will. This would give him the chance to prove to Sheri he wasn't a failure. *Ah, Sheri.*

He pulled his wallet from his back pocket. The leather had survived his tumble into the river, but the contents, not so much. With careful fingers, he pulled out the water-damaged picture and stroked his ex-wife's grainy image. "Not much longer, my love, not much longer."

Chapter Twenty-One

Demir stood outside the carved wooden double doors of the king's Throne room, Aramie at his side. Cool air drifted along the corridor, and the smell of the morning repast made his stomach rumble. A trip to the Grand Hall after this meeting was on his agenda. First, though, he had to eat some crow.

Apologizing to Noeh and Melissa was not something he could put off. He'd been a world-class ass to both of them. Hell, he'd tried to steal the crown and the queen. Such a great guy, huh?

He glanced at Aramie. She held her head high and squared her shoulders. Her lips were still reddened and plump from their kiss, and his lips tingled at the memory. She wouldn't meet his gaze, but she gnawed her bottom lip with her teeth. *She's more nervous than I am.*

He hadn't wanted to strip her of her role. She was damn good at leading the Pride under his direction, but he'd had no choice. He couldn't show mercy. She'd broken one of the old laws. He should've punished her more, but he couldn't bring himself to do so.

"You ready?" he asked.

She gave a curt nod. "Whenever you are."

His knuckles rapped against the worn grain of the old oak door.

Footsteps approached on the other side. The double doors opened wide, creating their own draft. Aramie's perfume raced by, tickling his nose.

Jax, Noeh's personal attendant, and one of the Jixies in the Keep, stared at Demir. His eyes widened, his mouth rounded, and his little body shook. "Y-you're awake? Oh, my." He turned his back and peered into the room. "Oh, Your Majesty, you won't believe who's here. Oh, my, no, you won't. It's Demir, it's really him. He's alive. Well, I mean…he was always alive, but now he's awake…and Aramie is here, too."

A moment of silence, then Noeh's deep chuckle emanated from within the room. "Yes, Gaetan mentioned something along those lines. Please let them in, Jax."

Jax stepped aside, his body shaking with nervous energy. As Demir walked by, Jax tracked him with large, round eyes full of wonder.

Two wooden statues of ancient Stiyaha warriors guarded the entryway. Cuffs surrounded their forearms and short swords dangled from their waists. The figures looked menacing and signified the strength and power the Stiyaha possessed. Carved centuries ago, the aged wood still smelled of oak from the constant polishing they received.

Noeh sat in his ornate wooden chair at the back of the room, Melissa and their son, Anlon, by his side. Per Alora's and Veromé's decree, the Stiyaha King was the leader of all the Lemurian species.

"Your Majesty." Demir bent on one knee and bowed his head. Aramie followed suit and kneeled beside him.

"Demir, Aramie, rise. It is good to see you again." The old chair creaked as Noeh rose from his seat. The King stood well over six and a half feet tall and had the typical muscular Stiyaha build. He wore the traditional black slacks and white button-down shirt that all the warriors wore, tailored by the Jixies. The sunstone ring on his middle finger set him apart as king along with the gold crown coiled around his head. His unique marking circled his right eye—three straight, black lines over his eyebrow connected by a thin line around his eye to two swirls over his cheek.

Melissa, the queen, had the opposite marking surrounding her left eye. From what he'd heard Aramie say while he was in his coma, the marking was part of the bonding between mates. Melissa seemed so small next to Noeh. As a female Dren, she used to be one of his slaves. Her red hair shone in the light, and her green eyes glittered with happiness. She held the new prince in her lap.

Guilt stung Demir in the gut. He fought the urge to flinch. In his madness, his obsession over her had driven him to nearly force her to become his concubine. He'd almost crossed the line when he'd confronted her about the pregnancy, but Aramie had stopped him. Good thing she had.

"King Noeh, I offer my sincerest apology." The words were bitter on his tongue. As much as he really meant them, bowing to another male fought against his alpha tendencies.

"To what do you refer?" Noeh asked.

Damn. The male wasn't going to make this easy for him. Well, that's what he deserved, wasn't it? *How's that crow tasting?* Even his own sarcasm didn't help the situation.

"I've…been an ass, plain and simple. I should've trusted you from the start. The gods knew what they were doing when they selected you as the Lemurian king." He held his head high and focused on Noeh's blue eyes. The guilt in his gut twisted tighter.

"You saved my life by taking the dart. That makes up for any past transgressions you may have done, real or imagined." Noeh raised his hand, palm facing outward in the traditional Lemurian greeting.

Demir smiled. He'd been down this road before. This time, he wouldn't make the same mistake of challenging the king. Demir approached Noeh and placed his palm against the king's hand. He put a mild amount of pressure to signify acceptance, then dropped his hand first in deference to the king's authority.

The king returned to his seat on his throne.

Now, the difficult apology. Demir glanced at Melissa. His chest constricted. He bowed his head to her, but the hair on the back of his neck stood on end. He'd apologize, but the shame of his behavior had already ripped out a chunk of his ego. The pain in his chest was still raw.

"Melissa…my queen. I owe you an even bigger apology. I was out of line. You looked so much like Elean—"

"Demir. Please. Enough. Let the past stay in the past." Her soft words broke him, and his throat tightened, rendering him unable to respond.

"Aramie, I'm sorry for your loss." Noeh changed the subject, giving Demir the opportunity to recover his pride.

"Thank you, Your Majesty." Aramie choked on her words, the pain evident in her strained voice.

Demir peered at her. The glimmer of a tear caught in her eyelashes, and she blinked. The droplet rolled down her cheek. His hand jerked, and he had the sudden urge to wipe away her tear. He stopped himself and ground his teeth.

"Sidea was well liked among our kind. She shall be missed. I don't mean to rush you, but I'd like to hear about the blue sunstone…and Ram. Gaetan filled me in as best he could, but please, tell me what you know of my enemy." Noeh leaned forward in his chair and took the babe Melissa offered to him. The little guy gripped a handful of Noeh's shirt in his tiny fist. The king rubbed his son's back, a slight smile interrupting his serious expression for a moment.

To see Noeh holding his son made Demir still. The king had changed since he'd last seen him. He wasn't so imposing this way. The babe, too, seemed to be larger than he would've expected. Maybe that was due to Noeh's Stiyaha build. Demir shook his head in wonder.

"Sidea and Kitani patrolled the area while Jonue and I searched for the stone. The crystal was in a small cave under the waterfall. When we resurfaced, the

Gossum battled against them." Aramie held her head high, her eyes focused on the king.

Demir admired her strength and ability to hold herself together. Her toughness under the circumstances made him respect her all the more.

"They were too far away, we couldn't help them." Aramie pressed her lips together. She peered at the sunstones in the ceiling before returning her gaze to the king. "Ram emerged from the trees with a couple of his brood. They killed Sidea, but not before they took some of her blood. I saw the vial, and the glint of success in Ram's eyes." Aramie's words grew in intensity until she hissed their enemy's name.

Demir pulled in a deep breath as a sense of pride filled him. Despite her pain, she was a warrior through and through.

"He intends to use her powers, just like he did Melissa's." Noeh glanced at his queen.

Melissa nodded in agreement. "He'll attack soon. When he stole my shield power, it only lasted a few weeks before it weakened, and I regained it."

"But Sidea died. She can't get her panther back. What then?" Aramie scrunched her brow.

Demir didn't like this new twist. Until now, he hadn't known Ram had taken Panthera blood. The ramifications boggled his mind. What would a mix between a Gossum and a Panthera be capable of? Goosebumps rose along his arms. "Good question. We need to kill him before *he* or *we* find out."

Aramie tensed beside him. "I'll go. I can track him from Blue Pool. I want revenge for Sidea and Kitani."

"You're not going alone." Demir wanted to forbid her to go at all. If she were his mate, she'd stay here, protected within the walls of the Keep. He jerked, suddenly aware of where his mind had gone.

She inhaled at his command. Her face reddened, but she didn't speak. She wouldn't contradict him in front of the others. Loyal to him from the start, his heart clenched at the pain in her eyes.

He looked at Noeh. "We'll take a small scouting party—find out where he hides. We'll let you know what we find."

Noeh assessed Demir. A tic started in his jaw, but then he nodded. "As you wish. I expect a full report."

One thing hadn't changed—Demir's hatred of authority. His muscles flexed beneath his shirt. "Naturally. I'd expect nothing less."

Noeh glanced between Aramie and Demir. "Get some rest. You look like you need it."

Rest? That's what he'd been doing for weeks. One look at Aramie, though, and he could tell she was tired by the dark, puffy skin under her eyes and the waxen hue to her skin.

"You want something to eat before you go to bed?" He wasn't sure which enticed him more, food, or the idea of Aramie in bed. A tingling sensation started in his crotch. Well, that answered that question. Unmated Panthera could have casual sex, but Demir had too much respect for Aramie as a warrior to pursue that option.

"I could use a bite to eat, but then a shower and a quick nap sound good." Her smile didn't quite light up her eyes, but a spot of redness on her cheeks erased some of her exhaustion. "Thank you, Your Majesty."

Noeh nodded then peered at his son. Anlon slept peacefully in his father's arms.

Demir turned to leave. Jax pulled on the doorknob. The double doors glided open with ease. As Demir and Aramie left the king's chamber, a drop of doubt and fear crept into his mind. What if they couldn't find Ram?

Chapter Twenty-Two

Tanen sat at one of the empty chairs around the magistrate's table. The familiar scent of oak and furniture polish calmed his nerves. He was in his favorite room, the council chamber, the one where he ruled. As council leader, he dealt with the petty grievances and squabbles between the residents at the Keep allowing Noeh the flexibility to lead the warriors in battles against the Gossum.

After the morning repast, Tanen had headed to his quarters for the day's rest when he'd received the call through the sunstones. Noeh had summoned him here, but the king was late. That wasn't like him and a nugget of worry worked its way into Tanen's stomach, flaring his recent bout of heartburn. He traced the outline of the silver pin attached to his shirt pocket. The "M" stood for "Mu" the nickname for Lemuria and was his most precious adornment.

He stood and paced by the stacks of books lining the shelves. One text caught his eye. The heavy tome stuck out a bit further from the rest. A bead of irritation creased his brow. With care, he pressed his thumb against the spine until order was restored. The tension in his shoulders eased.

Footsteps approached. The familiar cadence was one he recognized—Noeh.

A babe's shrill cry pierced the air.

"Is he hungry?" Noeh's words echoed off the stone corridor.

The royal couple entered the room. Noeh ran his hand through his hair. His sunstone ring reflected the light in a cascade of brilliance. The queen's long red hair cascaded over her shoulders, and the babe in her arms gripped a handful of the silky strands in his fist. Tears glistened in his eyes, but he'd stopped his incessant wail, at least for now.

Tanen bowed. "Your Majesty. You requested to see me? Is something wrong?"

Noeh's gaze searched the room. "Have you seen Gaetan?"

"No. I take it he's to join us. What is this about?" He placed his hand on the back of his favorite chair, his fingers digging into the cushion. Usually a comfort, the soft material didn't ease his anxiety.

Tension lines formed on Noeh's forehead.

Tanen's heart skipped a beat. *The king has bad news to share.*

"I'm here. Was delayed..." Gaetan hobbled into the room, his cane clacking against the stone floor. Ginnia, his sister, tagged along.

"Hi, Tanen. When are you going to clean the books? I want to read them." Ginnia's smile was all innocence, but her words hit a soft spot inside him.

Noeh had commissioned him to restore the Hall of Scriptures. Its neglect wasn't his fault, but it was his responsibility now. He'd procrastinated. His face heated. "Soon, Ginnia, soon."

Noeh grabbed one of the chairs from the magistrate's table, turned it around, and sat down. His forearms rested across the back. Melissa pulled up a chair next to him, Anlon cradled in her arms. The young prince cooed softly.

"Ram is alive," Noeh said.

"What? How is that possible? You killed him." The idea of meeting their enemy sent a shiver down Tanen's back. He was glad he wasn't a warrior, but he couldn't suppress his inner beast's growl at the mention of their opponent.

"Guess he survived after all." Gaetan sat in one of the chairs against the wall. He rubbed his knee. His face contorted into a pained wince.

Noeh turned toward Tanen. "Have you pulled any useful information out of Mauree?"

"Nothing worth noting. She insists she doesn't know anything." Locked in a holding cell, she awaited trial. As Council Leader, his job was to prosecute her and mete out her sentence. He'd searched through his papers and the stacks of books in this room, but hadn't found anything covering the unusual circumstance of treason. Disloyalty of that magnitude had never occurred. He'd have to visit the Hall of Scriptures soon. Her trial date was fast approaching.

The muscles in Noeh's jaw tensed. "Maybe I should give her a visit."

Tanen's mouth went dry and his heartburn flared. "Let me talk to her again. She's warming up to me. I'm sure I can get something out of her."

Tanen's gaze caught on the red and green sunstone necklace Melissa wore around her throat, and the familiar sensation to pocket a trinket prickled his fingers. He cracked his knuckles. Over the years, he'd learned to pop the joints as a way to curb his anxiety and his destructive obsession. He hadn't lifted anything in decades.

Noeh focused his attention on Tanen's face. His eyes narrowed. "You're running out of time, her trial is in three nights. Get the information from her and find the ruling on treason, or I will deal with her on my terms."

"As you wish, Your Majesty." Tanen rose from his chair and headed out the door. There must be something in one of those ancient texts that covered treason. He clenched his fist at his inability to find the old law. He'd pored over the scriptures in the council chamber for weeks, delaying his search in the Hall of Scriptures. Stopping in his tracks, a sense of foreboding ran over his shoulders. He padded his pockets. *My keys.* He'd left them in the room with Noeh and the others.

With a heavy sigh, he reversed course. As he approached the room, heated voices rang into the hallway. The corridor was empty. He didn't want to eavesdrop, but couldn't resist the overwhelming urge. Slowing his pace, he took quiet steps. As he got closer, the conversation became clearer.

"The stone should've worked. It healed Demir. Try again." Noeh's voice was tense.

"I've tried several times already. Do you really think this time would be any different?" Gaetan's voice cracked as he spoke, and his cane tapped against the stone floor.

Was something wrong with Noeh? Tanen's heart pounded. That would be devastating.

When Gaetan spoke again, his words were softer, more relaxed. "In the old legend, the blue sunstone healed the warrior that sacrificed himself for another. The stone restored Demir from his coma because he took the dart intended for you. That could be why it's not working—not the right circumstances."

A loud exhale echoed from the room. "Point taken. How much longer do I have before I'm completely deaf?"

Tanen froze and held his breath. Every Stiyaha had one weakness, maybe this was Noeh's.

"I don't know. I'm not a seer." Gaetan sounded tired, resigned.

Ginnia giggled. "Silly brother. Seers don't exist, right? Just like sacred sunstones."

A chair creaked as if someone had stood.

"Ginnia, do you know anything about this?" Noeh's encouraging voice whispered into the corridor.

"When I gave Aramie the book, she read to me the part about the blue sunstone. That's my favorite part. I knew she'd find it." Her light laughter was like a soft melody to Tanen's ears.

They'd found the sacred blue sunstone. His fingers itched with the need to take something that wasn't his. He cracked his knuckles. The sound echoed down the hall.

The conversation in the room stopped. They knew he was there. Before he could think twice, he entered the room.

Feigning a look of surprise, he raised his eyebrows. "You're still here?"

He walked over to the small desk in the corner, his movements fast, deliberate. "I forgot these." He held up the keys to the containment cell.

The blank look on their faces was a dead giveaway. His stomach tightened. He hadn't fooled anyone.

"Tanen. How long were you out there?" Noeh's gaze bore into him.

Blood pumped through Tanen's veins. "Not long. I heard Ginnia mention a favorite story. Did you read one to her?" He pasted on a smile and did his best to appear casual. He wasn't sure he'd be successful.

"Not recently. I think you were headed somewhere, weren't you?" Noeh raised an eyebrow.

"Ah…yes, Your Majesty." Tanen bowed one last time. He glanced at Gaetan. The old male sat in a chair, rubbing his leg. His pocket bulged.

As Tanen headed into the hallway, he couldn't get the image of a rare blue sunstone out of his mind.

Chapter Twenty-Three

After a good meal and some sleep, Demir was rested and ready to head out to search for Ram. He glanced around his room. The bed, the table, and a dresser were his only furnishings. As Pride leader, he deserved better. He furrowed his brow. Sooner or later, he'd have to fix that.

He closed the book, the one Aramie had read to him while he'd been in a coma. The cover was soft to his touch, and he brushed the worn leather savoring how it tingled his skin.

Memories flooded his mind, of her fingers caressing his face as she trimmed his beard. His heart rate picked up speed. A need to see her brought him to his feet. Without another thought, he left his room, desire spurring him along the corridor.

He stood outside her door. When he'd left her here earlier, she'd avoided him, her body stiff, defensive, as if their kiss had never occurred. He'd never forget what happened between them. His jaw tightened, and a low growl crawled up his chest.

He knocked.

Her room was quiet.

He knocked again.

Silence permeated the air.

A ball of unease lodged itself in his gut. He grabbed the doorknob. It twisted in his grasp.

"Aramie?"

Her faint scent filled his nose. He pushed open the door and peered around the small room. Her bed was empty. A chill raced up his spine. She wouldn't have left without him, would she?

She might, and that galled him. He couldn't ignore his sense of emptiness, as if she'd left *him*, instead of having her own agenda. Eleanor would never have gone against his wishes, but the truth didn't ease the void in his chest. It bothered him that he imagined Aramie as his mate. Despite their passionate kiss, she was a warrior to him and nothing more. Still, he couldn't get the determination in her beautiful eyes out of his mind.

He turned and left the room, following her scent. His boots pounded against the stone floor as he ran down the corridor. He passed several Stiyaha merchants and Jixies starting their nightly activities. No one paid him any attention.

She'd purposefully left without him. Tension raced along his nerves.

On his way to the Portal Navigation Center, he passed the Grand Hall. The smell of the evening repast—eggs, bacon, ham, fresh bread—covered Aramie's scent. He stopped. The crowded room swarmed with the Keep's inhabitants. She'd said she was hungry. Maybe he was overreacting. Maybe she was here eating her meal.

He entered the room and scanned the crowd. A group of Stiyaha warriors sat at a nearby table. Saar, Noeh's Commander of Arms, caught Demir's attention. Saar nodded in greeting.

Leon sauntered over to him. The male, one of Demir's Pride, gave a short bow then met Demir's gaze. "Welcome back. I'm glad to see the rumors are true. You're well."

"Have you seen Aramie?" Demir scanned the mob standing in the food line, but he didn't see her shiny dark hair or her sleek frame.

Leon curled his lip. "No, I haven't seen *that* female."

Of course, he would blame Aramie for Kitani's death. A wave of guilt raced over Demir's shoulders. In his effort to find Aramie, he'd forgotten about his Pridemate's loss. Demir placed his palm on Leon's shoulder. "I'm sorry, my friend. Kitani was a good female."

Leon's eyes shifted back and forth as he studied Demir. "She was, and now she's gone. I heard you stripped Aramie of her status. Why didn't you banish her from the Pride?"

Demir's hackles rose. He puffed out his chest. "Your pain clouds your judgment. I forgive your insolence—this time."

Leon lowered his gaze, but didn't speak.

"If you see Aramie, tell her I'm looking for her."

"As you wish." Leon bowed low in front of Demir.

Demir turned to leave and plowed right into Bet.

The small Jixie landed on her rump and skittered several feet across the floor. "Oh, my."

Blood rushed to Demir's face. He hadn't seen Bet since she'd washed his body. The memory made him flinch. He composed himself and offered her his hand. "Forgive me. I didn't see you there."

Her cheeks reddened, and she wiped her hands on her stained apron. "Oh, I guess the rumors are true. You're awake." She dropped her gaze then quickly glanced at him again. She took his proffered hand, and he helped her stand.

His own desire to escape flared to life, but he ground his feet in place. He would not run from this tiny female. She'd seen his scars, and like the adult females when he was a child, she'd pitied him. Bile rose in his throat. Pity was the last thing he wanted or needed from anyone.

"You're in time for the first repast. Is there anything special you'd like?" She'd recovered her composure and was the attentive Jixie he'd known before, not that he'd treated her well.

"I'm looking for Aramie. Have you seen her?"

"No, not this evening. If I do—"

He didn't have time for niceties and left before she could finish her sentence. A quick bang of regret hit him between the eyes at his sudden dismissal of the small Jixie. At the Grand Hall's entrance, he stopped and turned. She met his gaze, her mouth downturned in a sad frown.

He raised his voice to be heard above the din of the crowd. "Thank you, Bet."

A grin broke across her face, and her eyes glinted with amusement. "Hurry now, Demir!" She shooed him on. He raised his hand and raced into the corridor.

Although she seemed happy at his acknowledgement, he couldn't forget she'd seen his scars. His encounter with her brought back memories, ones he didn't want to revisit, but couldn't seem to avoid.

Demir hated the training sessions with his father, the throwing stars in particular. He'd failed to hit the mark, yet again.

His father grabbed him by the back of the neck and raised him off the ground. He shook Demir, his feet tangling together from the force.

"You're an embarrassment to me." With a shove, his father tossed him to the ground. "Go find a switch."

Demir choked back a sob. He headed into the underbrush, searching for a stray branch. If he didn't find a suitable candidate, his father would give him extra thrashings for the error.

Demir didn't speak, but handed the young hazel branch he'd found to his father. Their gazes met. Demir longed to see some kind of compassion in his eyes, but there was only the glint of disappointment.

"Pull down your pants. Assume the position."

Demir did as he was told. His bare ass exposed, he bent over and grabbed his ankles.

His father's feet squeaked on the wet grass when he backed up. The switch whistled through the air.

Pain registered in Demir's brain, and he couldn't stop the sob that escaped his mouth.

His father let out a bellow so fierce, it echoed off the pine trees.

The next lashing was stronger than the last. Each strike to his buttocks was another reminder of his weakness. He'd never be good enough and in his pre-pubescent mind, he wondered if he'd ever live up to expectations. The beating stopped when drops of blood coated the damp leaves at his feet.

"Pull up your pants and run home to your mama."

Demir yanked on his trousers with as much dignity as he could and ran. Now that he was away from his father, the tears flowed down his cheeks. When he entered the small cave they used as their home, a group of females turned from their food cleaning duties to stare. The pity on their faces almost broke him.

He ran to his small blanket at the back of the room and lay on his abdomen, face turned away from inquisitive eyes. His wounds would heal in a few minutes, but the scars, those would be added to the others already there and last a lifetime.

The hair at the back of his neck stiffened. He curled his lip. His constant disappointment and punishment—an endless cycle in futility, one he vowed never to repeat.

A soft glow emanated from the entrance to the Portal Navigation Center. Demir arrived to see Rin cleaning sunstones at his workshop table. The little Jixie turned in his seat, the old wooden chair creaking in protest.

"Eh, ya woke up, did ya? What brings ya here?" Rin wiped his hands on a cloth and tossed it onto the bench.

Demir flared his nostrils. A trace of strawberry fragrance lingered in the air. "Where did you send Aramie?"

Rin narrowed his eyes. "She told me not ta tell ya."

A burn raced through Demir's veins. The predator in him took over. He stalked closer to the little male. His fear for Aramie brought out his aggression. "Open the portal to her location."

Rin backed up until his butt hit the porte stanen. "I don't know where she is."

"Not now, maybe, but you know where you sent her. Open a portal."

Rin turned around, his back to Demir. The little male ran his hands over the stones. They brightened, and the mist formed.

The outline of evergreen trees, ferns, and moss materialized before them. The smell of dew and pine carried into the room on a stiff breeze.

"Very good. You've done well." Demir changed into his panther and jumped through the gateway.

Chapter Twenty-Four

Aramie stopped by a small lake. Douglas fir trees surrounded the edge and looked like upended pencils in the darkened forest. She'd left right at nightfall, as soon as the sun had set. Although she'd searched for hours, she still hadn't found Blue Pool again. If she hadn't seen the magical place for herself, she might've believed it didn't exist.

What she needed was a moment to catch her breath, to think. She exhaled and stared at the stars.

A rare snowy owl flew over the lake, its brilliant wings reflecting the moon in an eerie dance. She wanted to be free like that bird, to live without emotional pain and worries—to live without fear. She and Sidea had always been on the run, escaping or running from something, and Aramie was tired.

This was the first time she'd actually been on her own. Aramie's chest constricted. The raw wound of losing Sidea cut deep, opening a giant chasm of agony. It was times like this she ached for the father she didn't know. She craved a strong, supportive influence in her life, someone to help her navigate the waves of loss that tossed her around.

Before the tears could start, she shook her head, clearing her mind of what would never be. Heat flushed through her body as her anguish turned to anger. She wallowed in the emotion, using the energy to drive her temper. If she couldn't find Blue Pool and locate her enemy's scent, she'd find Ram some other way.

With the quickness born of her species, she shifted into her panther and headed deeper into the forest. Lithe and strong, her muscles moved in a graceful rhythm as she prowled. Her sense of time and place fell away, and the raw instincts of the animal took over.

Forest scents infiltrated her senses—rabbit, deer, pine, ferns, moss, dampness—she enjoyed every one. The bitter tang of astringent burned her nose, the first sign of Gossum. Turning toward the smell, she doubled her efforts.

So focused on her goal, she didn't hear the snap of a twig until it was too late. A heavy weight landed on her back. She hit the ground face-first, damp soil cushioning her fall. Air whooshed from her lungs. Panic welled in her mind, sending a flush of adrenaline through her veins.

Her attacker pinned her to the forest floor, his body covering her in an instant. Instinct kicked in and she lashed out with her feet. Her claws raked down skin.

The pressure in her lungs finally relented, and she took a large breath. Musk and incense. The familiar essence made her heart skip a beat. *Demir.*

A deep male growl reverberated into her chest.

She froze.

His feline nose nuzzled against her ear, his breath tickling the fine hairs. With a low growl, he nipped the back of her neck. The dominant display was his right as Pride leader, but the sensual nature of it sent tendrils of excitement through her body. She responded against her will, secreting her unique strawberry scent.

His muscles tensed, becoming rigid. His own pheromones filled the air in response to hers. The growl he emitted was deep and sensuous. With deliberate movements, he rubbed his whiskers against her cheek, marking her with his scent.

Her pulse raced. She didn't want this. The urge to break free, to get away from him drove all her thoughts, and she changed into human form. Adrenaline surged through her body, and she pushed against him with all her might, but she couldn't break his hold.

When she'd changed, he'd done the same. "Stop. I won't hurt you."

She fought him all the more. Twisting and turning, she managed to get her knees underneath her. He used her momentum to flip her over, and then engulfed her in his arms.

She pushed against his biceps bulging beneath his black T-shirt. His strength overwhelmed her, and she had a conflicting desire to bite him on the shoulder, both to cause him pain and to mark him in her own way. The contradictory yearning made her cry out in frustration.

He pulled her tighter, closing the distance between them. "Relax, Aramie, relax." He practically purred her name.

The vibration rattled over the skin on her back, tickling her bottom. She couldn't stop her body's natural shiver.

"Please, let me go." Even as she said the words, the deepest part of her didn't want him to ever let her go.

He glanced at her mouth, and his pupils dilated. The memory of his kiss raced through her mind. Unbidden, her tongue slid over her bottom lip, moistening it.

The muscles in his jaw tightened, but his hold on her remained gentle in its control. "Did you really think you could escape me?"

Yes. She'd left the Keep intent on her mission—to kill Ram. Had she intended on returning? Even she didn't know the answer.

He raised an eyebrow. "Indeed, your expression says it all."

She squirmed under him and awareness of his desire caused her to still once again. A warm wetness dampened her panties, and the scent of strawberries thickened. Her body's betrayal made her angry, and heat rose to her cheeks.

Demir was the epitome of an alpha male. Her desire for him grated against her independent and willful nature. Most Panthera didn't mind casual sex, but she couldn't—not with him. Even as much as she cared for Demir, she wouldn't allow any male to get that close. Her chest tightened as adrenaline born of frustration raced through her body.

She bit him on the lower lip, as much a warning as a need to taste him again.

The guttural sound he emitted was a mixture of desire and anger.

"Why did you come after me?" She said the words with such force, spittle landed on his face.

A small smirk pulled at the corner of his mouth, and the diamond stud above his lip glinted in the moonlight. With quick reflexes he released her and stood. Like a splash of cold water, a draft of cool air replaced his heated body. He grabbed her hands and yanked her to her feet.

"You knew I would. I protect my Pride." He scrutinized her, his brow furrowing, accentuating his deep brown eyes. With the back of his hand, he wiped the drop of blood from his lip. "It's a good thing I did. Had I been the enemy, you'd be dead."

He was right. She'd been distracted. Demir had approached her from downwind. In her anger and grief, she hadn't paid attention, and he'd caught her easily. She wouldn't make that mistake again.

His features softened, and he trailed his fingers over her cheek, his palm cradling her face. "I never told you how sorry I am—for Sidea. She was a great warrior, a vital member of our Pride. She will be missed by many."

Tears welled in Aramie's eyes. She couldn't stop them as they spilled onto her cheek.

His thumb caught one on the way down, and he wiped it away. His tender care brought on a fresh round. She couldn't do this, not with him, not with any male. She pulled back and raised her chin.

His hand remained in the air for a moment, as if hesitant to let go. He studied her, his assessing gaze roaming her face. His brow furrowed, a pained expression crossing his features. "I never apologized to you—for backhanding you."

She blinked. His words were unexpected.

He closed his eyes for a moment and swallowed. When he opened them, a fire burned in their depths. "You stood up to me. No female has ever done that before."

Her heart skipped a beat, but she refused to speak, giving him the chance to come clean.

"You were right to do so. I was out of line with Melissa. As a promise to you, I swear I will never hit you again." He stood tall, proud, his head held high, but his eyes tracked her. Was he waiting for her reaction to see if she would accept his assurance?

Memories of her mother dominated and controlled by male after male raced through her mind. Fear weaseled its way into her heart, erecting the familiar barriers, strengthening them. The urge to bolt overwhelmed her and her leg muscles tensed in anticipation. She backed up, putting distance between them.

He gripped her arm, but his touch was gentle. "Talk to me…"

Her dry mouth prevented her from swallowing the lump in her throat. She trembled, but a strange anger burned inside. The old wound ripped open, and before she could think better of it, she blurted the words. "I never knew my father. My mother left him and every other male in her life."

Demir blinked and released his hold on her arm. If she hadn't known him better, she wouldn't have caught the slight flinch that crossed his face. "You didn't have a good male influence in your life. I understand, but not all males are bad, Aramie, not all."

Her face heated as a rush of blood raced up her neck and into her cheeks. "My mother abandoned us—me and Sidea. I can't be like her...I won't *ever* become a mated female."

Tension lines appeared on his forehead and around his pursed lips. "You're passionate about that, aren't you? Don't worry, you're safe with me."

An empty hole grew in her chest. As much as she would never bow down to a male, a part of her longed for the love and companionship the mating would bring. Against her will, she imagined what it would be like to be his mated female. Tears threatened to form, but she clenched her jaw and wouldn't give in to the emotions roiling through her.

"You'll return with me to the Keep. Once we have assembled a proper search team, we'll look for Ram." He expected to be obeyed, that much was obvious in not only his tone, but also his firm stance and rigid posture.

Before he stripped her of her rank, she'd have followed his command without question. Now, though, she considered herself a Pride of one. "I came out here to find Ram and avenge my sister."

"You'll have your opportunity, when we return." He nodded toward the way they'd come.

"I'm not going with you." She held her ground, challenging him with her steady gaze.

He raised an eyebrow and a low chuckle escaped his lips. "You are ever a surprise, aren't you?"

Her mouth fell open. She'd expected him to get angry, demand that she return. Instead, he'd laughed. She shook her head, trying to understand him.

"I can't force you to return to the Keep, you'd run again. That would be pointless." He stepped closer, invading her personal space. His unique scent skittered across the sensitive nerves in her nose, pulling her in. "Instead," he moved a few stray hairs from her face, his fingertips trailing over her ear and down her neck, "I'm going with you."

"What? No." She stepped back, away from his gentle touch that made her ache to say yes.

"I can't force you to return to the Keep. You can't prevent me from following you." He smirked. The old Demir she knew so well was back in his unique, rare form.

She crossed her arms. "Fine, but I want the kill. Ram is mine." She wasn't sure what she'd signed up for, but a part of her, deep inside, couldn't wait to find out.

Chapter Twenty-Five

Zedron stared at the open bottle of chantelberry wine perched on the edge of the table. His gut twisted and bile rose in his throat. Expensive and hard to obtain, the wine was from his favorite collection, reserved solely for special occasions. His attention focused on Carine—his new problem. "Next time, bring me the correct bottle."

Carine raised her gaze to meet his. The skin around her lips tightened, and fight gleamed in her eyes. "That *is* the bottle you requested."

Her determination and will sent a shiver of excitement along his nerves. "Surely, you don't mean that. I requested the muldoberry wine. The difference is hard to mistake." He took a step forward, invading her personal space.

She flinched, but held her ground.

He smiled. "You've made several, similar errors. I suspect you choose to spite me."

The tips of her hair flew around her head, sparks crackling with her indignation. She glanced at the door and nibbled her bottom lip.

"Try it. See what happens." He peered at the irremovable gilded arm bands he'd placed on her soon after they'd arrived home. Built with the finest new technology, he controlled her whereabouts through the link to his personal communication device. The current setting—only his home.

Her attention narrowed on the door, and the muscles in her arms visibly tensed.

His pulse raced. *Do it, do it.*

She bolted for the door, gripped the handle, and yanked. Warm, fresh air wafted into the room. With a grace and beauty he had to admire, she ran for freedom and bounced against the invisible barrier. Her small cry rang in the air.

She landed on her rump. A loud whoosh escaped her lips.

He laughed, the sound bubbling up from his chest.

She glared at him, her brow furrowed, her lips pursed. The air around her head sparked with the electricity from the ends of her wild hair.

He couldn't help the smile that formed on his face. He stepped toward her and offered his hand.

The intensity in her grey eyes spoke of her fight. A thrill skittered along his arms.

She refused his offer and stood unaided. On her feet again, she turned to face him. "Shall I get you the *muldoberry* wine?"

He smiled. Although she'd given in this time, they were far from through with their training. "That won't be necessary, Carine. Why don't you," he pointed to her shirt which had ripped during her fall, "change, and then prepare for dinner. My guests will arrive soon."

She peered at the bottle of wine and the briefest smirk crossed her face. When her gaze returned to him, she spoke, her words contrite and overly sweet. "Of course, master."

As she walked past, he chuckled. Breaking her in was more entertaining than he'd anticipated, but he'd spent far too much time with her the past few days. So much so, he'd neglected to check in with his characters in the war on Earth. Time to rectify that issue.

*****

Ram ran his fingers along his chin, stroking the bare skin. He picked up a half-full Smirnoff's bottle from the warped wooden table and poured two fingers of alcohol into the bottom of his empty cup. The liquid hugged the inside lip of the mug as he swirled the contents. With one swift move, he tilted back his head and the vodka raced down his throat. The burn made him shiver. He closed his eyes in delight.

"My lord." Jakar's strained voice broke through the silence in the old cellar.

Ram's moment of peace ended. The scales on the back of his neck flared. He opened his eyes and glared at his first lieutenant. A piece of translucent skin hung from Jakar's arm, catching Ram's attention. Ram pointed to it and raised an eyebrow.

"What?" Jakar asked.

"You're shedding."

"Oh. Yessss." Jakar tugged at the skin, pulling a large chunk that ran from his forearm to his shoulder. He held it up to the light. "Perfect." His tongue whipped out of his mouth and wrapped around the skin, which disappeared into his mouth.

The vodka in Ram's stomach threatened to come up. He grimaced. "You're disgusting. You do know that, don't you?"

Jakar smiled, his serrated teeth lining up like knives in a chopping block. He retrieved a couple of the empty vodka bottles strewn across the table. With a full armload, he put them back in one of the boxes lining the dirt walls.

A spark fizzled from the overhead lightbulb, causing Ram's body to cast a strange shadow against the wall. The electricity in the room prickled his skin. Sweat beaded along his upper lip. "Oh, no."

The current in the air could mean only one thing. *Zedron.*

Jakar turned to stare at Ram.

A cool breeze filtered down the stairs, turning the banister white with frost. The small crystals stood at odd angles and reflected the ceiling light with a strange beauty. Ram's nose and ears numbed under the sudden drop in temperature.

At the bottom of the stairs, a nebulous blue mist took the shape of their god, Zedron. He wore a fine Italian suit with patent-leather wingtip shoes. His brown hair cascaded around his shoulders. He stood with his head held high.

Zedron held Ram's gaze with his piercing blue eyes. "You failed."

Ram's blood froze. The weight of his failure sent him to his knees. Good thing, since it was grovel time.

"My Lord, Zedron. It is a…pleasure to see you again. Your choice of Earthling clothing is…stylish." He swallowed and almost couldn't get the lump in his throat to go down.

Zedron glanced around the room and his lip curled in distaste. "You live in squalor. Well, not for much longer." He wiped his hands over his sleeves and sent a disgusted glare around the room.

"My lord. To what do we owe the pleasure of your visit?" Ram's voice wavered.

"Noeh is still alive. Do you know what happens to my characters when they fail?" Zedron smiled, but his eyes were hard and unfeeling.

The contradiction sent a chill along Ram's scales and over his back. "Lord Zedron. I have some news, something that will ensure we will win this war."

"Do tell. I'd like to hear why I shouldn't kill you now." Zedron walked over to the table cluttered with empty cups, used syringes, and beakers. Selecting an empty syringe, he brought it to his nose, taking a large whiff. He turned and stared at Ram. "Panthera blood."

A glimmer of hope formed in Ram's mind. He stood and faced his god. "Yes, I used it to create a new serum. All of our brood has the ability to shift into panther form." He clapped his hands together, unable to contain his giddiness.

Zedron raised one eyebrow. "Really?"

Ram looked at Jakar. "Show him."

"As you wish, my lord." Jakar took one look at Zedron then dropped his gaze. He crouched on all fours, his hands grinding into the dirt, brow furrowing as he concentrated. His back arched. A hiss escaped his lips. To his credit, he didn't cry out like the first time he'd changed.

His body contorted, clothing disappeared underneath his skin. Jakar resembled a Panthera without hair, blue and red veins visible under the translucent skin. He growled and bared his serrated teeth. His tongue whipped out of his mouth, coming close to Zedron's shoes.

"The brood has practiced in their new form and is ready to fight, Lord Zedron." Ram closed his eyes for a brief moment. He didn't want to see the expression on Zedron's face. If the god wasn't pleased, this would be Ram's endgame.

A low chuckle filled the room and grew until it shook the earth. Pebbles and dust filtered from the rafters. Muffled grunts and shouts erupted from above as Ram's brood reacted to the mini-quake.

"Well done." Zedron wiped a tear from his eye. "You've earned another chance. I won't be so forgiving next time."

Ram bowed his head. "Thank you, Lord Zedron. I'll make you proud."

The lines in Zedron's face tightened and his focus narrowed on Ram. "I have a certain…" Zedron waved his hand in the air, "*animosity* for Demir. If the opportunity arises, be sure to make him suffer before you kill him."

Ram's pulse increased. "My pleasure, my lord."

A flash of blinding light lit up the room. The coolness in the air retreated. Zedron was gone.

Chapter Twenty-Six

Demir pushed through the dense undergrowth, the blackberry brambles catching along his pant legs. Like giant spiders, the dead, brown vines rose from the ground, eager to trap him in their grasp. Even the animals seemed to avoid this stretch of land. The dense canopy of trees blocked the moon, but his cat-like eyes adjusted to the dimness.

He turned to glance at Aramie. Determination lined her eyes. A lock of her hair snagged on a blackberry vine, pulling the fine strands over her ear. She jerked her head. "Damn it."

Despite the cold winter night, a bead of sweat rolled down his back, cooling his skin. His teeth ground together and caused his jaw to ache. He should've dragged Aramie back to the Keep. Instead, he'd given in to her wishes. Now, he trekked through the forest, in search of his enemy, with Aramie. His father was right—he was weak. He hated himself all the more.

"Why'd you stop? We can't pause, we have to keep going." She placed her hands on her hips, her hurried breaths easing in and out of her parted lips.

He focused on them, remembering their luscious appeal. With effort, he pulled his gaze up to her eyes. "We're not searching for Blue Pool. We hunt for Gossum. One will lead us to Ram."

She huffed and crossed her arms. "Blue Pool exists—"

"That I stand here before you is proof that it does," he gripped her elbow, the skin on skin contact sending all kinds of sparks over his fingers, "but you won't find it—not again."

She focused on his hand and with a slow ease, she pulled away. The loss of contact sparked a bout of frustration in his chest, causing him to grind his teeth. She bit her lip and exhaled. "Blue Pool is where we last saw Ram. We have to find him. I won't give up."

He looked into the dark cover of evergreens. "We take to the trees."

Aramie pursed her lips and surveyed their surroundings. She seemed unwilling to give up on her chosen path. He'd have to try harder to convince her.

"You know as well as I they are cunning and elusive. Did you expect them to let you waltz right into their lair?"

"No, of course not." She closed her eyes for a second. "I need revenge—for Sidea."

"I have no doubt we'll find our enemy. Let's go." He changed into his panther form and climbed the nearest pine tree. His claws dug into the bark, giving him the grip he needed to scale into the branches.

Aramie followed.

They travelled among the trees for several minutes before they came upon evidence of their enemy. A shriveled Gossum skin hung from one of the branches. The thin membrane flew like a flag in the soft breeze. The faint astringent reek burned Demir's sensitive nose.

Aramie's fur rose between her shoulder blades.

Demir crept down a couple of branches, then leapt to the forest floor. His paws landed on the soft pine needles that muffled the sound.

Aramie joined him, and as her soft fur rubbed against his, a quiet mewl escaped her lips.

His heightened senses focused on her. The scent of strawberries cascaded over him, easing its way into his heart. Her coat shone in the dim light. He wanted to rub himself all over her and mark her with his own scent. The predator in him took over, clouding his thoughts.

He panted as he circled her. His cat would launch himself at her at any moment, taking her down, dominating her into submission.

A low warning growl emitted from her throat, announcing her intention. She'd fight him. That spurned him all the more. She'd been driving him crazy all night, he couldn't hold back any longer.

One moment, a female black panther taunted him with her yellow eyes, the next—Aramie stood before him in human form. She held out her hands in supplication. "No, Demir. Please."

The rejection stung, like a verbal slap to the face. He took a step back, shaking his head, trying to clear the lust that had consumed him.

What was he thinking? So unlike Eleanor, Aramie would fight him, challenge him over even the smallest decisions. He didn't need that in his life, not now, not when he already felt weak.

He transformed into his human state. To maintain some semblance of dignity, he straightened his shirt, even though it already molded to his chest. "Now we have their trail. Tracking our enemy should be easy."

Her hand curled into a fist. "You are so infuriating. Why do you play games with me?" She raised her hand. "Never mind, I don't want to know. It doesn't matter, anyway." Her brown eyes bore into him, piercing him with her gaze, but her mouth quivered and betrayed her pain.

A lump formed in his throat. *She cares for me, not just as her Pride leader, but as a male.* He couldn't speak, the words trapped in his throat.

"Let's go." She headed upwind, the Gossum's stench growing stronger with the breeze.

He followed close behind. "Aramie," he tsked, "don't mistake me for something I'm not—a refined, genteel male." He hid behind his cynicism, the barrier like a familiar blanket.

She whirled around. Her about-face caught him off guard. He gripped her arms as much to prevent their collision as his need to touch her. The anger evident in her red face and pursed lips made her all the more attractive.

"Maybe I don't want a *genteel* male."

"Is this what you'd rather have?"

His own frustration and desire broke through his thin veil of control. He didn't wait for her permission, but pulled her into his arms. Without thought, he cradled her head in his palm. Her short breaths panted from her mouth. He kissed her lips, bruising her with his need. She fought him at first, but then relaxed, snaking her hands through his hair to rest at the base of his neck.

She returned the force of the kiss, shocking him with her intensity. He licked the inside of her bottom lip, requesting entrance. She opened to him, and the taste of her delicious strawberry flavor was sweeter than he'd remembered. He pulled her closer. Her firm breasts pressed against his sweaty shirt. Beneath her blouse her nipples hardened, driving his need to claim her.

He released her from the kiss, their heavy pants loud in the night air. Running his fingers through her hair sent a chill up his arm. The softness of those dark strands teased the sensitive pads on his fingertips. He wanted to touch every part of her body, experience all the soft places he could imagine.

"Demir—" The sensual way she said his name sent a jolt of male pride right to his groin. A guttural moan escaped his lips. At this point, he'd do anything she asked of him.

She grabbed his bottom lip with her teeth and pulled. The combined sensation of pain and pleasure rippled along the nerves in his mouth. She let him go, and a gentle growl reverberated from her chest and into his.

The coppery taste of blood filled his mouth. She'd bitten him good. A rush of adrenaline raced to his cock, and he hardened at the realization of how rough she'd be as a lover. He wanted to find out, right here, right now.

"Hey, tough stuff," his words were low and rough, "do you really want to tempt me?" As much as he didn't want to, he'd give her one last chance to walk away. He pulled back and ran both his hands through her short, silky hair, prepared to kiss her once again.

Her hand raced to her hair. She patted the spot where her barrette used to be. Her eyes widened, and a frail gasp rose from her throat. "My barrette, it's gone."

Her face drained of color. The pale hue set off all kinds of warning bells in his mind.

She pulled away from him completely, and with a frantic pace, searched the ground. "Please, help me find it." With quick and shaky hands, she patted the ground where they stood.

He kneeled next to her and placed a hand on her shoulder. "We'll find your hair pin. Don't worry."

After searching for several minutes without success, he glanced at her. She paced the area, her movement frantic. "Aramie, why is this barrette so important to you?"

She stared into his eyes, her brow furrowed. His gut twisted at her anxiety, but he had to know the answer.

"It was a gift from my gran'ma. I have to find it." The slack expression on her face along, with the slight glisten in her eyes, brought the pain into his chest. Her anguish over the lost hair clip was the worst kind of torture. "We have to go back—to the place where we first changed into our panthers. It must be there. It has to be."

Her command was not something he'd challenge. To bow to anyone's will was not his style, but for her, he would. She gave him a new purpose, a new goal—to retrieve a small red barrette. The absurdity of it wasn't lost on him, but he was lost to her, and that was all that mattered. The Gossum would have to wait.

Chapter Twenty-Seven

The walls narrowed in this portion of the Keep, forcing Tanen to turn sideways to squeeze through the passage. Several large boulders lay scattered along the path, aftereffects of the Keep's last outburst when the Gossum had tried to enter their sanctuary using a portal. Good thing they hadn't succeeded.

The sharp edge of a rock scraped the back of his arm, leaving a long scratch. Blood welled in the injury. *Craya!* A twinge of irritation flashed through his mind. He wiped the red fluid on his trousers and kept moving.

The Strong room hadn't been occupied in hundreds of years. Stiyaha were steadfast in their loyalty to the royal family. The unused dungeon had sat in empty silence, as far back as he could recall. Not anymore.

The scent of mildew, wetness, and earth brought back memories of nights when he'd roamed the land outside the confines of the Keep. He hadn't been outside in over a century, not since a Gossum had nearly taken him down. As a council member, he had all the same training as the rest of the warriors, but his skills were rusty from lack of use. After his little bout with the enemy, he'd elected to stay inside from then on.

As he walked along the corridor, Mauree's sweet scent of roses merged with the other smells. There were nights when he wished he wasn't council leader.

"Tanen, I hear you coming. Let me out of here!" Mauree grasped one of the bars and peered at him. Her blue eyes flecked with gold, and her greasy, matted hair hung limp around her shoulders. The dress she wore had a rip up the thigh, displaying one long elegant leg.

An open tome lay on the stone floor, face down, the spine broken. His cheeks heated. He loved his books and all the knowledge they contained. Narrowing his focus, he glared at her. She smiled, as if enjoying his discomfort and agitation.

"If you can't treat the ancient texts with respect, then you can't have any." He spit the words at her.

She laughed. The high-pitched snicker reverberated off the walls and into the corridor. Goosebumps raced over his arms. *She's lost her mind.*

He wished that were true. The lucid look in her eyes revealed she was as sane as anyone else in this horrible war. He shuddered and bile rose in his throat.

In direct contrast to her loud laughter, he lowered his voice. "How do you like your cell?"

She stared hard at him. Her chipped nails and scuffed shoes were so unlike her. She liked to be pampered, and had seemed to enjoy how the males tracked her with their admiring gazes whenever she walked by. Short skirts and tight blouses were her traditional outfits. He'd noticed every one.

She gripped the bars with both hands, her fingers turning white from her exertion. "Let me out and I will repay you…like you want me to."

Her eyes twinkled, her smile all mischief. She opened her mouth. With a slow sweep of her tongue, she wet her bottom lip. She positioned her face next to her hands, and then glided her moist tongue along one of the cell bars.

He curled his lip, but despite his outward display of disgust, blood raced to his genitals. His own scent of musk and pepper deepened, giving away his desire. Against his will, he focused on her mouth.

"C'mon, Tanen. I know you like what you see." The soft lilt in her voice drew him in further. He'd been down this road before. Over the past few weeks, she'd used her sensual nature to encourage him to release her. So far, he'd been able to resist.

He moved closer and gripped her hands, the skin on skin contact like a drug to him. "Maurce."

Grinding his teeth, he fought his inner beast who wanted to do exactly what she wanted. "Tell me…where is Jakar's hideout." There was no way he'd tell her Ram was still alive. He could play this game just as well.

Her eyes bore into his. "Let me out, and I'll tell you." The warmth of her breath teased the skin on his clean-shaven face.

"Tell me, and I'll let you out." What he'd do with her then, he wasn't sure, but his beast had ideas.

She closed her eyes, parted her lips, and whispered. "Too bad you're nothing like Noeh."

The mention of the king's name brought reality rushing back with a wallop. He pushed away from the cell. Raw energy burned through his veins, hot and fast. She'd been after Noeh for centuries, and they were all lucky Noeh hadn't selected Mauree as queen.

"Nice try." His ragged breaths were loud in the empty corridor. "You're fortunate the king hasn't authorized torture to drag the information out of you."

She stepped back into the darkness of her cell. Moistness made her eyes sparkle in the meager light. She grabbed the book, riffling the pages with the edge of her finger.

"Find anything in these precious books of yours, yet?" She goaded him, but he wouldn't talk to her about his failure to find any guidance on how to prosecute her. King Noeh wanted to sentence her to death. Unless Tanen could find anything in the scriptures that said otherwise, she would die. Not that he cared about Mauree, per se, but he was responsible for upholding the laws. It wouldn't look good if someone found the law later and realized he'd made a mistake by sentencing her to death. A bead of sweat rolled down his back.

"Give me the book." He held out his hand. Because of his love for books, he wouldn't let her continue to damage the old text.

It slipped through her fingers. The ancient tome landed on its back with a thud. "Oops. So sorry." An eerie giggle eased from her throat.

"This is a waste of my time." He turned and headed back the way he'd come.

"Wait! Please...don't go." The pleading in her voice almost broke him.

He stopped. His breathing and the small sobs coming from her cell were the only sounds in the Strong room. *Craya!* He'd regret this, he was sure.

He returned to her. The lines around her eyes softened. Her pert nose and full lips reminded him she was still a beauty.

"Mauree. Your trial date will be in three days. You will stand before the council for treason, kidnapping, and attempted murder." He studied her, waiting for her reaction.

She remained passive. Her gaze traveled over his body and back to his eyes. An alluring smile formed on her lips. His skin crawled, and he took a step back. She was a seductress, and he was in her crosshairs.

"Tanen." His name rolled off her tongue, sending a strange mixture of delight and disgust along his arms. "You want me, I can tell. Come in here. No one has to know. I would—"

"Stop. Right. There." What did she think? That he was stupid enough to open the cell door? He sniffed the air, exaggerating the movements. "You could use a bath. Maybe I'll send Bet. Then, again, maybe not."

Her mouth pursed, the bitterness and anger returning in the lines on her face. "You do that. Think about me taking a bath, Tanen. Be gentle. Don't hurt yourself when you come in your own hand."

Her taunting laughter followed him all the way back to his room.

Chapter Twenty-Eight

"Where is it?" Aramie pushed the wet ferns out of the way, searching for her precious missing barrette. She held her breath, holding in a sob. If she let the wail escape, the tears would start, and she couldn't let that happen. Not here, not in front of Demir. Water from the damp foliage splashed against her face, creating the tears she didn't want to shed.

The familiar scene started again, the one that played over and over in her mind. She couldn't stop it even if she'd tried, so she let the memory consume her.

"Gran'ma, I'm home." Warm air assailed Aramie as she stepped into their makeshift home. The small shelter they'd built over the summer kept the sun out during the day, but the stifling heat remained long into the night and made living here difficult.

"Aramie, did you bring home a kill? We're out of meat again." Her mother strolled into the room, the smell of her recent coupling oozing from her pores.

"Chantre, come back to bed." Her lover's voice boomed from the adjacent room.

Aramie winced. The male was the latest in a long string of step-fathers, none of which she'd liked. With a glare that could scrape fat from a hide, her mother's gaze travelled over Aramie's small frame. The older female shrugged and disappeared to be with her latest mate.

"Aramie, where's Sidea?" Gran'ma wiped her hands on her apron. Dark circles ringed her eyes, and lines creased her cheeks. She'd reached the age where youth had let go of its hold. Time was short for her gran'ma, but as a child, Aramie had no clue how little time she had left with the one woman who loved her.

"Out back. She's coming." Aramie ran into her gran'ma's arms. The warmth of her embrace was like a salve for Aramie's rough childhood.

Gran'ma pulled back and looked into Aramie's eyes. Her round face twisted into a devilish smile, and her eyes flashed with amusement. "Aramie, I have something for you." She rummaged around in her pockets and pulled out her closed fists, palms down. "Pick one."

Aramie's chest constricted, and she clapped her hands. She glanced from one hand to the other and pointed to the one that had a small mole on the back.

A soft chuckle emanated from the older female and she opened her palm to reveal a bright red barrette, carved in the shape of a strawberry. "Take it, sweetheart. I made it for you."

Aramie picked up the beautiful barrette. She held it to her chest then hugged her gran'ma with all her strength.

"Let me put it in for you."

Aramie handed her gift back to the female she loved more than anyone. Gran'ma placed the jewelry in her hair and leaned back. She scrutinized her work. "That ought to keep the hair out of your eyes."

"I love you, Gran'ma." Aramie hugged her again, squeezing the older female tight.

"You're welcome, sweetheart."

That was the last memory Aramie had of her gran'ma. She'd passed away that day while they'd all slumbered. Her soul had returned home to Lemuria, and she'd left Aramie in her mother's care.

Aramie's heart pounded. Adrenaline surged through her veins. To lose Gran'ma's gift was to lose the one happy part of her youth. Her hands shook with the need to find the precious piece of jewelry. The plants, the trees, the moss, all painted the forest in different shades of green. Finding the red barrette should be easy.

She paced where Demir had tackled her. The trampled ferns and bent saplings were evidence of their previous encounter. An image of his body pressed against hers vied for attention in her mind. She pushed the bittersweet memory aside. A knot formed in her stomach as grief over the loss of her gran'ma's barrette overrode all other thoughts.

No sign of her barrette anywhere. The weight bore down on her. She plunged her hands into the broken ferns at her feet. The wet foliage slipped through her fingers before her grip took hold, sending a pungent earthy smell into the air. She pulled. The roots resisted her efforts, but not for long. Dirt clods clung to the long strands, as if unwilling to let go of their prize. The destruction eased the ache in her heart, but didn't uncover her treasure. She ripped, again, and again, flinging the underbrush into the air.

"Aramie, stop." Demir's hand on her shoulder made her jump. "Is this what you're looking for?"

A jolt raced through her body. She whipped around to face him.

The red barrette, her most cherished possession, lay atop his outstretched palm.

The ball in her gut released its tension. She exhaled, and looked into Demir's eyes.

"Where did you find it?"

"Close by. It must've fallen out of your hair when—" He stilled.

His gaze roamed her face, stopping for a brief moment at her lips, before returning to her eyes. "Let me put it in for you." His statement was half question, half demand, and bounced against the memory of her gran'ma.

Gran'ma had loved her, and Aramie had trusted her Gran'ma without question. Demir? She didn't know on either count.

"I'll do it." She reached for the barrette, and he closed it in his palm.

The yellow slits of his eyes burned with smoldering desire. The tip of one fang protruded over his plump bottom lip in a shielded display of authority. His body shook, and his jaw flexed with controlled tension. He closed his eyelids, and inhaled.

She held her breath and took a step back.

He opened his eyes. His pupils had returned to their normal chocolate brown. He uncurled his fingers and tossed the barrette into the air. "Take it."

She caught her favorite jewelry in her palm. The familiar wood against her skin warmed her heart. As she clipped the barrette into her hair, a feeling of wholeness and peace crept into her heart. She had her gran'ma back, or at least her parting gift.

Demir glanced at the ground. The shadows from the trees grew longer in the moonlight. Sunrise wasn't far away. "We must return to the Keep."

She inhaled, her pulse rising. "No…not yet."

By going against his command, she'd challenged him. A sour taste formed in the back of her throat, and she steeled herself for the repercussions.

Demir's nostrils flared and his eyes flashed yellow, but he didn't respond.

Downwind, the trees rustled. *Hisssss.*

Gossum.

Several yards away, Ram dropped from the limbs of a pine tree. The tip of his tongue snaked from between his lips. His mouth turned up at the corner. Bright, serrated teeth gleamed in the darkness.

One by one, three other Gossum dropped from the trees.

Aramie crouched, muscles coiled as she prepared for the upcoming fight. They'd found Ram after all.

Chapter Twenty-Nine

Demir tensed and moved in front of Aramie. Blood pounded at his temple, as he eyed his enemy. Four Gossum stood among the trees, their black orbs glittering from the remaining rays of the moon. Two circled around, enclosing Demir and Aramie into a confined space.

"My, my. Fancy meeting you here." Ram shifted to the side, to gain a better view of Aramie. "Well, if it isn't the young gal from the pretty blue pool. By the way, your stench was easy to track from downwind."

"You killed my sister!" Aramie pushed against Demir, trying to get to their enemy.

Demir wrapped his arm around her waist and pulled her backside against him. "Wait. Be smart."

He didn't want her emotions to cloud her judgment. She'd always been cool, calculating. To see her this way sent a jab of fear under his skin. It raced along his nerves, fueling his anxiety.

The Gossum compressed the circle, inching closer.

A piercing, guttural laugh filled the air. "She went down easy, as shall you." Ram's long tongue whipped out of his mouth, the sharp tip cracking in the calm night. His spittle flew through the air. A drop landed on Demir's boot.

Demir growled and curled his lip. With his free hand, he unclipped a throwing star from his belt. The smooth metal of his once-hated, now-favorite weapon caressed his palm.

"Sweet thing that she was, she gave us a parting gift." Ram glanced at one of his comrades and nodded.

Cracking and popping sounds filled the air. The ugly creature transformed, its body contorting into something grotesque, yet familiar. Smooth, hairless skin covered the shape of a Panthera. Dark eyes shone from its head. Serrated teeth gleamed in the moonlight. The beast panted, the guttural grunts reminiscent of its Gossum origins.

Demir held his breath. *No.* This couldn't be, but the evidence before him couldn't be denied.

"Sidea—"

Aramie's soft whisper broke Demir out of his trance. He launched his throwing star, piercing the creature's eyeball in one swift move. The Gossum fell to the ground, black goo coating the underbrush.

Battle screams pierced the air.

Aramie's fur grazed across Demir's arm as she leapt to battle one of the Gossum.

Ram crouched, the muscles bulging under his filthy jeans. He launched himself, changing into a hideous version of a panther.

Demir transformed and met Ram head-on. Claws scraped down his forearm. Throbbing pain raced into his shoulder, but he didn't stop. He used the ache to drive him. They tumbled to the ground, rolling over and over the ferns and small boulders that pebbled the ground.

Demir's back hit a tree trunk. He failed to take in air. Spots clouded his vision, but he used the power in his hind legs to kick out. His nails dug into tissue and he ripped, shredding the tender flesh. Blood splashed on his fur.

Ram skidded away, the injury forming a line on his chest, next to a long pink scar.

Where was Aramie? He glanced to his left, in the direction she'd gone, but he didn't see her. A cold chill raised his hackles.

As Demir stood, he caught sight of the remaining Gossum heading his way. The creature leapt before Demir could fight back. The animal knocked him down, tearing into his shoulder with his knife-like claws. A new agony raced along his nerves. He head-butted the faux cat.

The sound of their skulls colliding reverberated through the trees. The animal lost its grip. Demir used his strength to flip the creature over, gaining the advantage. He was about to slit its throat when a heavy load descended on his back.

The weight of his adversary pinned him between the two males. A tongue snapped next to his face, the spur dangerously close to his ear. Before he could retaliate, serrated teeth pierced the skin on the back of his shoulder. Intense pain radiated through his arm, across his back, and into his skull. His mind blanked at everything but the agony.

A growl pierced the night air.

The weight lifted from his body, the freedom a welcome relief. The creature still pinned underneath him struggled to gain a purchase. Using his remaining strength, Demir slashed the creature's throat with his claw. The animal heaved one last breath and disintegrated.

"Demir!" Aramie's hand traced across his back. Her soft touch set off little bombs of agony from the venom racing through his system.

Somehow, he managed to change into his human form. Warmth radiated from the bite, pulsing with each heartbeat. He'd been bitten before, but the pain had never been like this. A Gossum bite could be lethal, good thing Aramie had removed the threat.

Aramie. She had a cut on her cheek and blood stained her shirt, but otherwise, she appeared fine. His stomach rolled at the thought of her injured. "You ok?"

"It's not me I'm worried about." Her voice broke, and she coughed.

He rose to one knee. "Where's Ram?"

"Fled…the coward." Aramie jutted her chin.

He inhaled and warmth filtered into his lungs. Despite the pain in his shoulder and back, a strange sense of pride filled him. This female standing before him was a fine warrior. She'd make a formidable mate, one that wouldn't bow down to him, one that would make him toe the line. Maybe that was what he needed—a strong, powerful female.

Cupping his face with his hand, he rubbed his eyes. As he stood, little white dots expanded in his vision, nearly dropping him once again.

Soft, strong fingers gripped his forearm, steadying him. She placed one of his arms over her shoulder. The scent of strawberries tickled his nose. He moaned in delight.

"Rin. Open a portal." She steadied him, and they walked toward a small boulder situated next to one of the larger evergreen trees. She eased him onto the stone. "Here, sit."

He needed to clear the fog from his mind. Trouble was, there was only one thing on his mind—Aramie.

"Damn!" She paced in front of him, her well-muscled legs and firm bottom attracting his attention like a beacon. He traced his gaze up her body, stopping for a moment to enjoy the firmness of her breasts until he reached her face. The smoothness of her skin taunted him, and he longed to capture those soft lips with his own. The features of her face blurred and tiny white dots formed in his vision.

Snap. Snap. Long, sensuous, feminine fingers drew away from his face.

"Demir. Wake up." She shook his shoulder, sending a new bout of pain through his body. Had he fallen asleep? Was he hallucinating?

She cupped his cheeks in her palms, forcing him to meet her gaze. "The portal won't open. We have to find shelter." She glanced upward. "The sun will be up soon. Can you walk?"

He looked into the brightening sky. The light blue was something he'd only seen a few times in his life. He smiled, mesmerized by its beauty. Somewhere in the back of his mind, his cat screamed.

Chapter Thirty

Aramie's fingers stung from the force of her blow. She'd struck her Pride leader, but she'd had no choice. He needed to rouse out of his daze.

Demir shook his head. He massaged his cheek, and his brows furrowed. With a quick glance, he focused on her, his eyes burning with contempt. "You hit me."

"At least you're aware of it." She peered at the lightening sky. Dread's cold fingers skated over her arms. "Can you walk? We have to find shelter."

He stood, but he couldn't maintain his balance. His body slumped onto the stone.

With great effort, he pushed himself to a standing position. He wavered, but remained upright. "Why do we need shelter? Didn't you call for a portal?"

"I sent Rin a mental request. The portal won't open. He didn't know why."

He scanned their surroundings, focusing Aramie's attention back to the world around them. A robin chirped its morning call. A squirrel ran up the trunk of a nearby tree, its tail flipping back and forth. The forest creatures woke around them. Aramie's restless legs ached to move, for her to run, and find some kind of shelter before it was too late.

"The mountain we passed a while back may offer some shelter." He touched the back of his shoulder. Blood coated his fingers. He wiped them on his pants.

"Can you shift?" Aramie bit her cheek, anticipating the worst.

He closed his eyes. The muscles in his face tightened, and he frowned, but he remained in human form. He looked at her and shook his head. "We go, now."

The pain in his body must be intense to prevent him from changing, but he didn't complain, didn't utter one sound. A deep rooted respect for his inner strength caught Aramie off guard, and she caught her breath. There was a reason he was her Pride leader, and he'd proved it once again.

She followed him into the thick forest. The tree branches pulled at her hair, snagged her clothing, but that was part of the experience. She'd run from the sun before.

Boulders lined the area, reminders of the force of the now dormant volcano. A morning fog rose among the trees, cooling her skin. The sign was another reminder the sun would be up in minutes.

They broke into a small clearing. Demir stopped, causing Aramie to run into him.

He gasped and visibly stiffened. She'd hurt him, and her heart ached in response.

A meadow ran to the edge of the mountain, the grass wet from the fog. Through the mist, the snow on the mountain crags gleamed with the light of the morning sun. She'd never seen anything so beautiful.

He turned to her, his eyes intensely scanning her face as if this was the last time he'd see her. A tendril of fear raced into her heart. He cupped her cheek in his palm, the movement gentle and intimate.

"Aramie," the way he purred her name sent a shiver of delight down her spine, "shift, you can make it before the sun hits the meadow. Find shelter."

A lump formed in her throat. He wanted her to leave him here. She couldn't believe it. Tears formed in her eyes, and she shook her head. "N-n-no. I...won't go without you."

"You're wasting time!" His jaw tightened, the muscles flexing under his skin.

"We can make it together. I know we can." She wouldn't give up on him—she couldn't.

"You're so stubborn." He grabbed her hand and pulled her along as he ran for the mountain's edge. The wet grass slapped against her pants, her shoes soaked from the damp soil. The fog dissipated into the air. The sun peeked over the tips of the trees casting strange shadows across the meadow.

They were out of time.

A bunch of boulders surrounded the mountain's edge, evidence of a recent rockslide. Demir crawled over the rubble, inching closer to both the mountain and the sun's encroaching rays.

Aramie followed, certain they'd find an outcropping of rock or some form of shelter. She couldn't believe it would end this way—death by the sun. What had she accomplished in her life? She'd raised her sister and stayed away from any true relationship, her fear of being controlled ruling her in its vice-grip. She peered at

Demir as they crawled over the rocks. His inner strength and sarcastic wit had

crept into her heart. Had she missed out on what could be? Maybe she'd never

know. A knot formed in her stomach, squeezing, clenching her insides tight.

They reached the mountain as the sun crested over the trees. The rocks right

above her head brightened from the light. She crouched, away from the deadly

sun.

"Do you see anything?" Demir glanced at her.

His pale face and red-rimmed eyes reminded her of his injury. He didn't look

good, not that it would matter now.

The solid rock face before them had no opening, not even the slightest

overhang from a protruding rock. The sun's warm rays moved over the rock,

forcing them to crouch lower. They only had a few seconds left.

"Demir—" Aramie placed her hand on his shoulder, careful not to touch his

injury.

He looked over his shoulder at her and his eyes turned into yellow slits.

"Aramie—" He pulled her into his embrace as they crouched against the

mountain. His warm scent cascaded over her, and she couldn't imagine a nicer way

to go.

A rumbling shook the ground. Boulders loosened with a loud crack and fell.

Demir covered her head and shoulders with his body, protecting her from the debris. Small pebbles pelted Aramie's arms and legs. Dust rose into the air, shielding them momentarily from the sun.

In the shadows, a small opening appeared. Their salvation. Demir pushed dust and pebbles out of the way, widening the shallow cave's entrance. He turned to her, pulling her close. "Go."

She dived into the cave, the sharp rocks scratching her arms in the process. The smell of her own blood permeated the air. She inhaled. Dust coated the back of her throat and she coughed.

Demir! Adrenaline spiked through her system. She scrambled onto her knees, heading for the opening.

A figure filled the entrance to the cave, blocking out the light. The scent of musk and incense competed with the smell of burnt flesh. He slid into the cave, coming to rest by her side. He lay motionless.

Her heartbeat pounded. With shaky hands, she rolled him onto his back. He was still alive, or he'd show signs of disintegration. His pale face was unmarked, his eyes closed. The diamond stud above his lip glittered in the dim light. He seemed at peace.

She glanced over his body, looking for the source of the burn she'd smelled. Black, charred skin on his left hand and forearm made her wince. He'd recover, but the pain would be excruciating.

She shook him gently. "Demir."

He didn't respond. She shook him harder this time, but to no avail. He was out cold.

She dragged him over to the soft dirt at the back of the small cave. The shelter itself was barely big enough to contain them. There wasn't room to stand, so she sat cross-legged, cradling his head in her hands. She'd do whatever she could to make him comfortable. Until nightfall, they were stuck here.

Chapter Thirty-One

"Get me another." Zedron held up his glass and glanced at Carine.

Her hand clenched around the washrag. Drops of water landed on the deck and soaked into the wood. She didn't comment, but lowered her chin in a slight nod.

A tratee fly with its brilliantly lit wings buzzed around his head. He grabbed a nearby cloth and swatted at the annoying creature, but it eluded him. The fly circled his head once more before fleeing into the branches of the Rolmdew tree. He looked at Carine and caught the smirk on her face. His cheeks heated.

He tapped the edge of his manicured fingernail against the fine grain of his armrest. The noise would annoy Carine, as Arotaars had extra sensitive hearing. That was fine by him, he enjoyed taunting her. The lounge creaked as he adjusted himself to a more comfortable position.

She wiped her hands on her apron and grabbed the pitcher from the bar. With deliberate strides, she approached, her defiant attitude etched in the fine lines in her face. The orange spots on her skin pulsed lightly, confirming what he'd seen in her expression.

She snatched his drinking glass and poured him some judona ade. The juice in the container didn't quite fill the glass. She peered at him.

He raised an eyebrow, and smiled. "More would be nice." If nothing else, he was ever polite and cultured.

The strands of her blue hair crackled.

He had managed to irritate her. A laugh burst from his lips. She couldn't hide her emotions from him, and he loved that about her.

While he waited for her to return, he studied his surroundings. Leaves whispered in the trees, the dryness a reminder the forest this time of year was a tinderbox. The brief rain they'd had a few days ago was long gone, and the coolness of the night was a gentle reprieve from the relentless Lemurian sun.

"Master, come quickly." Carine's soft voice filtered out the open door.

That she called him 'master' warmed him on the inside. He bolted from his chair and ran across the deck. A growl from below alerted him to the presence of rhondo beasts. He stopped at the back entrance to his home. A shiver ran over his back. Good thing he was one hundred feet up in a Rolmdew tree.

"What is it, Carine? Don't tell me the rhondo beast scared you." He rolled his shoulders and entered the sitting room with a casual air.

"Look!" She pointed to his *visus bacin.*

The scrying bowl was his tool for searching out new planets to supply Lemuria with needed resources. It was also used to watch activities unfold when two colonizers battled over the right to colonize a planet. Events could be displayed as they occurred, and sometimes he could get a glimpse of a possible future. The invaluable information could alter the course of the game. His current battle was with Alora, over Earth. Although he couldn't spy on her directly, he could watch the characters, or see through their eyes.

"Well done, Carine. You are dismissed."

Her lips pursed, but she did as he asked and left the room.

The water bubbled on the surface of the large stone, froth spitting over the edge and onto the polished wooden floor. This was an indication something had changed in the game.

He skimmed his hand over the surface, allowing the water to guide him. Outlines of tall evergreen trees, shrouded in fog, coalesced in the water. The smell of pine and wetness filtered into his senses. *Earth.* His skin tingled with anticipation. A meadow spread out between the trees, the sun cresting over the pointy tips.

Two figures, a male with brown hair tied in a queue and a female with short, dark hair, ran for the safety of the mountain. Zedron tensed. *Demir and Aramie—* Alora's characters. Their frantic pace indicated the depths of their anxiety for getting caught in the waning moments of daybreak.

The vision shifted. A pale hand with knife-like claws gripped the edge of a branch. The hairless arm and the intense astringent smell were a dead giveaway. *Ah, one of my own.*

Unlike Alora's warriors, who suffered the same punishment as their goddess and couldn't go out in the sun, his fighters had no such restriction. That gave him an advantage in the game, one he exploited every chance he could. He willed the creature to glance back at its prey. It complied.

The couple climbed over boulders and huddled close. Demir stroked Aramie's face with his hand. *How touching.* They crouched, away from the impending sunlight. Zedron looked forward to watching them fry.

A loud rumble echoed from the *visus bacin.*

The mountain shook, and a hole formed in front of the couple. Demir pushed Aramie into the cave. A shaft of sunlight caught his hand and part of his arm. Smoke rose in the air.

The smell of burnt flesh wafted into the room.

Demir hunched over, in obvious pain, and then dove into the cave.

The image vanished.

Zedron inhaled and stepped back. The way the cave opened right in front of the couple was no accident. Alora did this—he was sure of it. He smiled. One of the benefits of the visus bacin was the recording device. Everything displayed was saved for future reference. She'd cheated. He had her. How would he use the information?

As for Demir and Aramie, he had faith Ram would take care of them as he'd instructed.

The floor creaked.

Zedron glanced toward the sound. Over the years, he'd come to know every nook and cranny of his home, including every squeak and groan. He rolled his head and eased the stiffness in his neck.

"Come out, Carine. It's no use hiding."

Carine stepped out of the shadows between his ornately carved cases. His trophies and favorite collectibles from his colonized planets lined the shelves. Her eyes glowed with her defiance.

"I thought you'd learned, but apparently not." He stared at the ceiling and tapped a finger next to his chin. "What new task shall I give you? What would be fitting punishment?"

She jutted out her chin.

He chuckled. "I know how much your kind detests chilopods." He had a colony of the small, multi-legged creatures as pets. They secreted venom from tiny fangs. Although the sting wasn't deadly, the bite caused discomfort. "Come, I have several that need attention."

She furrowed her brow, but obeyed. He'd break her yet.

Chapter Thirty-Two

Tender fingers stroked Demir's goatee and the fine hairs over his lip. *Aramie.*

He inhaled, eager to soak in her feline fragrance, the one he'd grown so

accustomed to. Her strawberry scent filtered into his brain, along with the stench

of burnt flesh. A dull throb started in his hand and raced up his arm.

He wasn't in a coma, not anymore. Memories crashed down on him. *Gossum—*

sunlight—cave.

He opened his eyes and jerked to a sitting position.

Aramie gasped. "Demir, you're awake…are you ok?"

He flexed his fingers. The burn had healed, but the pink skin was still sensitive.

"I'm fine."

With a glance, he took in her features, assessing the damage. A few cuts and

bruises in the last stages of regeneration marred her face and arms. Dark circles

rimmed her eyes. She needed rest and food. He wanted to provide for her, but

with the burning sun outside, all he could do was ferment in his own frustration.

He peered around the small cave, their safe haven for the day. They were lucky.

If the rockslide hadn't uncovered the cave, they'd be dead.

"You're not *fine*." She narrowed her eyes, evaluating him. "Your shirt is damp from blood, do you want me to take a look at—"

"I said I was fine." The last thing he wanted was for her to see the skin on his back.

She sighed and rubbed her eyes.

The bite mark over his shoulder burned, the heat so intense, spikes of pain pounded into his brain. He touched the spot through the torn shreds of his shirt. Blood leaked onto his hand, and he wiped it onto his pants. "How long was I unconscious?"

She swallowed and turned her attention to him. "A few hours, I'd guess. I cat-napped a couple of times, so it's hard to tell." As she pushed to a kneeling position, she stretched her arms over her head, her fingers pressing against the cave's ceiling.

He couldn't help but admire how her firm breasts strained against her tight shirt. The smooth skin of her abdomen peeked from beneath the hem, and he longed to run his hand over the concave flesh, stroking her until she purred. He swallowed and forced himself to return his attention to her face.

Her cheeks reddened. She shivered, visible goosebumps forming on her arms. "I can't wait to leave."

Demir glanced out the cave's opening. The sun's rays still penetrated the rocks at the entrance. "Looks like we'll be here for a while. Got any cards?"

Her strained laughter filled the small space, and her shoulders relaxed.

The sound penetrated into his chest and warmed him on the inside. At least his joke had helped relieve some of her stress.

"Nope, not a one." The smirk on her face erased some of the tiredness from her eyes. Her lips quivered with amusement. Memories of their kiss and her warm, soft body pressed against him made his heart pound. Blood rushed through his veins.

She must've sensed his intense stare, for her smile faded, and she pulled at her bottom lip with her teeth. Absolutely irresistible, he couldn't resist her. He tensed, eager to take control.

She focused on something over his shoulder, and her eyes widened. A tremble started in her chin. "No—noooo."

He turned to look. Nothing but the cave wall.

"I-I've got to…" She bolted for the entrance, crawling on her hands and knees. Dirt from the soft earthen floor kicked up in her wake.

"Aramie, no!" Demir grabbed her ankle just in time.

She fought him, kicking her feet with a force he had to admire. Although she was strong, powerful, and full of tenacity, she couldn't match his strength. He grabbed her other leg and pulled her toward him. "Stop—fighting."

She landed a heel to his head. The ringing in his ears sounded like a swarm of bees, and he loosened his hold. She bolted for the entrance once again.

He regained enough sense to snag her pant leg. She landed on her side, the air escaping her lungs with a whoosh.

In her effort to escape the small cave, she flailed on the ground, scratching at the dirt floor. Her head hit a rock near the entrance. The coppery scent of blood permeated the air.

Fear gripped his chest. His breath squeezed from his lungs. *Aramie!* He crawled over her back and trapped her legs, capturing each of her wrists in his palms. With tender care, he cradled her in his embrace and protected her from further harm.

A small sob escaped her lips and wedged itself into his heart.

"It's ok, tough stuff. I've got you."

Her chest hitched, her body still trembling. Several seconds ticked by. Finally, her tension subsided, and she relaxed in his arms. Soft strands of hair caressed his face and caught in his goatee. The sensation tickled his skin, teasing him.

"Did you…did you kill it?" The words were a mere whisper, a soft plea.

"Kill what, Aramie?" She feared something, and every male fiber in his being wanted to protect her.

"The s-spider." A bead of perspiration rolled down her nose and dripped onto the soil.

A wave of understanding hit him in the chest. He'd never known about her fear. She'd always put up such a strong front, he didn't think she feared anything. A spider, of all creatures.

"I'll take care of it." His voice sounded raspy, but he couldn't hold back his compassion for her. "I'm going to let you go. You won't run from me, will you?" He needed to be sure she wouldn't bolt if her anxiety took hold again.

"No. I-I promise."

His shoulders relaxed. He crouched on all fours and helped her to sit. Small bits of rock clung to her palms. He wiped the dirt away, cleaning her, massaging her skin to take away the sting. Her brown eyes tracked his movements with catlike precision.

"Where did you see the spider?"

She pointed into the dark corner. "It ran under that rock."

As he moved to take care of the little predator, her hands trailed along his arm, her touch lighting up his nerves.

Demir lifted one of the rocks. Nothing. He looked at Aramie. Crouched near the entrance to the cave, she visibly shivered, her eyes wide. To see her so scared burned a hole in his gut, and a determination to protect her raced through him. It didn't escape him that the threat was her own fear, but he'd find the spider, of that he had no doubt.

He returned to his search, moving rocks out of the way, one by one. At last, he came upon the small arachnid. He was in agreement with Aramie—he'd never much liked the hairy, multi-eyed critters.

Demir took off his boot. The movement must've caught the creature's attention, because it skittered across the soft dirt.

Squish.

With great care, he checked the entire cave, every nook and cranny. He'd killed two more before he was done. "Justice has been served."

"Thank you." Aramie's gaze bore into him. "I don't like spiders."

A smirk crept across his face, and he raised an eyebrow. "You don't say."

Her own smile turned into a wide grin. She'd always liked his sarcasm, and he enjoyed her response.

The pain in his hand and arm subsided to a minor ache, the skin knitting back together with his powerful Lemurian blood, but his shoulder pulsed with agony. Distracted by Aramie's anxiety attack, he'd forgotten about his own injuries, but not anymore. A bead of sweat rolled from the tip of his hairline down his face.

"Demir?" Aramie crawled next to him. She wiped away the moisture from his brow. The arc of tension between them spiked, the pull almost physical in its intensity.

"Aramie—" He touched her barrette and traced his fingers through her thick, glossy hair.

"Shh…" She placed her finger over his mouth, pushed him down, and straddled his lap.

A strange thrill coursed through his body at her brazen attitude, and his stiffening shaft told him how much he was on board with this little exercise.

She tugged his shirt out of his waistband, her eyes focused on her task. The material bunched around his abdomen as she pulled. He lifted his arms, eager for her to eliminate this barrier between them. With one swift move, she ripped the shirt over his head.

Cold air hit him, cooling the sheen of sweat that coated his skin. The bite mark still pounded, but he was much more interested in the blood pulsing in his cock.

Aramie leaned back, her palms resting on his forearms. Her admiring gaze roamed over his chest and abs. A sly smile pulled at one corner of her mouth. She grazed her hands up his biceps, her nails scratching his skin, sending a thrill along his nerves that made his shaft jump.

When she reached his shoulders, he grabbed her hands. A warning growl erupted from his chest. "No further."

Chapter Thirty-Three

Demir's warning lifted the hackles on the back of Aramie's neck. His firm but tender grip around her wrists held her in place. An ache of rejection clenched her chest, and tears welled in her eyes. She glanced away, pulling against his grasp. Instead of releasing her, he drew her hands to his lips.

Tender kisses along her knuckles woke up her nerves, the sensitive skin alive and aware of every brush. The intensity of his gaze bore into her, roaming her face before returning to her fingers. "Don't misunderstand, Aramie, I want you...I want you very much."

She swallowed the lump in her throat. "Why did you stop me?"

He sat up on his elbows, and focused on her eyes. "Call me old fashioned, but I like to be in control."

Her heart skittered a beat. She'd spent her whole life avoiding this very situation. To give up control went against everything she believed, but when she looked into his eyes, she didn't see the burning need to dominate her into submission. What she saw was compassion, and his own need to be strong.

Unsure what to do, she remained tense. She wanted to give herself to him, yet she didn't know if she could. A tear slid down her cheek.

He let go of her hands and traced the tear with the back of his finger. She leaned toward him, and his other hand cradled her head, his tender fingers massaging the base of her neck. Relaxing under his ministrations, her body's hyper-sensitive senses reacted to his every touch.

An uncontrollable purr radiated from her chest. The whiskers of his goatee tickled her skin as he smiled, and a warm chuckle filled with masculine pride eased from his throat. Her traitorous body shivered in response.

Without warning, he lay back down, pulling her with him. She hissed and her hands landed on his firm pecs. An appreciative growl reverberated from within him, the vibration causing her fingers to tingle. His breath smelled of mint and tea and mixed with his own masculine scent. Washed along by his tide, she couldn't resist him.

His powerful kiss was tender, yet demanding. The electric current between them spiked, pulling her further under his spell. Strong, sensual fingers tracked through her hair and down her back. He gripped the edge of her shirt and pulled it over her head. With practiced skill, he unhooked her bra. The confining material fell forward, revealing her breasts. He studied her for a moment before his gaze met hers.

"Beautiful Aramie."

The words came out on a slow purr, and she loved how his voice resonated within her body, intensifying her own desire. He traced a finger over the side of her face, along the contours of her neck, and to the small "V" of her breasts, leaving small shivers of delight in his path. Cupping one of her mounds in his palm, her pert nipples stood at attention, ready for his touch.

His cock jerked below her as she straddled him, his firmness making her wet with her own need. He raised his head, his breath tickling her breast. When he licked the fine bud, she shivered. Tension built within her, and the tips of her claws extended, digging into his arms.

Gently, he pulled her nipple into his mouth, circling the hard point with his tongue. The warm wetness and his nips brought her close to her climax. She'd never experienced anything this intense before, and a whimper born of need escaped her lips.

Without thinking, she trailed her hands up his arms to his neck, eager to touch every firm muscle under his taut skin. Before she knew what had happened, he flipped her onto her back. Dark and predatory, he consumed her with his yellow eyes. His hungry gaze sent a rush of pure, feminine pride through her body.

With quick hands, he removed her shoes. She unbuttoned her jeans and he grabbed them by the waist, pulling them off in short order, panties included. He straddled her, placing his firm legs on either side of her thighs. She quivered with anticipation.

"Strip." The word came out a command, and she didn't regret it. She wanted him as naked as she was.

His eyebrows shot up and the skin around his eyes creased, his eyes glowing with admiration. He smiled, and the diamond stud in his upper lip glinted in the dim light.

Her heart constricted. *I love him.* She'd fallen for this strong, proud male, and fallen hard.

They couldn't be together, though. She wouldn't bow down to a male, not even him. A deep cut shaved off part of her heart, and she'd never felt such a mixture of pain and regret. Her eyes moistened, but she gave him her best smile. They had today and she'd record every moment in her memory.

He unlatched his buckle, his abdominal muscles tensing against the pull of the belt. She traced her finger over each taut ridge, up to his pectoral muscles where the slightest tinge of dark brown hair curled between her fingers.

His ragged breaths raced over the back of her hands, tickling the fine hairs. A low moan emanated from his chest, echoing off the rocks in the enclosed space. In a physical response to his call, her skin heated as a rush of desire overwhelmed her.

He moved away from her long enough to kick off his boots and shed his pants. Careful in his movements, he seemed to hide something. She didn't get time to think on it. A glimpse of his manhood and the heavy sac that hung below caused her to inhale. She'd fantasized about him for a long time, and the reality was more than she'd ever imagined.

He must've noticed her attention because his cock pulsed. His low, sensual chuckle sent a rush of wetness to her core. She glanced at his face. A tic in his jaw and a furrowed brow indicated his fierce concentration.

He was all male—tough, lean, and firm.

She purred in admiration, aware that doing so invited him in.

Chapter Thirty-Four

Aramie's scent cascaded over Demir's senses, into his lungs and his bloodstream. She'd revved up his drive, good and hard, with that sensual purr. The pulse pounding in both his cock and his shoulder vied for attention, but with sweet Aramie sprawled naked before him, the pain faded.

A sheen of sweat had broken out on her body, her skin glistening in the dim light. She was beautiful, from her smooth dark hair to her crooked little toe. He admired the view and longed to make her comfortable, but the fine dirt lining the cave floor was all they had.

"Gorgeous Aramie." He liked the way her name rolled off his tongue as he accentuated the "r," drawing it out.

She shivered under his attention, and her purr increased in volume, an open invitation. Pulling gently on his arm, she encouraged him. He straddled her hips once again, the length of him jutting out over her soft abdomen. With a firm grip, she squeezed the tip of his shaft.

He hissed.

Her touch lit up his nerves, and he leaned in to kiss her, pulling himself out of her grasp. As he captured her mouth, their bodies brushed together. The skin on skin contact short-circuited his brain and his animal instincts took over. She responded under his onslaught, their tongues dancing together, their passionate kiss all about what was right between them. Tracing her fingers along his arms and into his hair, her nails dug into his scalp. Her rough claiming drew out his predator, and a low moan eased from his chest.

She arched into him, pressing against his arousal, driving him insane. When they came up for air, the tips of her fingers grazed down his neck. He ran his hands up her arms, entwining his fingers with hers. As he brought her hands over her head, he kept them away from his back, and the evidence of his weakness. He held both her wrists in one hand, locking her there.

Her body tensed. She seemed frightened, and that wouldn't do. He ran his fingers over the soft skin on the inside of her arm, tickling her. "What is it, tough stuff?"

She shook her head and smiled, but the sly grin was forced. He looked into her eyes, searching for an answer. A fine warrior, not much scared her—except spiders and him, apparently. He stilled as the answer dawned on him. *She's afraid I'm going to make her my mate.*

His cat cried out. *Yes.* That's what he wanted to do, but he would never hurt her, never force her to bend to his will. The realization hit him like a punch. This high-spirited female with the dark hair and brazen attitude had crawled under his skin and touched his heart.

I love her.

His chest expanded, and he longed to make her his mate, but in doing so, he'd strip her of her identity, her need to be a warrior, and that would rip out everything he loved about her. He swallowed. *No!* There was no way that would happen. He'd show her what was in his heart, even if he could never give it to her.

"I won't hurt you, Aramie, and I won't…bite you. You have my word."

She stared into his eyes for a long moment. Would she trust him? His heart raced. Suddenly, the question became the most important one he'd ever had. He held his breath. His heart pounded as he counted the seconds.

She exhaled and her body relaxed beneath him. "Kiss me," she whispered.

He ravaged her mouth, pouring all his emotions into their embrace. She returned his kiss with a passion all her own. As her body moved beneath him she rubbed against his skin, sending sparks of desire to his balls. His cock hardened, the skin taut, straining with the rush of blood.

Kissing her cheeks, chin, the dimple in the crook of her neck, he savored every bit of skin he could reach. His free hand stroked the side of one breast, teasing her with his soft caress. She moaned under his assault.

He glanced at her face, eager to see the pleasure in her eyes. The usual brown color was gone, replaced with her yellow feline eyes. Her lips parted on ragged breaths.

With one knee and then the other, he spread her legs, opening up her core. The scent of strawberries intensified, and he breathed in her unique bouquet. The need to please her overwhelmed him, and he wanted nothing more than to make her come.

He glided his hand to the opening between her legs. Soft curls tickled the sensitive pads on his fingers. He twirled the fine strands enjoying how she squirmed beneath him. A tenderness filled him, and he vowed to make this a day Aramie would never forget. With utmost care, he rubbed his finger between her slick folds.

"You're so wet for me." He ground the words out through clenched teeth.

She bit her lip, soft pants escaping her mouth.

He growled his appreciation. Using one finger, he eased into her sheath. She shuddered beneath him and spread her legs wider, giving him easier access. A sudden urge to bite her overwhelmed him and his teeth elongated. He pursed his lips together, hiding them from her.

Her hips arched beneath him and his focus returned to her needs. He rubbed her firm clit with his thumb while he moved his fingers in and out of her passage. Her breaths grew ragged as he worked her. His focus remained on her face, soaking in her pleasure.

She stilled for a moment then bucked against him in a wild frenzy, her hands pulling against his grip. Her sheath tightened around his fingers as she came. He kept up his pressure, wringing out every last drop. When she quieted at last, he eased his hand from between her legs. A satisfied glint formed in her eyes, and she gave him a cute little smile. She raised her hips, rubbing herself against his member.

He closed his eyes and shivered. Good thing they weren't human. Disease wasn't an issue for Lemurians, and since the females were infertile, they didn't have to worry about pregnancy.

Her slick folds washed over him, coating him with her wetness. A deep-seated need to claim her raced through him and his body shook. He briefly closed his eyes and clenched his teeth, unwilling to give in to his desire. When he opened his eyes, the devotion and trust reflected in her gaze melted his heart completely.

With a feral groan, he plunged into her warm passage. She gripped him, squeezing her inner muscles, coaxing him along. They established a rhythm and moved together in a sensual motion. As his desire increased, so did their speed. He gripped her hip with one hand, steadying her as best he could.

His balls tightened. White dots formed in front of his eyes. As he came, he stared into the eyes of the female he'd fallen for. Her gaze locked with his, and he swore she loved him, too.

When he was spent, he lay on top of her, his free hand stroking her cheek. His other hand still held her wrists, her hands captive over her head. As much as he wanted to give her his heart and soul, he couldn't even give her access to his full body.

The dire thought wasn't what he needed right now, and he shoved it into the back of his mind. His inability to open fully to her burned in his gut. *I'm not worthy of her.* If she saw his scars, she'd think him weak just like his father.

Rolling off her, he pulled her against him, cradling her head in the crook of his arm. They didn't speak, each lost in their own thoughts. He couldn't tell her what he wanted. It would only make things uncomfortable between them. He caressed her hair and glanced to the cave entrance. Shadows over the rocks indicated the sun was still high in the sky.

A spot of red caught his attention. Her barrette had fallen out of her hair during their coupling. He picked it up, and then handed it to her.

She stared at her trinket then looked at him. Her gaze darted between his eyes. She studied him for a long moment. When she spoke, her words were soft. "Would you put it in for me?"

This barrette was so important to her. For her to ask him to do so was a great honor, a sign of trust.

"How could I not, my Aramie." He choked on the words, and they came out rough, strained.

She held open her palm, and he grasped her most precious object. With gentle care, he smoothed her locks, and clipped the strawberry-shaped jewelry into her hair.

A warm, shy smile broke out on her face. He was lost to her now. She was nothing like Eleanor, no, nothing at all. Aramie was so much more. Unlike submissive and quiet Eleanor, Aramie exuded strength and determination—and he loved her for it. There wasn't anything he wouldn't do for Aramie now.

"We should try to get some sleep." He kissed her hair, taking in her scent, the one he'd never be able to forget.

She snuggled up to him. Within minutes she snored, the little yips weaseling their way into his heart.

The skin on the back of his shoulder burned. He touched the bite mark. Wetness squeezed from the open sore. He glanced at his hand. Instead of red blood, a vibrant shade of blue coated his fingers. His hackles rose.

He rolled Aramie over and covered her with her clothes as best he could. Picking up his pants and shirt, he threw them on. He didn't want her to see the wound, or the scars on his back and buttocks. A sense of unease rippled over his shoulders and down his arms. The bite still burned. Why hadn't it healed already?

He lay next to Aramie. Placing his arm over her body, he spooned her, drawing her close to him. Her warmth and unique scent calmed his racing nerves. As he slept, strange thoughts of vodka, razor-like teeth, and an intense desire to kill became his nightmare.

Chapter Thirty-Five

The headache started again. Typically, Ram enjoyed pain, even when it was his own, but not this time. He sat on the rickety, whitewashed deck swing that graced the farmhouse's porch—the one made for two lovers to gaze at the moon on a warm summer's night. *Please, poke me in the eye with a stick.*

His vision blurred. Images of a small cave and Aramie in the throes of an orgasm flashed across his mind. Adrenaline surged through his body in a purely male response. He stood in a panic, the swing crashing into the back of his calf. A bruise he could live with, visions of sex with his enemy, not so much. Gossum had no need for sex. Ram wasn't quite sure if it was one of the benefits of the transformation, or maybe it was a disadvantage.

The female purred under him, and a male hand, not his own, stroked her cheek. He fell further into the vision, the smell of strawberries stirred his desire, something he hadn't experienced since his days as a human. Adrenaline pumped through his veins, and he swayed on his feet. He gripped the chain that held up the swing to steady himself.

The vision faded for a moment, and he regained some semblance of his location. He was on the front porch. A strange warmth emanated from his crotch.

He blinked and glanced down. His sweatpants tented, the material straining against his cock. Wasn't that nice—he had a boner.

The front door creaked as it opened.

"Ram, the new recruits…" Jakar gaped like a fish.

"What's the matter? Never seen anything quite this big before, have you?" If his first lieutenant stared any longer, he'd give him a close-up shot.

"My lord…please excuse me." Jakar bowed his head and retreated into the farmhouse.

Ram removed his cap and wiped his brow with the back of his hand. What the hell? These strange visions had started a few hours ago, and they had increased in frequency and duration. It was like he was in someone else's head—Demir's. A kernel of excitement spread through Ram's chest.

He'd bitten Demir on the back of the shoulder during the fight, but with his comrades dead, it had been two against one, and he hadn't liked those odds. So, he'd fled, tracking the two from afar. They'd holed up in a cave which seemed to materialize out of the side of the mountain.

Ram had wanted to attack them during the day, but decided not to because of a nearby hiking trail frequented by humans even in the winter. He'd weighed the option of converting any humans he'd encounter, but he couldn't risk them having connections, family—and the questions that would come. Tonight, he'd bring back his minions to finish off his enemy.

He walked down the three steps into the front yard. The setting sun warmed the back of his arms. Although he could go out during the day, he much preferred the night, and the opportunity to tangle with his enemy.

The neighing of horses floated by on the breeze, along with the stench of manure. In addition to the mares, a couple of pigs and an old goat inhabited the barn. The pesky billy had a habit of sneaking out of his stall. He'd already chewed up Ram's favorite hammock. Jakar seemed to have an affinity for the creatures, so they had remained. Ram ground his teeth. *Those animals will be the death of me yet.*

With a loud exhale, he continued, his boots crunching over the frost encrusted grass. If Sheri could see him now, she'd laugh at his accommodations. A longing to see his ex-wife expanded, twisting his insides like an old rag, but he didn't dare seek her out, not yet. He needed to prove himself worthy first, and that meant bringing down Noch, the Stiyaha king. This time, he would succeed. If he didn't, he'd never see her again, never get the chance to prove himself to her. His heart ached, and the ragged scar that ran over his chest burned.

A cobblestone path led off to an old, forgotten garden. Maybe a walk would clear his mind. Cages from last year's tomatoes still dotted the soil, the wire bent at odd angles from years of use. A handful of shriveled, moldy Better Boys still clung to the stems. The scent of loam and rotten fruit permeated the air.

He bent over to right one of the cages, the lone sentinel out of line. A wave of pain radiated from the back of his shoulder. The intensity brought him to his knees. Soft, moist soil cushioned his fall.

His tongue lashed out and struck the tomato cage he'd straightened, flipping it into the air. The wire pen bounced on the ground and stilled. One tomato landed next to Ram's knee. Red juice, like blood, soaked into the soil. Wetness coated the edge of his mouth. More from an old instinct than anything, he lapped up the rotten juice. He retched, his body no longer able to handle human food. Spittle dripped from his mouth onto the moist Earth.

With effort, he pulled himself to a standing position. A wave of dizziness caused him to sway, and he stumbled over the uneven lawn as he returned to the porch. Sweat coated his arms and the cool breeze raised goosebumps. He sat on the rickety swing and covered his face in his palms. His body shook and he stayed that way for several minutes, resting, calming his racing heart.

Before he could regain his composure, the vision of the cave returned. Aramie lay on her side, breathing the deep rhythmic breaths of sleep. The male's hand stroked her arm. She stirred, and rolled onto her back. A slow smile curved from her mouth.

"Demir…" His name rolled off her tongue in a gentle purr.

Demir looked out the cave entrance, then back to Aramie. He took her hand and kissed her fingers. "It will be dark soon."

I can see through his eyes. How could this happen? He wasn't sure, but his mind raced with possibilities.

Aramie tugged on her pants, but Demir had other ideas. He pulled her into his embrace and kissed her on the mouth.

The taste of strawberries and sweat filled Ram's mouth. He spit on the ground.

Ugh. Break away already.

The kiss ended, and Demir pulled back.

Aramie's eyebrows furrowed. "What's wrong? Demir?"

Ram stilled. Did he cause Demir to end the kiss?

Glance outside. Ram pushed the command toward Demir.

The vision shifted from Aramie to the cave's entrance. Sunlight no longer shone on the rocks. Instead, shadows filled the small opening.

Ram gasped. He could control Demir. Maybe he could use this as an opportunity to get back into Zedron's good graces.

Demir's hand moved past his eyes, toward his back. A moment later, his hand reappeared. A blue wetness coated his fingers.

That's where he'd bitten Demir, on the back of the shoulder. Could his bite have given him control over Demir? Was this an unintended consequence of taking the female Panthera's blood or was that a coincidence? Ram would have to find out.

He focused on the couple. Demir cradled Aramie's face in his palm.

Her eyes searched his, her penetrating gaze full of worry. "You're injured. Your blood...it's blue. Let me help you."

Such a touching couple. Their tenderness made Ram gag.

A cruel idea crossed his mind. Energy surged through his body. He clapped his hands like a child, giddiness getting the best of him.

Bare your fangs. Growl. A shiver ran down Ram's spine.

Demir's hand, which had supported Aramie's head with such tender care, tensed. Her skin dimpled under his thumb.

Grrrrr.

Aramie's eyes widened, her attention riveted to his mouth.

Ram chuckled. *Kill her.*

*****

The voice in Demir's head compelled him to kill Aramie. His cat screamed. He didn't realize he'd made the sound until his ears rang.

"Demir. What are you doing?" She backed up, putting distance between them.

He tried to speak, to tell her to run. The sun would be down in minutes. She could stay in the shadows until the sun dropped below the horizon. His growl was the only sound from him.

Kill. Her. The insistent voice left no room for argument. His body responded, tensing for his attack.

She changed into her panther form. A low, eerie growl erupted from her throat. She'd fight back.

He changed as well. Long, pointed claws extended from his paws. Taut muscles bunched beneath his skin.

Her hackles rose, the raised fur a warning to stay back.

A ball of pain grew in his chest. He'd rather die than harm Aramie. He used the energy to fight against the voice in his head. An internal struggle brewed, twisting

214

his insides as he fought for control. The bite mark on his shoulder burned with such intensity, white stars flashed in his vision. He shook his head, trying to clear his mind.

Aramie took a tentative step toward him, her yellow eyes searching his face. She tilted her head and nuzzled his nose. Her desire to help him broke his resolve. He didn't deserve her support and commitment. His father was right—he was weak.

Imaginary cuffs wrapped around Demir's soul, binding him to his new master.

You belong to me now. Kill her and come to me. Demir recognized the voice—Ram. He pulled against the restraints, but they were iron clad, immovable.

Demir focused his gaze on Aramie. His large body blocked the exit. Trapped in the cave, she had nowhere to run. He tried to choke out a warning, but only a snarl emerged from his throat. Hackles raised, he bared his fangs and lunged at her. He ripped into her haunch, his sharp claws penetrating deep into the flesh.

She snarled and scratched his face. Blood trickled into his mouth, the harsh taste nothing like the bitterness in his heart.

His sharp teeth ripped into her forearm, tearing away a piece of skin. He attacked her again, biting her on the thigh. She drew her claw down the skin over his ribcage. The snarl she emitted was filled with sorrow, and the look in her eyes was a hurt he'd never forget.

He backed up, looking for another opportunity. Blood dripped from both her arm and her rump. His throat constricted. He'd inflicted those wounds.

She swiped at him, and he bit her paw. Blood oozed from her leg and onto the dirt, staining the earth with her life force. Her back leg wobbled, but she didn't back down. The strength inside her made his chest tighten.

Finish her!

Demir couldn't ignore the command. He bared his fangs and snarled. His muscles bunched, tensing for his launch. He fought against Ram, but couldn't budge the evil creature's control over him. After propelling himself into the air, he landed on her back, taking her down.

She fell on her side. A loud whoosh burst from her lips. She bit him on the chin, the ear, the nose. The pain was nothing like the ache in his heart.

He slashed his claws over her hip and thigh, his nails digging into the soft flesh. Blood seeped from the wound. Through the haze in his mind, his heart fragmented with every lash he gave her.

Battered and torn, she fought him until the end. He pinned her on her back and crawled on top of her. Her paws were over her head, and the image reminded him of their lovemaking only a few short hours ago. It seemed like a lifetime.

She mewled softly, her breaths ragged. The scent of blood filled the cave, reeking of the battle and portending her upcoming death. When he killed her, his heart would break.

He opened his mouth, and a guttural growl born of anguish filled the cave. Against his will, he looked into her eyes. Expecting to see resentment, anger, and bitterness, all he saw was confusion and sadness.

His heart clenched and for a brief moment, the shackles loosened. A fleeting niggle of hope raced along his nerves before the manacles tightened once again.

Finish her then come to me.

Compliance was the only option. His enemy controlled him, reinforcing his weakness and his own belief he wasn't worthy of love.

He bit her at the base of the throat, in the soft spot between the neck and the shoulder. It wasn't a coincidence this was the very place a male chose when marking a female as his mate. Aramie had already won his heart, and this was his parting gift to her. He'd mourn her as his mate for the rest of his life, brief as he prayed it would be.

As her body relaxed, he let her go and raced into the night.

Chapter Thirty-Six

Tanen entered the Throne room and stopped in his tracks. His heart raced. He'd found the scripture describing the punishment for treason. He dreaded telling the king.

Noeh leaned back in his chair, and tapped his ring against the massive chair's engraved arm. He raised an eyebrow. "What news do you bring?"

Melissa placed her hand over Noeh's, and he grasped her fingers with a gentle squeeze. The intimate contact was something Tanen had never experienced. As council leader, he didn't have time to deal with a female. Besides, he was too uptight, and the females confused him with their mixed signals and wild moods. *I'm better off alone.*

Anlon sat on Melissa's lap. The little prince's blond hair and blue eyes were the spitting image of his father's. The babe had grown so much over the past few weeks. Perhaps his growth was due to Melissa's quick Dren metabolism. In any case, the happy family brought much-needed hope to the residents of the Keep, and for that, Tanen was thankful.

He raised his chin and approached his king and queen. "I pored through many ancient tomes in the Hall of Scriptures. Stacks and stacks—"

"Tanen..."

"—of books on the old law—"

"Tanen!" Noeh's raised voice was a clear warning. "Get to the point."

A small rumble shook the Keep.

Noeh peered at Melissa, and she shook her head. The small interchange seemed as if more than a glance had passed between them.

"My apologies, Your Majesty, but I thought you'd want to hear how—"

"I care not for how, only what."

"Tanen, please forgive Noeh. Demir and Aramie are missing. Noeh is worried about them." Melissa looked at Noeh and pursed her lips.

Noeh ran his hand through his hair. "Please, Tanen...continue."

Tanen bowed before his king. "According to the scriptures, one hundred years in the Strong room is the sentence for kidnapping and attempted murder." He cleared his throat. "For treason—death."

"So it shall be done." Noeh rose from his chair and strode over to his ornate desk. The monstrosity stood in the corner. A small carved owl hung from a nearby post, as if watching over the Keep's best kept secrets.

Noeh grabbed a piece of parchment from the stack of papers and a quill pen from the carved burl holder. The scratching of stylus on paper echoed in the room. Tanen stepped closer to receive Mauree's death sentence.

Noeh set down the pen and opened the desk drawer. On the end of the carved inner tray, a giant blue sunstone glinted in the light. *The sacred stone. Gaetan must've given it to Noeh.*

Tanen's fingers twitched and his mouth went dry. The sudden urge to snatch the mesmerizing crystal raced along his nerves. He swallowed, but the lump that had formed in his throat wouldn't go down.

Noeh pulled out his seal and an ink pad. He raised the marker above the paper and brought it down with a loud bang. With great care, he cleaned the seal with a small cloth, put it back in the desk, and closed the drawer.

Although the sunstone was no longer visible, Tanen couldn't pull his eyes away from its home. Why had Noeh left such a valuable crystal in his desk drawer?

The temperature in the room heated. Tanen's collar seemed tight around his neck, choking him. Unable to handle the discomfort any longer, he unclasped the top button. The fresh air did little to cool his skin. He hadn't reacted to a bauble like this in years. A shiver of dread raced over his arms.

Lines of determination ringed Noeh's eyes, and he tightened his lips. "As king, I proclaim Mauree guilty of treason and issue a death sentence."

Tanen accepted the official parchment. As council leader, his duties included enforcing the laws. He'd soon be on his way to deliver the news. The flapping of paper caught his attention. He peered at his shaking hands. In an effort not to call attention to his turmoil, he folded the paper then placed it in his coat's breast pocket.

Noeh returned to his chair and tickled his son's cheek with his finger. The babe's giggles and coos were sounds Tanen hadn't heard in centuries. "I assume you still haven't pulled the information about Ram's lair out of Mauree."

Memories of his latest encounter with the traitorous female filtered through his mind. Cunning and dangerous, she'd used her curves to taunt him, enticing him to let her out. She'd almost succeeded. That wouldn't happen again.

"Not yet, but I'm making progress." His face heated, and a drop of sweat rolled down his back. *Craya!* An urge to rip off his sweaty shirt and throw it on the ground increased his frustration.

"You're out of time. We'll find Ram some other way, or we'll wait until he finds us." Noeh shook his head. "Bring Maurec to the Grand Hall. I'll sanction her in public before the execution."

"As you wish, Your Majesty." Tanen bowed to his king, glanced once more at the desk and its hidden treasure before racing out the door.

*****

Pain, numbing pain. The throb in Aramie's neck burst through her consciousness, waking her into a nightmare. Her entire body ached. She stared at the ceiling, trying to focus on her location. Although the rocks looked like those in the Keep, no sunstones lined the walls. She moved, sending a new wave of agony through her muscles.

Raising herself onto one elbow, she peered around the small cave. Dried drops of blood and tufts of fur littered the soft soil, reminders of her encounter with Demir.

Demir! A trace of his scent still lingered in the air, but he was long gone. Her chest ached, sending a new round of pain through her body. Blood oozed from a deep gash in her thigh and three long scratches still marred the skin on her abdomen, but the rest of the marks were pink scars.

The last image she remembered was Demir's face, his yellow eyes penetrating into her soul. Although he'd attacked her, his pained expression belied his intent. Instead of killing her, he'd marked her as his mate.

Heat raced up her neck and into her face, but at the same time, a deep sense of peace enveloped her. She bit her lip as her mind spun, confusion warring with her pain.

Moonlight cascaded on the rocks at the cave's entrance. By the looks of it, she'd been out for several hours. Where was Demir?

Strewn across the ground, her clothes were another reminder of their time together. Her chest constricted as a new pain enveloped her heart. Although Demir had bitten her, she hadn't submitted to him so they hadn't completed the mating ritual.

She pulled on her pants and shirt, careful to avoid the tender cuts and bruises, and crawled on her hands and knees to the cave entrance. The wind picked up, catching the ends of her hair, flipping them against her face. *My barrette!* She touched the empty spot where her hair clip normally held back her strands. Always so careful with her precious piece, she hadn't had time to deal with it when Demir had attacked her.

She ran back into the cave. On the floor, next to the place they'd made love, the spot of red stood out from the dark colors in the cave. She clutched the hair piece to her heart. This time, though, it wasn't the memory of her gran'ma that crossed her mind, but of Demir. She'd asked him to put the barrette in her hair. He'd swallowed, his serious gaze searching her face. He wanted to make sure this was what she'd wanted. She'd wanted nothing more.

The ache in her chest competed with her other injuries, the pain raw and new. She couldn't believe for one moment Demir had intentionally attacked her. Not after his gentle touch, and the tender way he stroked his fingers over her skin the look of reverence and love in his eyes. *No, Demir wouldn't do this.* Yet, he had. Tears formed in her eyes.

After their brief nap, Demir had rubbed his back. Caught up in their lovemaking, she hadn't paid close attention before, but a thin blue liquid had coated his fingers. Blue—like the sacred sunstone. Aramie sat on her haunches. Her heartbeat raced, ringing in her ears.

What did the stone do to him besides bring him out of his coma?

His attack was so out of character, she didn't think he'd hurt her of his own free will. He was their leader, protector of all of their kind, and would rather die than kill another Pridemate unprovoked. Something else was at play here, and she needed to find out what it was.

She sniffed the air, searching for his scent, but the bitter winter wind had erased Demir's tracks. Not that she was in any condition to hunt him down. She needed to see Gaetan, get some medical attention and find out more about the sacred blue sunstone.

Chapter Thirty-Seven

The gash on Aramie's leg still burned, as much from the injury as the fact that Demir had done this to her. A surge of adrenaline rushed through her veins, her need for information hurrying her along the corridor. She knocked on the infirmary door, and then pushed it open without waiting for a reply.

"Ent—" Gaetan focused on her. His eyes widened. "Aramie, I'm so glad to see you. When you didn't return to the Keep last night, everyone figured you were dead."

"Gaetan, I need to know more about Blue Pool." She stood in front of the old healer, searching his face for answers.

His cane clattered against the stone floor as he raised himself from his stool. Gaetan's measured stare roamed over her face, stopping at her neck for a moment before continuing on. When his gaze landed on her torn pant leg with the dried blood, he tsked.

"Let's get you fixed up first, shall we?" He rubbed her shoulder and gave her a gentle squeeze. Nodding at the closest carved stone medical bed, he studied her, his blue eyes rimmed with concern. "Hop up here."

I don't have time for this. A loud huff escaped her lips, but she did as he asked. She couldn't rush the determined healer. Once on the bed, she gripped the edge so tight, her knuckles ached. "What does the blue sunstone do to someone after it's healed them?"

With the tip of a knife, Gaetan cut the ragged material away from her injury. The shredded fabric hung loose at her sides, exposing the half-healed cuts.

He blinked and glanced at her. "These aren't Gossum marks. Who did this to you?"

Her face reddened and a lump formed in her throat. The evidence of Demir's betrayal stung her heart more than her thigh. Could she verbally acknowledge he'd done this? *No.* Unwilling to say the words, she closed her eyes and shook her head.

"Are you hurt anywhere else?" Gaetan grabbed some white paste from a jar and wiped some over her cuts. A lime and mint aroma filled the air. The cool medicine relieved the ache, and her skin began to knit together.

A vision of Demir formed in her mind, his eyes wild as he attacked her. Where was he? Was he injured? Her stomach churned, tightening with anxiety. She gripped his arm, the black lines of his marking pulsing beneath her touch. "I *need* to know about the blue sunstone."

He met her gaze. "I can see it's important to you, but I *need* information as well if I'm to treat my patient."

She clamped her jaw, the instant ache helping her focus. Giving in, she exhaled. "Fine. The side of my hip could use some of the salve, to make the cuts heal faster."

"Well, that's a start. This side?" He pointed to her shirt.

She lifted the material, exposing the sore. A long ragged sigh eased from her lips.

He applied the soothing lotion, and she longed for such an easy fix for her soul.

He walked over to the counter and replaced the vial among the racks of herbs and remedies. "Now, tell me. Why did Demir attack you?"

She inhaled. "How did you know?"

A brief half-smile flickered across his face. "It's not hard to figure out. When Demir found out you'd left, he went after you. Now, you're asking about the stone."

Gingerly, she slid off the medical table and approached him. His presence was a warm, calming influence. She believed she could trust him, rely on him to help her. "You're right. Demir…did this." She choked on her words.

He turned to face her, empathy lined in the creases around his eyes. "Tell me what you fear."

His words were like turning on a floodgate. She couldn't stop now. "Something's wrong. Ram bit him on the back of the shoulder. His blood turned blue. He would never attack me unprovoked, yet he did. I have to know more about the blue sunstone. Please, tell me what you know."

Gaetan raised a finger. As he headed for the corner, the tip of his cane tapping against the stone floor echoed around the room. He touched a sunstone lining the cave wall, and it brightened beneath his touch.

Other Stiyaha communicated this way. She hadn't tried it herself...yet.

He turned to face her. "Ginnia will be here soon. She knows more about the ancient scriptures than anyone."

"She's the one who showed me the book, the one with the legend of Tenida." Aramie paced in the space between the two beds to relieve some of her pent-up energy. Where was Demir? A shiver ran over her shoulders.

"Do you want anything for the bite mark?" Gaetan waved his finger at her throat, his demeanor nonchalant. Did he know the meaning behind the purposeful wound?

She eyed him, trying to read his body for non-verbal clues. He appeared to be a master at hiding his emotions, and she couldn't get a good read on him. She touched the tender flesh at her neck. A thin film of skin covered the punctures, the first evidence of the scars that would mar her throat in the tell-tale sign. She was a mated female.

Reality crashed down and her vision narrowed. Demir had bitten her, doing his part to claim her as his mate. The sound of her own heartbeat pounded in her ears. Good thing she hadn't submitted to him, for if she had, she wouldn't be able to fight.

Gaetan's hand wrapped around her arm, steadying her. "Hey, you ok?"

She raised her chin and met his gaze. "Yeah, I'm fine." She wouldn't let anyone see her fear.

The door creaked.

Strands of stray brown hair flew around Ginnia's head as she peeked around the door. "Hi, Aramie." Her giggle was a welcome diversion.

Ginnia bolted for her brother, who wrapped her in his arms. He rubbed her back, the gesture heartwarming and attentive. She pulled away, and he lifted her chin. "Angel, I'm glad you're here. Aramie has some questions for you about Blue Pool."

She turned to face Aramie, her eyebrows scrunched together. "You already went to Blue Pool. Did you not like it?"

Aramie approached the strange seer. She held her hands, as much in a sign of goodwill as the need for her own comfort. "Tell me more about Tenida and why he threw the sacred stone into the waterfall."

A glint of intelligence and understanding flashed in Ginnia's eyes before the childlike film returned. She pouted her lips. "We already read the best part of the story. I like to end it there."

Gaetan placed his hand on Ginnia's back. "From what I remember, Tenida threw the stone in the waterfall so the Gossum wouldn't get it. Is there more?"

Ginnia pulled away from Aramie and hid behind one of the tables. "I'm afraid to tell."

Aramie's heart raced. She didn't want to scare Ginnia, but she desperately needed to know. She peered down at the large adult female crouched behind the table. Aramie's chest clenched. This poor female didn't ask to be a seer, but ever since the childhood accident that damaged her brain, she couldn't stop the visions.

Gaetan peeked over the top of the table. "It's ok, Ginnia."

Ginnia glanced at Aramie. "I'm sorry. I don't like that part, so I didn't show you."

Aramie grasped Ginnia's shoulder and gave her a gentle squeeze. "Please, tell us."

Ginnia nodded and came out from behind the table. "The stone was good, but it was also *baaaaad.* After the stone healed Grian, the warrior got in a fight with a nasty Gossum. Icky Gossum blood coated Grian's body, seeping into his cuts. The creature called to him, and he became a weapon for the enemy. When Tenida found out, he threw the stone back into the waterfall."

A kernel of dread formed in Aramie's stomach. Bile rose in her throat, and she wanted to hurl. "What happened to Grian?" she whispered.

"He died. Killed by another warrior." Ginnia stared at her feet, pushing the toe of her leather shoe against the edge of the table.

Aramie tensed. *Not Demir.* She wouldn't let that happen. "Was there a way to save him?"

The seer nodded, her straggly hair covering her eyes. "The legend said if another made an equal sacrifice to save the warrior, the power could be broken. But no one did."

Gaetan touched his sister on the shoulder. "Is there anything else?"

She met his gaze and shook her head.

"That's okay, angel, you did good." His warm smile made even Aramie's pulse calm.

Ginnia hugged her brother, her hands wrapped around his chest in a tight grip.

Aramie tapped her finger against her lip as the pieces fell into place. "Ram bit Demir on the back of the shoulder. Do you think Ram can control him because of the sacred stone?"

"You haven't told me exactly what happened, but if the legend is true, then…yes." Gaetan nodded.

"Where's the stone?" Aramie asked.

"I left it with Noeh. It's in his Throne room." Gaetan grabbed his cane, his fingers white from his tight grip. "Ginnia, come with me. We need to tell Noeh what's happened and get the stone. I need to throw it back into Blue Pool."

"I have to find Ram's lair." A new determination rose inside. She knew who had the information and she'd get it one way or another.

Chapter Thirty-Eight

Zedron stared into the night sky. Teres, one of Lemuria's two moons, was a giant orb, illuminating much of the landscape. In the dense canopy above, branches moved in the breeze, casting strange shadows like small stick figures dancing in the night. Every fifty-seven days, Teres circled Lemuria. Colonizers met once every lunar cycle to discuss new galaxies and the possibility of colonizing recently discovered worlds.

A slow smile pulled at Zedron's lips. Tonight he'd see Alora at the meeting, but better yet, she'd see his new slave. Zedron had kept Carine from shopping at the market until the stores were almost closed. She'd hurried along, placing the fruits and vegetables in her basket with quick fingers. To see her in such a rushed state had sent trickles of excitement over his skin. He'd planned her delay, so he'd have to bring her with him to the meeting.

Carine walked with him along the platforms and stairs that linked the Rolmdew and Etila trees together in an extensive network. Zedron gripped a gnarled branch, using the stick as leverage to pull himself to the next platform. He glanced over his shoulder. Despite the two heavy bags she carried, Carine didn't ask for assistance, but her glare was confirmation of her irritation.

Tucked away in a corner of one of the large Rolmdew trees, an open doorway beckoned with a warm and comforting light. Zedron straightened his jacket, and he adjusted the small gold pin on his lapel. He raised his chin, closed his eyes, and inhaled a calming breath, but his fingers twitched.

Passing through the doorway, he noted several co-workers deep in their own discussions. They didn't seem to notice him, but that changed the moment Carine entered the room.

All conversations ceased.

Quill, one of the older Colonizers, stepped away from his small group. He glared at Carine, his lip curling at the corner. His attention focused on Zedron, and he crossed his arms over his chest. "You know the rules. Why did you bring a slave to our meeting?"

The orange spots on her face darkened, and the ends of her blue hair snapped loudly in the quiet room.

Murmurs of assent from others rippled into the air.

Zedron had anticipated such a reaction, and he had to force himself not to smile. He lowered his head in a slight bow to supplicate the elder Colonizer. "Forgive me, Quill. My slave delayed us. I had no choice but to bring her along."

"She can't stay. Send her home." Quill's voice was tight.

"I wish I could, but I haven't loosened the range on her arm bands, yet. We are still in the midst of training. She must stay close to me outside our home." Zedron pasted on his best contrite grin. He looked around the room, searching for Alora. He'd expected her to raise a fuss.

Quill exhaled and pursed his lips. "I'd ask you to leave, but we need your input on one of the new worlds Clayor discovered. Have her wait in the corner."

"Of course." Zedron bowed once again. He gripped Carine's elbow, his fingers pressing into her flesh harder than was necessary, and shoved her into a chair against the far wall. "Wait here. Don't give me any trouble."

Her brows furrowed and her lips tightened, but she sat. The packages landed at her feet with a loud thump.

Conversations resumed. Colonizers carried on discussions in small groups of two or three. Zedron scanned the room. Alora was nowhere in sight. A tic started in his jaw. He'd staged this whole performance for her benefit, and she wasn't here. A painful pulse pounded at his temple. He rubbed his forehead, but the familiar movement didn't relieve the tension.

The click of a door caught his attention. On the far side of the room, Alora exited from a small washroom. She straightened her dress and drew a stray curl around her ear. Their gazes locked. Her shoulders visibly stiffened and her beautiful features turned sour. Not the reaction he'd longed for, but the one he'd expected. His chest tightened.

Her focus drew past him to Carine. With a quick flinch, her mouth opened and her eyes widened. She clenched her fists at her side, her body quaking with anger.

From the moment they'd met, he'd been drawn to her, their relationship like fire and water. The arguments had been brutal, the reconciliations passionate.

Alora approached him, her mouth pursed, her strides purposeful. "What have you done?"

Here was the confrontation he'd expected. He liked her spunk, her determination. The way she moved, all grace and power rolled up in a perfect package. Her energy fueled him, made him feel, and he delighted in her attention, even if it was her hatred for him.

Raising his eyebrows, he extended his hands, palms up. "What bothers you, Alora?" He accentuated her name, drawing it out the way she used to like when they were together.

She narrowed her eyes, and a single fang protruded over her lip. "You did this on purpose to taunt me."

"Whatever do you mean?" He couldn't resist the jab.

She leaned forward, into his personal space. Her perfume, like the sweet venom from the Tralum plant, assailed his senses. "The female Arotaar. Why do you bring an innocent soul into our battle?"

"There are many innocent and not-so-innocent lives affected by our game." He breathed in deep, savoring her scent for as long as he could. "Why should *she* make any difference?"

Alora visibly swallowed, her disgust written in her downturned mouth. "You know very well why."

He nodded toward Carine. "I bought Carine as I needed a slave to tend my home. That she reminds you of your father's favorite pet is none of my concern."

She stepped back, the color draining from her face. Her pain was not something he'd expected.

A brief flicker of guilt lodged in his throat, but he pushed it aside. Instead, he focused on his own bitterness and anger at her rejection of his bonding offer.

She whirled on her toes, heading back the way she'd come. He gripped her arm, stopping her flight. A gold bracelet grazed the skin on his arm. The fine strands were made from the most delicate and rare metal on the planet. Feigning ignorance, he frowned. "What's this?"

Her eyes narrowed on him, and a smirk broke across her face. "An anniversary gift from Veromé, my *beloved* mate."

Even though Zedron already knew of the bracelet, to hear her speak of Veromé that way sent him over the edge. A wave of anger rushed through his veins. "There's something between *us*, Alora. I know you feel it, too."

Her pale blue eyes flecked with silver. "I will win this war, and when I do, you will free Carine."

He responded with mocking laughter. "What if I win the war? What shall you give me?"

She glanced at his hand, his grip still tight around her arm. "What do you want?"

He sneered. "You know what I want, Alora—you."

"No." She yanked her arm from his grasp.

He gave her his best smile, the one she'd fallen for in the beginning of their short, yet passionate relationship. "Have you broken any rules of the game lately, my dear?"

Alora visibly swallowed, her stare locked with his.

He leaned in, her unique scent infiltrating his senses once again. With a slow and gentle touch, he ran his finger over the soft curve of her cheek. "I think you like small caves," he whispered.

The creases in the skin around her eyes flinched ever so slightly, but she held his gaze. He wanted to pull her to him, kiss her until she relented, and remind her of the passion between them. But he held his ground. To give in to his impulses would weaken his position in the game, and he was all about winning this war.

A slow, forced smile curved her lips, and she stepped back. With a grace that drove him mad, she turned around, her chin held high. As she walked away, he couldn't help but admire her spunk. His pulse raced. He ached to win her back, and one way or another, he'd do just that.

Chapter Thirty-Nine

The picket fence was not what Demir expected to see. The farmhouse with its white paint, floral drapes, and porch swing reminded him of humans. Thick in the air, the scent of Gossum stung his sensitive nose. In human form, he strolled across the overgrown lawn, fighting against the new bonds that bound him. As much as he tried, he couldn't break free. His feet marched on.

The front door opened on a squeaky hinge. Ram stood in the doorway, a broad smile exposing his serrated teeth. "Welcome, welcome, welcome, Demir. Such a pleasure to have you join us."

Bile rose in Demir's throat, but he couldn't stop himself from walking up the stairs. Crossing the threshold, he passed within inches of Ram's putrid hide. His pulse thrummed in his veins, and he wanted to slay the creature that had forced him to murder Aramie.

My mate. His stomach grew heavy even as his chest expanded. Although the word sounded odd to his brain, the rightness in it was something he couldn't deny. The lone day they'd had together was the best one of his life.

Ram's brood sat in chairs and on the sofa, some asleep, some nursing a bottle of Smirnoff's. One by one, they roused, their noses twitching.

Jakar stood. His gaze raked over Demir.

"Stay calm, everyone. He's my new right-hand man." Ram slapped Demir on the back.

Pain radiated from the bite mark on Demir's shoulder, and a wave of dizziness nearly dropped him.

Jakar's eyes narrowed on Ram. "What's going on?"

"Demir and I," Ram twirled his hand in the air, "are joined at the hip, shall we say."

Demir wanted to growl, but Ram's control was like a rival Panthera who had him pinned, biting into his neck, forcing his submission.

"What's that supposed to mean?" Jakar's words were laced with ice.

Ram raised his eyebrows then furrowed them, his attention focusing on Jakar. "A bit jealous are we? Don't fret. He's a means to an end, nothing more."

One of the brood inched closer to Demir. The creature's stench made him gag, and he couldn't stop the natural reflex. He crouched and puked on the floor, remnants of his last meal dripping from his mouth.

"Ugh, I forgot what it was like to have a cat in the house." Ram curled his lip and pointed to the Gossum that had approached Demir. "You, clean this up."

The creature scurried away and returned with a cloth.

"Come, Demir. I have plans for you." Ram placed his arm around Demir and led him toward a doorway on the far side of the kitchen.

Jakar raced around them and opened the door. The smell of damp earth and decay wafted up the old wooden stairs. With the tip of his razor-sharp fingernail, Ram flicked on the light switch. A muted glow bathed the staircase in amber light.

The hair on Demir's nape rose, as instinctually, he knew only pain awaited him there.

Ram nodded to Jakar. "Please, lead the way."

Jakar headed through the open doorway and down the stairs.

Ram held out his hand. "After you."

Demir wanted to rip his claws through Ram's jugular, but instead, he marched down the staircase.

The decrepit wood creaked under his feet. Cobwebs blew between the railings as a gust of wind pushed him onward. With each step, the room and all its contents became more visible.

A workbench filled with bottles and lab equipment hugged the closest wall. Scattered in the corners, old garden tools and equipment lay against rickety shelving. The smell of moist, recently unearthed soil intensified, and a large hollowed out section of the basement came into view. An old, empty table top, the legs removed, took up the majority of space. Four shackles, one attached to each corner, sat on top of the wood.

Ram shoved Demir over the last few steps, tripping him at the ankle. Demir rolled on the dirt, but landed on his feet.

"You see this table? It's for you…if you fail me." The smile on Ram's face lit up, eagerness etched in the fine lines. "For your sake, you better succeed. On second thought…I'd be just as happy to see you fail."

Jakar selected a nail from the workbench and twirled the small implement between his fingers. "What's he going to do for us? Besides cause trouble."

Demir agreed. He'd cause trouble if he got the chance.

Punch Jakar.

The command was firm, insistent, and not something he could ignore. Demir fisted his hand and hit Jakar on the jaw. At the flesh on flesh contact, a burst of energy sent a thrill of enjoyment into his heart. The small bit of satisfaction eased the ache in his chest, but it was merely a drop of retribution for losing Aramic.

Jakar's tongue snapped at Demir's shoulder, but Ram blocked it with his arm.

"That's quite enough. I figured you'd rather enjoy the demonstration. My bad." Ram snickered.

Blood dripped from Jakar's nose onto the floor. The dirt soaked up the blood, leaving a red stain. He grabbed a rag from the countertop and wiped at the injury.

Ram placed his finger over his lips and whispered. "I can control what he does."

Jakar's body shook, his hand clenched tight around the towel. "Yesssss…noted, but how?"

"Good question. Maybe it's because we transformed into their likeness." Ram rubbed his chin and stared at Demir. "I bit him, too. Could that be related?" He focused his gaze on Jakar. "We'll try again. Tell the brood next time we encounter another Lemurian, don't inject enough venom to kill, only to stun."

"As you wish, my lord." Jakar nodded and pointed toward Demir. "What are your plans with him?"

Ram chuckled. "We'll send our good buddy Demir back to the Keep as an assassin…to kill Noeh."

No. Demir couldn't let that happen. Once, he'd wanted the king dead, now, he'd honor his commitment to the Stiyaha leader. Hatred over what they planned boiled inside. He tried to extend a claw, but his fingernail wouldn't cooperate.

One side of Ram's mouth quirked into a grin. "Open a portal."

Demir fought against the bonds, straining with all his might, but he sent out a call. *Rin. Rin. Open a portal for me.* Demir's stomach tightened like a giant coil, reminding him of when he was in his coma. Unable to move, he'd thought that was the worst thing he'd ever endured. He'd been so wrong.

Nothing. No response.

Try again. A pain in his head made Demir wince. He concentrated and sent out another request.

The Keep senses y'er with the enemy. Entry not granted, ya mangy cat. Demir wanted to laugh at Rin's taunt, relief flooding his system, but Ram clamped down on his spirit, squashing the brief flash of victory.

Ram fisted his hand so hard his knuckles cracked. The edge of his lip twitched. "Do you know another way into the Keep?"

"The Keep recalibrated the manual entrances after the last battle. Other than the portals, I don't know another way in." *Thank the gods for small miracles.* Demir appreciated the Keep's ability to protect her inhabitants, now more than ever.

"Well, then, you are of little use to me…except as a *toy.*" Ram glanced at the table and returned his attention to Demir. Another smile, this one more evil than the last, broke across his face. "Strip and lay face down on the table. You'll wear the chains, just in case. I can control you, but why take chances?"

Demir's gaze wandered to the shackles. Ram's reputation preceded him, and Demir had no doubt he'd be tortured. A part of him didn't care. After killing Aramie, the punishment was justified. He prayed death would be swift.

His shoes were the first to go. He made quick work of his pants and shirt. Naked in front of Ram and Jakar, he felt as exposed as ever. He'd endured plenty of torment at his father's hands. He ground his teeth as a wave of anger roiled in his gut. This would be another lesson in humility and prove he was weak once again. Demir headed for the table and lay down, spread eagle.

Ram inhaled. With his finger, he traced a long trail from Demir's back and over his buttocks. "My, my. You've got some worthy scars there, boy." The chains rattled as they bound the shackles to Demir's wrists and ankles. His skin burned along the edge of his bite mark, fogging his brain. Ram whispered in Demir's ear. "We'll give you a few more to add to the collection."

Demir's cat strained to break free, causing a frenzy in his head. One image replayed in his mind—Aramie's face as she exhaled her last breath.

Chapter Forty

The dampness in the lower levels of the Keep crept into Aramie's lungs. The heaviness made her pant. Hundreds of feet underground, the walls closed in around her. She placed her hand against the wet rock for stability and rubbed her eyelids. Rushing water sounded like a torrent, but when she opened her eyes, only a small rivulet ran along the path.

There was a reason the Strong room was here—to torture anyone unlucky enough to be put there. Aramie pushed away from the wall and straightened her shoulders. The clumping of her shoes preceded her down the corridor.

"Cat. I can smell you from here." Mauree's taunt echoed from her cell.

Aramie ground her teeth. She wouldn't give Mauree the satisfaction of letting her know she'd hit a nerve. "I'd think you'd be nicer to visitors, since you don't get any."

A soft chuckle filtered through the bars.

Aramie's hackles rose on the back of her neck. Carved within the rock, the walls and ceilings of the dingy cell were musty and damp. The only means of entrance or exit—through the door made of iron bars.

Mauree, the lone inhabitant in the cell wore a tight skirt slit up the side, exposing her long slender legs. Her bare shoulder poked through the rip in her shirt. Short, blond hair hung in strings around her face, unwashed and unkempt. Pale, blue eyes reflected the meager light, intelligence and madness evident in their shine.

"What brings you to my humble abode, cat? I'd offer you some milk," she glanced around and shrugged her shoulders, "but, as you can see, I'm fresh out."

"I'm not here to play games with you." Aramie's jaw ached from her clenched teeth. "Where's Ram's hideout?"

Mauree's burst of laughter raced down the hallway, as if it could escape its owner. "Please...you're so funny." With cool abruptness, her laughter stopped. "Forget it." She tsked and flicked an imaginary piece of dirt from her arm.

Aramie grabbed the bars, twisting her hands on the smooth, hard metal. "Your choice, easy way or—"

"Others have tried and failed. What makes you think I'll tell you?" The female's arrogance knew no bounds.

Mauree stood and stretched. A book lay on her cot. The title *Basic Self-Defense* made Aramie smirk.

Aramie raised an eyebrow. "You'll tell me, one way or another."

"Go find something else to do." Mauree waved her hand in a dismissive gesture. "You're bothering me."

Aramie trailed her fingers over the bars, assessing the space between them. Made for Stiyaha, they were several inches apart. That would do. Aramie glared at Mauree and raised her lip, exposing one sharp, pointed fang. "I'll be right back."

Mauree's eyebrows creased, and a glimpse of uncertainty crossed her face. "Wait. Where are you going? Please don't leave me here alone. I was so enjoying our conversation."

Aramie stood out of Mauree's view and changed into her panther. The idea of giving this female a close up view of her "cat" sent a thrill down her back. Aramie's muscles bunched under her skin as she prowled back down the hallway.

She growled, and the warning sent a flash of adrenaline through her body. Pacing in front of the bars, she made sure Mauree got a good, long look at her firm muscles.

Mauree grabbed the iron and pressed her face against the bars. With a quick inhale, she opened her mouth and spit.

Wetness coated Aramie's fur on her shoulder. The stench of eggs and bad breath filtered into her sensitive nose.

Grrrr. Aramie bared her fangs.

Mauree laughed and sat in her rickety chair. "Strut all you want, cat. You can't touch me in here."

Mauree was wrong about that. Aramie rubbed the metal with her nose, and the scent of iron and age replaced Mauree's stench. With a bit of effort, Aramie pushed her head and shoulders between the bars, all the time keeping eye contact with her target.

"No…" Mauree's eyes widened. She stood and the crash of the chair against the stone floor echoed into the hallway. With a firm grasp, she picked up the chair, using the furniture as a barrier. "Stay back."

Aramie squeezed her entire body through the bars and lunged at Mauree, knocking her down. The chair flew through the air, hit the wall, and broke apart. Mauree kicked out, landing a foot on Aramie's shoulder.

Aramie batted at Mauree, careful to keep her claws retracted. As much as she didn't like the female, she didn't want to hurt her, just get the necessary information. Mauree gripped her shoulder and even through the fur, her nails dug into her skin. The slight pinch was more of an irritation than anything else.

Aramie pushed forward, pinning the larger Stiyaha under her. She clamped her jaw around Mauree's throat, but didn't bite.

Mauree stilled beneath her.

Grrrrrr.

"Kill me and you won't get the information you seek," Mauree hissed.

Aramie tightened her jaw, pinching the irritating female's skin between her teeth. Blood trickled over Mauree's neck. The Stiyaha female kicked and punched, but Aramie had her pinned tight. Mauree stopped her attack, her body tense.

Grrrrr. The guttural sound reverberated in Aramie's throat.

Mauree swallowed. Her shallow breaths sounded loud in the enclosed space. "Let me go."

Aramie held her ground.

Several seconds ticked by, the two locked together, neither giving way. Finally, Mauree relaxed. "Fine. I don't know his exact location, but I overheard Jakar mention a farmhouse he was interested in…somewhere off Shadybrook Road. It's on the east side of Mt. Hood, near the outskirts of Tygh Valley. The place is white, with a picket fence."

Aramie released Mauree and squeezed through the bars before the deranged female could come after her. With the needed information, she raced down the corridor. *I'm coming, Demir.*

Chapter Forty-One

Tanen adjusted his collar, straightening the folds to perfection. As he walked into the Grand Hall, he scanned the crowd in line for the evening repast. These were the early birds, the ones who liked to get in and get out before the masses really filled up the place. Not that there were many Stiyaha left anymore, not since the great scourge, but with the addition of the Panthera and Dren, mealtime was a bit crowded most evenings.

The scent of fresh basil and garlic bread filled the air. His mouth watered in anticipation. He snagged a plate and stood in line. *I shouldn't be here.* A bite of regret landed in the pit of his stomach. Avoiding his responsibility was so unlike him, but he couldn't bring himself to visit Mauree and relay her death sentence. Not that he cared about her, per se, but the idea of having a hand in her death didn't sit well with him. Mealtime was a valid excuse.

He raised his chin, pinning his shoulders back. He was Noeh's council leader and had the right to enforce and dictate the law in his own manner. She'd have to wait until after he'd eaten.

He dumped a spoonful of peas onto his plate and a few raced to the edge. An image of Mauree's head rolling across the floor flashed through his mind. To think of her execution made the ball in his gut harden, flaring his heartburn.

His appetite deserted him.

He left the plate on the table and turned to leave.

"Tanen!"

The muscles in his shoulders tensed. Gaetan hobbled toward him, his deformed leg bulging out to the side with each step. His cane tapped along the stone floor, the rapping sound working its way into Tanen's brain like a pick.

Tanen put on his best smile. "Gaetan, what can I do for you?"

The haelen placed his hand on Tanen's shoulder. "I...I need a favor."

Interesting. Gaetan never asked for a favor. Tanen leaned toward the old male. "How can I be of service to you?"

"I left my healing bag in Noeh's Throne room." Gaetan winced and rubbed his knee. "I'd go back for it, but I'm not having one of my better evenings."

"Worry not. I'll retrieve your satchel." He studied the old male. For Gaetan to forget his medicines was unusual, to say the least. "Shall I bring it here...or?"

Gaetan rubbed his brow. "Leave it in the infirmary, on the counter next to the elixirs." His attention focused on Tanen. "Thank you. I appreciate it."

"Perhaps you should sit." Tanen pulled a chair out from a nearby table. "Here, please."

"Thanks." Gaetan plopped more than sat in the wooden chair. A bead of sweat rolled down the side of his face. He exhaled. "Ah, much better."

Tanen scrutinized him. "Maybe some rest—"

Gaetan raised his hand. "I'm fine." His eyes narrowed and a glint of tension raced across his features.

Tanen leaned back. "Ok, well, I'm on my way out." He nodded in respect and left the old male to deal with his own issues.

A slight breeze ruffled his hair, and he smoothed the stray strands back into place. His soft-soled shoes squeaked against the stone, but the familiar sound didn't ease his tension. He still needed to deliver the news to Mauree. His jaw clenched along with his fist. He didn't want to think too hard about why that bothered him, so he concentrated on Gaetan's request.

Good thing the king's Throne room was close by. He stopped outside the massive double doors and rapped his knuckles against the hard wood.

Silence.

He knocked again.

Nothing.

With an impatient huff, he crossed his arms. No one was allowed in the king's Throne room without specific authority from Noeh. He could always come back later, but that would be out of his way. With a quick whip of his head, he peered down the hallway, first to the left, then the right. Empty, except for him.

He raised his chin and inhaled. Certainly, as council leader, the king wouldn't mind if he entered to retrieve Gaetan's satchel. Convinced with that rationale, he pulled on the heavy doors.

As if in protest, the doors creaked at the intrusion. He entered the room, and the sunstones lining the walls brightened. The chamber contained a trace of pine and sage, Noeh's scent, and the only sound was Tanen's own breaths. Feeling like an intruder in his king's sacred room, his muscles bunched beneath his tunic. *Maybe I should leave.*

Glancing around, he focused on Noeh's desk. On the edge of the massive piece of furniture sat a small, brown leather bag—Gaetan's satchel. The tension in Tanen's shoulders relaxed.

He hurried across the room, his shoes swishing along the stone floor. With a quick swipe, he grabbed the soft leather bag and stowed it in the pocket of his overcoat. His gaze followed a path across the top of the desk, riveting to the spot where he'd seen the blue sunstone.

His back stiffened, and his fingers smoothed the material around his neck, straightening his collar. He cleared his throat, the sound loud in the empty room. Riveted in place by the memory of the magnificent blue sunstone, he couldn't move.

The sunstones lining the Keep's walls brightened, and a wave of heat filled the room. Sweat formed under his armpits. The old, familiar tingling started in his fingers. He cracked his knuckles, trying to ease the itch.

One peek, that's all. I want to see the crystal. The old wooden owl hovering in the corner seemed to watch his every move. His fingers trembled as he reached for the knob. Cold metal against his skin fed his need. The tingling in his fingers moved up his arms until his whole body vibrated with anticipation.

He yanked open the drawer. The blue sunstone of legend sparkled against the drab background of the dark wood. His vision narrowed. Focused solely on the object of his desire, the rest of the room seemed to disappear.

His brain fogged, white dots forming before his eyes. He held his breath, and his body shook.

Don't touch it. Don't touch it. But of course, he couldn't resist.

With a gentle caress, he stroked the edge of the crystal. The nerves along his fingertips tingled, sending tendrils of electricity up his arm. He cradled the stone and brought the crystal closer for further inspection.

Twirling the stone in his hand, blue rays landed on the desk, the walls, the ceiling. The light shone with an eerie glow and mesmerized him. He couldn't put the precious gem down, not now, maybe not ever. Endorphins flooded his bloodstream, and his inner beast roared, eager to break free.

Before he could think better of it, he put the sunstone in his pocket next to Gaetan's satchel. A strange warmth emanated from the cloth, warming his thigh through his trousers.

A sense of urgency raced through his veins. The last thing he needed was to get caught. He shut Noeh's drawer and headed for the exit. Closing the doors behind him, he had the sense to realize he'd started along the dark path once again. A part of him didn't care.

Chapter Forty-Two

The hallways of the Keep looked all the same to Aramie. Still learning to read

the sunstones that lined the walls, she headed along a corridor she thought led to

the Portal Navigation Center. If she could get out of here without anyone

knowing, all the better. The last thing she wanted was to run into anyone from her

Pride. They'd see her bite mark and know she was Demir's mate.

She passed a female Stiyaha headed in the opposite direction. The tall female

nodded. Her eyebrow arched and an inquisitive look formed in her eyes, but she

didn't stop to ask questions. Aramie's pulse pounded.

A passageway on the right didn't look familiar, and Aramie slowed down. Heat

escaped from the entrance, warmed by the sunstones that glowed from a large pit

in the center of the room. Several Jixies wore protective headgear and goggles,

apparent protection from the heat. Swords in various stages of creation lined the

walls. *A forge.*

A sense of wonder crept along her nerves. On a table, not far away, a pair of

throwing stars glinted in the light. Her chest expanded, and she touched her

favorite weapons lining her belt. She'd lost two in the encounter with Ram at Blue

Pool, leaving two remaining. After moving into the Keep, her supply of stars had dwindled away.

"Hey there, you need somthin'?" A stout Jixie removed his headgear and approached her. With bright red hair and a long beard, he reminded her of the human stories of elves. He wiped his hands on a cloth already blackened with grime. A broad smile crossed his face and set her at ease. "You lookin' for somethin' in particular?"

"Actually, I was looking for the Portal Navigation Center." Somewhere along the way, she'd made a wrong turn, and the diversion was not what she needed. She didn't want to be rude to the little male, but she needed to get to her destination.

"That's two levels up. Take the third right and you'll be fine."

"Thanks." She glanced at the throwing stars one last time and turned to leave.

The male touched her on the elbow. "Hey. You're a warrior, right?"

She stilled, afraid he'd try to stop her, prevent her from searching out Ram as any Panthera male would. She peered at him.

His smile and inquisitive eyes made her breath catch. He didn't hold her back and try to control her. On the contrary, he seemed willing to help.

"Y-yes."

"I saw ya eyein' them throwing stars. You want 'em?" His eyes twinkled and a shy smile graced his face.

The stars caught her attention once again. She'd love to have them, but she wasn't sure she should. "Really? They're not made for someone?"

He shook his head. "Naw, we make extras of different types of weapons. I saw several of you Panthera had 'em. Thought I'd give it a try. Here," he headed over to the table and picked them up, "you let me know how they turn out."

She accepted his gift, grateful for the finely crafted weapons. The light metal and etched edges were perfectly crafted. "These are exquisite. You've done a fabulous job."

He beamed at her compliment. "Thank you. Please, take them."

She hid them under the lining of her belt, underneath her old ones. Her gaze focused on the exit before returning to him. "Thank you for the directions as well."

He nodded and headed back to his work.

She ran down the hallway and took the third right. It wasn't long before the walls and the sunstones started to look familiar. She passed a few Stiyaha, some warriors, some merchants, all in a hurry going somewhere. Rounding the last corner, she bumped into Leon.

His presence filled the corridor, his scent of jasmine and spice sending warning spikes along her nerves. He glanced at her throat, recognition reflecting in his eyes.

"You're a mated female now. How…convenient." He looked behind him then returned his attention to her. "Where are you going? As if I don't already know."

"Demir and I aren't fully mated. I didn't submit to him. Where I'm going is none—"

Jonue strode alongside him, her short, dark hair pushed behind her ears. She wore her battle gear, the long pants and black shirt effective camouflage in the dark forest. "Be careful, Aramie. He's taken over the Pride."

Aramie's heart skipped a beat. "What? Demir is Pride leader."

"Rin spread the word about what happened…with you and Demir." Jonue's gaze flicked to Aramie's neck for a brief moment. "He almost killed you and went to the enemy."

Leon's eyes narrowed. "If Demir is aligned with the Gossum, then he's lost to us. Someone had to take over the Pride, so I did. Now, *you* will obey *me*."

"Ram is controlling Demir through the effects of the blue sunstone. We have to help him." Adrenaline surged through her body, her need to get to Demir burning in her chest.

Leon puffed out his chest, and the hair on the back of his neck visibly raised. "You will remain here at the Keep."

There was no way she'd stay here. She'd find Demir, even if she had to fight every male in the Keep first to prove her dominance.

"I don't have time for this. I know Ram's hideout. It's in a white farmhouse with a picket fence, east of the human town of Tygh Valley, near the river. I *will* save Demir." Her nostrils flared, and she had to resist the urge to bare her fangs. She didn't want a fight on her hands, not when she needed to save her energy for the Gossum.

Jonue placed her hand on Leon's shoulder. "Maybe we should help her...help Demir. You could round up the male warriors. I'd get the females—"

"No! Absolutely not." He grabbed Jonue's hand and pushed her away. "You are a mated female as well. I won't have Hallan end up a widower like me." A twitch in the skin around his eye betrayed his pain.

Aramie's chest constricted. Leon had lost Kitani. In the midst of her desire to save Demir, she'd forgotten that others were in pain as well. She bit her lip. "I'm sorry, Leon. Kitani was a good warrior. She helped Jonue and I escape with the blue sunstone that saved Demir."

He glared at her. "Like I said before, she died because of you. Mated females shouldn't fight."

"Mated females have a place on the battlefield." She shook her head. There was no winning an argument with this male, not in his current state of mind. "I'm leaving. Do I need to fight you?"

His eyes narrowed. The muscle in his jaw twitched. Silence stretched out for several seconds.

She'd bested him not long ago. Did he really think he'd be able to take her down? She didn't think so. She rose up, arching her shoulders in a display of dominance. "Move. Out. Of. The. Way."

Leon stiffened, but didn't attack her. He held his shoulders back, chest raised. They were in a standoff.

The temperature in the passageway dropped several degrees and their breaths became visible in the air. A low rumble emanated from the Keep and fine dirt and rocks sifted through the air.

Aramie slowly walked past Leon, careful not to let her guard down.

Jonue stepped aside and motioned with her hand in a gesture to proceed. "Good luck."

Aramie bolted along the corridor, eager to reach the forest and find Demir.

"Aramie!"

Jonue's shout stopped Aramie in her tracks. She glanced behind her.

"Gaetan…he said to tell you…the stone…it's missing."

A large ball of fear grew in her stomach, festering, spreading throughout her body. A fine sheen of sweat broke out on her arms. With renewed energy, she sprinted toward the Portal Navigation Center and a way out of this place.

As she rounded the corner, she skidded to a halt inside the portal room. The smell of pine and fresh rain still permeated the air. The portal must have opened recently. Somehow, she'd missed the chimes.

Rin polished a red sunstone in a rag. He stared at her, as if she had an extra eye. "I didn't expect to see ya here again so soon."

"Can you open a portal for me? Near the town of Tygh Valley?"

"Well, of course I can, but why would 'cha want ta go there?" He placed the stone in one of the inner rings of the porte stanen.

"I just…need to. Please, open a portal." She stood on the raised platform where the gateway would appear.

"Dern it, get off there. Ya have to jump through it." He motioned for her to move, his lips pursed.

If the situation weren't so dire, she'd find amusement in his reaction, but her heavy heart was too worried about Demir.

The little male circled his hands over the porte stanen, moving faster and faster with each round. A mist grew in the room, swirling until it coalesced into a ball. In the center, the forest solidified and the smell of pine and wet grass filtered into the room.

She didn't wait for his approval and dove through the opening, taking her fears and hopes with her.

Chapter Forty-Three

Aramie peered through the trees at the top of a forested ridge. A vast landscape of rolling hills filled with a patchwork of green lay before her. The sounds of domesticated animals—cows, horses, pigs—along with their stench, carried along the breeze. Human farmland.

She didn't like humans, didn't understand their motivations and their need to control and destroy their own home—Earth. Interaction with them wasn't forbidden, but highly discouraged. Homo sapiens could be transformed and turned into players in the game, but once changed, they couldn't return to their former lives. As long as they didn't find out Lemurians existed, they still had a chance of remaining human.

Aramie released the tree branch and let it fall back into place. The pine tree's pointy tips poked at her arm, as if pushing her along. She needed to leave the shelter of the forest to reach Ram's hideout.

Shaking her head, she followed a trail that led through the ever diminishing forest. A breeze kicked up. The familiar, unpleasant fragrance of Gossum set her on edge and fueled her excitement.

The farmhouse wasn't too hard to find. Surrounding the property was a stand of alder trees, the tall, skinny branches reaching for the sky. Closer in, a picket fence surrounded the house and gave it an air of innocence the home didn't possess. An old swing hung from cables attached to the ceiling on the wrap-around porch. Shadows stretched behind the curtains, the movement catching her attention.

She crept closer, using the trees for cover. To encourage herself, she traced her fingers under the lining of her belt and over her new throwing stars. The cold metal on her fingertips was a familiar comfort. She envisioned her fictional father giving her advice, helping her in the most basic of ways. The mental images fueled her with confidence, her slow breaths easing the tension in her chest.

Muffled voices, heated in conversation, escaped through the cracks in the walls. A loud laugh burst from the home, one Aramie recognized—Ram. She ran through an old garden and stepped on an overripe tomato. The fruit squished under the toe of her shoe. Hiding behind an overgrown rhododendron bush, she willed her heartbeat to slow.

Demir. She touched her throat where he'd marked her. The flesh had healed, leaving a ragged scar, evidence he still lived. If he'd died, the mark would've faded and disappeared when his heart stopped beating. Determination, raw and powerful, welled up in her chest. She loved him and would find him, no matter what.

While casing the house, she'd thought through her plan. She needed to create a diversion, something to draw out the Gossum.

The high-pitched squeal of a pig pierced the night air. She glanced toward the sound. Behind the house, on a spot of land next to the road, was a large barn. An idea formed in her mind and she smiled. Keeping close to the bushes, she approached the building and the animals within.

As she entered the structure, the animals quieted. A tenseness filled the air. Three pigs, a goat, and two horses called this place home. She didn't want to spook them, have them raise a ruckus and alert the Gossum, so she crouched to make herself as small as possible.

As she grew closer, the horses skittered in their stall, pounding the ground with their feet. With angry grunts, the pigs moved to the rear of their pen.

The goat placed its head over the stall door, its mouth moving in a rhythmic chew. White with a dark ring around one eye, the billy seemed interested. The goat would serve her purpose and maybe he'd enjoy the freedom she offered.

She removed her jacket. The material already carried her perfume, but she wanted to call attention to the coat, so she rubbed the sleeves against her mouth, marking it with her scent glands.

With slow movements, she opened the stall and grabbed the goat by his collar. The animal mewled, but he didn't fight her. She wrapped her coat around the small creature, securing the collar with the top button. After leading the goat to the entrance of the barn, she gave the small critter a whack on the behind.

The goat ran down the road, its loud bleat carrying on the wind. The other animals stirred at the commotion. Time to hide. She exited the barn and waited for the excitement to begin.

*****

"Those damn animals." Ram slammed his glass on the Formica countertop. Vodka spilled over the lip, coating his fingers with the fiery liquid. He squeezed the glass in his fingers. *Tink.* A crack ran up the side.

Jakar closed the pantry door, a bottle of Smirnoff's in one hand. He pointed at two of the brood who sat at the rickety kitchen table. The sound of shuffling cards was like an undercurrent to the noise outside. "You and you, go see what's spooked the animals. Find the others and take them with you. It's time to let off a little steam anyway."

As the males stood, chair legs scraped against the wooden floor. The screech made Ram wince. One ran outside, the other retreated farther into the farmhouse to find his brethren.

"Tell me again, why do we have these," Ram waved his hand in the air, "animals?"

"To blend in with the humans. Besides, they came with the property. The prior renters left them here to compensate the owner for unpaid rent, at least that's what he told me." Jakar shrugged.

"What do you think spooked them?"

"My guess—coyote. This is the third time this week."

The six remaining members of his brood raced out the front door. One male hung back, the largest of the bunch—Oliver. He gave Ram a quick nod, intelligence in his dark orbs. "We'll catch the critter this time. I promise you that."

Ram raised an eyebrow. "See that you do." He liked this new warrior he'd acquired. The male seemed to have more going on upstairs than many of the humans he'd turned.

Ram tsked. "I give the mutt credit. It takes balls to keep coming back here."

"Balls or stupidity, either works." Jakar folded his hands together, squeezing his palms tight. "Shall I supervise?"

"Not this time. Let's see what Oliver can do." A wave of dizziness crested over Ram. His vision wavered. The kitchen dimmed, and a smooth, flat surface, the color of day-old coffee, came into focus. His nerves tingled at the vision of the wooden platform. Ram shook his head to clear the scene from his mind. He glanced at the door to the root cellar then turned his focus on Jakar. He couldn't keep the sense of giddiness out of his voice. "Our guest is awake. Perhaps he's ready for another round."

Jakar nodded, a sly smile crossing his face. "Splendid idea, my lord."

Ram pushed away from the counter, leaving the cracked glass to swim in the spilled drink. The skin on his arms tingled with anticipation. Their new toy had provided endless hours of entertainment. Ram couldn't wait for more.

Chapter Forty-Four

Chains bound Demir. As he crouched on all fours, hard metal bit into his knees and hands. Pain radiated up his thighs and arms. He strained against the bonds, but only succeeded in reopening the cuts on his back and buttocks. The scent of his own blood filled his nose.

Ram had a penchant for torture. Demir had reached that conclusion early on. The countless tools on the workbench—screwdriver, pliers, hammer—seemed innocuous enough until used on skin, muscle, or bone. He'd endured the torment, refusing to scream even when the pain threatened to knock him out. At some point, thankfully, it had.

He'd awakened a short time ago. Thanks to his Lemurian lineage, most of the cuts and bruises had already healed.

Anger burned deep inside, festering, building in intensity, calling to his feline predator. With his cat's preternatural power, he tried to shift, only to have Ram take control of his mind. A feral growl erupted from his chest.

The door to his new prison swung open and crashed against the wall. Bright light from the kitchen illuminated the stairs and cast an eerie glow on the tool bench. This couldn't be good. Demir ground his teeth.

Ram poked his head through the doorway. His frame and the cap he wore blocked the light. The shadow of an ax appeared, and a deep chuckle filtered into the room. "Wendy, I'm home."

His stench preceded him as he sauntered down the stairs, the ax over his shoulder. "I'll bet you haven't seen that movie, have you?"

Jakar followed, like the little rat he was, slinking after his master.

Demir tried to wrench against the chains, but his body wouldn't cooperate.

Ram giggled. *Grab yourself and squeeze.*

Demir's hand reached to his crotch, and he fondled his nuts. A bead of sweat broke out on his forehead. His fingers clenched around his scrotum with a vise-like grip. Intense pain shot through his body and his vision faded.

No you don't. Stay awake.

A muffled groan escaped his lips as he slumped onto the cut-off tabletop. The chains on his ankles bit into the skin and blood trickled over his foot. He didn't even feel the cut, his body still reeling from his attack to his groin.

A part of him deep within accepted the punishment, considered it justice for killing Aramie, the one female that had ever stood up to him. As much as she made him feel whole, he didn't deserve her. A lump formed in his stomach, adding insult to injury.

Ram hefted the ax, sizing up Demir, but then he shrugged and placed the tool against the wall. "This would cause too much damage. It's not my intent to kill you…not yet, anyway."

With a smirk, he sauntered over to the workbench and pawed through the tools and debris. He selected a pick and pressed the pointed tip against his thumb. The skin dimpled, but the instrument didn't penetrate the tissue. He looked at Jakar and shook his head. Selecting a hammer, he hefted the heavy utensil in his palm as if testing the weight, then put it back on the table.

The evil Gossum hummed to himself. He glanced at Demir and winked.

Demir wanted to growl, to kick, to lash out anyway he could, but he couldn't break the hold Ram had over him. His frustration knew no bounds.

Ram grasped a box knife between his fingers and pressed the latch, inching the small cutting tool out of its case. The edge of the razor blade glinted in the light. "Such a simple implement." His tongue snaked out and cracked the air like a whip. "This will do nicely."

Naked and bleeding in front of his enemy, Demir didn't think his humiliation could get any worse.

He couldn't prevent the impending torture, so he searched for a distraction, something to concentrate on besides his pain. Visions of Aramie entered his mind, her last breath exhaling from her body as he bit into her shoulder. His chest ached, chasing away the physical pain, but spurring an emotional burden that was beyond compare. He deserved whatever Ram gave him. A part of him wanted to suffer, to pay for what he'd done to Aramie, but no amount of torture could ever be enough to erase his anguish.

"Let's start simple, shall we?" Ram trailed the edge of the blade across Demir's bicep. A thin line of blood pooled from the cut and a drop landed on the wooden table.

Ram's cackle raced along Demir's nerves, sending a new wave of anger through his body. He strained against the bonds, but couldn't break free. The evil Gossum wiped his finger through the blood and brought his hand to his face. He sniffed. "And you think we smell bad. Your kind reeks of…integrity and honor. How utterly revolting."

Integrity and honor? He'd never been described like that before. My, how he'd changed. Aramie had done that to him. The reminder of his dead mate caused a wave of anger to flood his system, blurring his vision. Demir gritted his teeth, and focused his attention on Ram's eyes. He longed to scratch them out with his claws and watch as the evil creature screamed under the torment.

"Ah, you have something to say, don't you? I can see it in your eyes." Ram smiled and loosened his hold on Demir's vocal cords. "Speak, cat, speak."

Anger burned deep in his soul. "I will kill you for what you made me do to Aramie. Your black sludge will be on *my* hands."

"Demir, Demir, you are such a comedian." Ram's smile faded. "Enough games. Let's get down to business. I want you to scream loud enough so Zedron can hear you on Lemuria. Besides, I get a thrill through our connection when I feel your…discomfort."

Demir hadn't realized there were so many ways a plain box knife could inflict injury. Even as the pain hit a new threshold, he refused to cry out. He'd honor his memory of Aramie and spite Ram in the process. His last vision before he passed out—Aramie's red barrette and her beautiful smile.

*****

Aramie hid behind the trunk of a tall alder tree. Downwind from the Gossum's lair, she peered around the tree—watching, waiting. The farmhouse was a far cry from the asylum, the Gossum's last hiding place. The old mental institution was creepy, but the building didn't hold a candle to the eerie vibe of cheerful and homey which radiated from the farmhouse. A shiver ran over her shoulders and up the back of her neck, raising her hackles.

The door opened and a single Gossum emerged. He jumped off the porch and headed to the barn. Not far behind, a group of his peers followed, some leaping over the porch railing, others bounding down the stairs.

One Gossum stopped in the unmowed lawn, the grass blowing against his faded jeans in a gentle caress. He sniffed the air. His dark eyes scanned the landscape. A quick rush of adrenaline sent her heart racing. Had he caught her scent? She leaned back and blended into the background.

The lone male's boots swishing through the grass floated by on the breeze. The sound faded as he followed his brood. She relaxed, the muscles in her shoulders releasing her tension.

Demir. Her chest constricted. He'd left her to die. How would he react when he saw her? She didn't know, but she couldn't leave him. He wouldn't hurt one of his own—especially not her—not without cause. Steeling herself, she unhooked the safety latch that bound her throwing stars.

The empty yard and still house beckoned, and she couldn't resist its call. The grass swished under her feet, slowing her down as if the long strands were fingers trying to hold her back. She used her preternatural vision and acute hearing to assess if anyone remained in the house. All seemed quiet within the structure.

She didn't have much time. Once they found the goat wrapped in her coat, they'd know she was here. She needed to find Demir before they returned. With soft footsteps, she crept to the stairs. The unpleasant scent of Gossum wafted by on the breeze.

Movement out of the corner of her eye caught her attention. The lone Gossum with the faded jeans hid behind a bush at the corner of the house. Their eyes locked.

The creature burst from his cover and raced full tilt toward her. She launched one of her old throwing stars. The creature dodged at the last second, but the metal piece lodged itself in his shoulder. Blood oozed from the wound, but her attack didn't seem to slow him.

His tongue lashed out, coming dangerously close to her face. She changed into her cat and let her animal instincts take over. Her claws slashed into his chest. The scream that rent from his mouth made her smile, but it also alerted the others to her whereabouts. That was bad news.

She might be trapped on the porch, but she wouldn't give up her ground. Backing toward the stairs, her claws found purchase in the worn wood. Hoots and hollers from the lawn raised her hackles. She growled, straightening her spine.

Three Gossum jumped on the porch, two to her right and one to her left. The male she'd fought pulled her throwing star from his shoulder and threw the weapon on the ground. He bared his serrated teeth and tensed, preparing to attack.

Unwilling to go down without a fight, she met him halfway.

The impact knocked the wind from her lungs. She scraped her claws over his torso, ripping into his flesh.

A weight descended on her, crushing her to the ground. Teeth bit into her shoulder, her leg, her haunch. She kicked and scratched, tearing into as much flesh as she could before a large fist hit her in the face. Darkness claimed her.

Chapter Forty-Five

Aramie woke to blood, sweat, and the astringent scent of Gossum. The pain in her shoulder competed with the ones on her leg and butt, but her left eye was the humdinger. The pain pulsed along with her increasing heartbeat. Gravel and bits of rough dirt bit into her face and arm. An awareness of the ground beneath her crept into her mind.

She opened her eyes and the dim light from a bare lightbulb was enough to make her squint. Earthen walls came into focus along with a tall staircase which ended in a closed door. Cobwebs hung between the railing posts. Goosebumps formed on her arm.

As she inhaled, a hint of musk and incense filtered through the other scents. *Demir!* She sat up, but a wave of dizziness forced her back down. Closing her eyes, she concentrated on breathing.

"Ah, welcome, Aramie. So good of you to join us." Ram's voice penetrated into her thick skull and sent a shiver of dread along her arms.

He bent down, his face mere inches from hers. "It's a good thing you showed up when you did. With Demir, I was getting…bored."

She tried to scratch him, but her pounding head slowed her reactions, and he moved out of the way with ease. A low answering growl filled the enclosure, one she recognized. She glanced around, searching for Demir.

He crouched on an old, sawed off table, his face contorted into a bizarre mask of anger and rage. One knee was on the ground, the other covered his bare chest. He was completely naked. Shackles enclosed his wrists and ankles. Open red cuts and dried blood ran over his arms and legs, evidence of his struggles. He straightened at her perusal, his backside hidden from her view. Blood coated the platform, more than what could've come from the manacles.

She looked into his eyes. Red-rimmed and bloodshot, he wasn't the male she'd grown to love. A lump formed in her throat. She placed her hand on her belt. Her old throwing stars were gone, but the new ones from the Jixie blacksmith were still hidden in the lining under her belt.

"Oliver. Can you see anything through her eyes?" Ram asked.

The male with the pale blue jeans sauntered over to her. He furrowed his brow, his gaze penetrating hers. "No. Nothing."

Ram knocked his hand on the counter and a screw fell to the ground. The small piece of hardware twirled back and forth a few times before coming to rest. "When she was captured, who else bit her?"

A Gossum with an oversized nose raised his hand.

Ram nodded. "You try. See if you can control her."

The male approached and crouched, but not close enough for her to reach him. He studied her face. She curled her lip and displayed her fangs.

The male flinched.

"I take it you didn't cause that." Ram tsked. He glanced at Demir. "Well, boy, it seems you and I have a special bond."

Of course they did, courtesy of the blue sunstone, but she wasn't about to tell her enemy. Let him think he had a chance to control others.

Aramie peered at her mate. His pale face remained expressionless, his eyes distant.

"Demir…" she called to him.

He didn't even blink.

"My, my, I think we could have some fun with this." Ram clapped his hands together, and the sound echoed around the room. "Oliver, take your buddies and go watch TV or help Jakar. I think he's tending to the goat, again." He waved his hand in the air in a dismissive gesture.

Oliver, the same male who'd taken her down, glared at her. His assessing gaze roamed her face. "The goat was a nice distraction, but it didn't work."

He looked at Ram and raised a hairless eyebrow. "You gonna be all right by yourself?"

Ram pursed his lips. "No need to worry your pretty bald head over me. Now, off with you."

The males raced up the stairs, their claw-like nails clicking on each wooden step. Alone with Ram, she didn't feel any better. His lip curled at the corner. Behind those dark eyes, he wasn't quite sane.

She struggled to her feet. A rush of adrenaline to her head nearly brought her down again, the white spots growing in her vision. With effort, she gripped the edge of the nearby counter to steady herself. The venom from the bite marks wasn't enough to kill her, but it slowed her movements. She'd mend—if she survived.

"Demir." She snapped her fingers, trying to get his attention. "You can fight this."

The look he gave her didn't ease her any. On the contrary, a kernel of dread formed in her gut. A grin of his own spread across his face. At that moment, a part of her died inside.

*****

Demir fought with all his strength, pushing against Ram and his relentless control. When they'd brought his female here, her sweet scent had filled his senses, and he'd nearly lost his mind. He'd thought she was dead. To find out she was alive had set off a protective reaction that was all mated male. Like an untamed beast, he'd fought Ram tooth and nail, but in the end, he'd lost. Ram's iron-clad control was complete.

Defeated, a failure—he didn't deserve her. In the end, his father had been right all along. He was weak and always would be.

Yes, you're weak. You'll prove that yet again before we're done. Demir tried to lash out at Ram, his frustration getting the better of him, but his hand remained on his knee, unmoving.

Ram strode over to Demir and patted his head, caressing his locks as if he were a pet. Heat ran up Demir's neck and into his face. The humiliation in front of his female was more than he could stand.

Ram bent down and stroked Demir's goatee. "How would you like to play a game? Hmm?" He glanced at Aramie.

"Well, sure, that sounds great." Ram's high-pitched tone was a mockery of Demir.

Ram turned and faced Aramie. "Are you ready, my dear?"

She spit on the ground at Ram's feet. "Go fuck yourself."

"Ah, child, I wish I could." His low chuckle reverberated around the room.

He unlocked the manacles at Demir's feet. The heavy chains fell away, but Demir didn't move. He stayed in his crouched position. Next, the locks at his wrists opened and clanked when they hit the floor.

Stand up. The command made Demir wince. He wanted to do more than stand, he wanted to fight. Although he strained against the invisible bonds, his body wasn't under his control. Against his will, he faced Aramie and his enemy.

Turn around.

No. Demir's hand fisted. He couldn't tell if he'd done that or Ram.

Turn. Around. The command screamed in his mind, bouncing against his skull. The pain was more than he imagined and broke his concentration. His body turned against his wishes.

He tensed. Aramie would see his scars—his weakness. Demir couldn't look at her. He didn't want to see the pity in the lines of her beautiful face. Not Aramie, it would kill him as surely as an arrow to his heart.

Seconds ticked by. The only sound, Ram's soft, grating cackle.

He couldn't stand it any longer and turned toward her. At this point, he wasn't sure if Ram controlled him or if he did this of his own free will, but in either case, he needed to see her face.

She stood rigid, her rapt attention focused on him. Her eyes widened for a brief moment, and then she met his gaze. Instead of pity, her eyes reflected a deep respect.

When she spoke, her voice cracked. "Demir...you are so strong, so powerful." Determination lined the creases around her eyes. "You can fight this—fight him. I know you can."

Ram's rough cackle filled the room. "Oh, Demir, Demir. Please tell the little lady how you got your beautiful scars. I'm sure she'd like to know."

Demir strained to keep his mouth shut, but he couldn't stop the words as they tumbled from his lips. "My father beat me...every time I failed to meet expectations." His chest ached at the confession.

Ram placed his finger next to his mouth. "Why didn't you meet expectations? Hmmm?"

Aramie trembled, and her eyes glistened with unshed tears.

"Because I'm weak." At the final admission, his self-respect died under the strain.

Finish what you started. Kill her. Ram's command blocked out all other thoughts.

A low guttural sound erupted from his chest. He tensed, his muscles bunching for his attack. Inside, he screamed. A torment he'd never known before eased into him, marking him as the weak, beaten male he'd always been. In the back of his mind, his father's disapproving glare stared down at him.

Chapter Forty-Six

Red welts and fresh cuts on Demir's back and buttocks couldn't hide the scars. The shock of what he must've endured to receive so many marks left Aramie speechless. Her face warmed as a sense of respect and admiration overcame her. To survive what those scars represented was a testament to his inner strength. She loved him all the more.

Demir's warning cry raised Aramie's hackles. Stepping away from him, she touched the spot under her belt which hid her new throwing stars. Her instincts told her to attack before he did, but she couldn't bring herself to do so.

With a quickness inherent in their species, Demir morphed into his panther. His muscles bunched under his sleek black coat as he approached, and his eyes never left hers. Even as he tracked her, she admired the strength and power his Panthera possessed. She elected to stay in human form, since it would be easier to maneuver in the enclosed space. His tell, the one she'd observed so many times on the battlefield, was the twitch under his right eye. Focused on his gaze, she refused to look away.

The skin under his right eye twitched. He charged.

She countered his moves, avoiding his attack. A single claw scraped down her arm. Red rivulets of blood bloomed on her skin. She glanced at him, but his eyes—those haunted eyes—burned with sorrow. He didn't want to attack her.

Ram's bright eyes glinted as he clapped his approval. "More, please."

Distracted by Ram's comment, she broke eye contact with Demir. He attacked, knocking her over. His heavy body pinned her to the ground. Still weak from the Gossum bites, she didn't have the strength to escape him. Soft fur rubbed against her arms, and her skin tingled at the contact.

"Bite her. Kill her." Ram egged Demir on, glee evident in his voice.

Demir's eyes glowed bright yellow. Pointed fangs extended from his mouth. A deep growl, one filled with anguish and regret, burst from his chest.

He seemed lost to her. Tears blurred her vision, and her chest constricted.

An image of Ginnia reading the ancient legend raced through her mind. *The stone had healed the warrior who'd sacrificed himself for another…and could be healed with an equal sacrifice.* An idea flashed through her mind—a crazy one. There was one thing she could do which might help him break Ram's hold—submit to him.

Her body chilled.

Everything she'd ever worked for, fought for, earned during countless battles, would be for naught. To submit to a male would break her spirit, but she'd do it—for him.

She bent her head in supplication. "I believe in you, Demir. You are strong—you won't hurt me. I submit to you, as your *mated* female."

He towered over her. His ragged, warm breaths brushed her hair causing the ends to tickle her neck. He nuzzled her red barrette. The gentle nudge made her throat constrict.

A low, needful cry escaped his lips.

"Kill her now or I will." Ram's tense whisper was so close, alcohol reeked from his mouth.

Demir bared his fangs.

Aramie's chest clenched. She hadn't reached him. A single tear tracked down her cheek. Unwilling to watch, she closed her eyes and braced for his attack.

*****

Demir understood all too well the courage Aramie put forth to submit to him. She would sacrifice everything that defined her as a warrior to become his mated female. Her loyalty humbled him and brought him to his figurative knees. Adrenaline pumped through his veins. His vision clouded. He fought for air. A plethora of emotions—regret, surprise, love—warred inside, jumbling his thoughts, scrambling his senses.

Ram spoke, but the words didn't register.

In the back of Demir's mind, his cat perceived a threat. He tensed, his muscles rock hard. As he finally processed the meaning behind Ram's words, anger built within him so great, it crashed over him like a brick wall.

Ram had threatened Aramie—his *mated* female.

The veil of Ram's control wavered, lifted for a brief moment. Demir glared at his true enemy and narrowed his eyes. A battle ensued within Demir's soul, both males vying for control.

Demir focused on Aramie's love and support. Her belief in him buoyed his own sense of self-worth. He remembered how she'd looked at him when she'd seen his scars, with respect and tenderness.

He pulled on the strength of her love, her faith in him. His confidence and dignity grew, giving him the courage and belief he was important, valued, worthy of love. With a new sense of self-respect, he pushed against Ram's control. The barrier stretched thin then broke apart.

Demir forced Ram out of his mind. The spot on his back ached for a brief moment then there was blissful nothingness, as if he'd never been bitten. Demir's heart pounded. Power and strength like he'd never known raced into his muscles.

Free from Ram's bondage, Demir pounced. Ram fell back, eyes wide, mouth open. The element of surprise gave Demir an advantage, and he bit Ram on the thigh.

Ram's eerie cry filled the room. Blood gushed from the wound. He lashed out with his tongue, stinging Demir on the ear.

Demir flinched, but kept his gaze on his enemy.

In panther form, Aramie launched herself at Ram. Her claws grazed over his arm, leaving a trail of blood. Ram howled and transformed into a grotesque hairless Panthera. In his altered cat-like form, he was twice as big as Aramie and twice as deadly. He raised his paw and batted her across the room. She hit the wall with a thud and slumped to the floor, returning to her human form.

Heat flushed through Demir's body, his need to protect his mate and kill his enemy fueling his anger. Demir snarled and attacked. He plowed into Ram, and they both fell against the counter. Glass from the beakers shattered. Pliers, hammers, and the box knife scattered onto the floor. An opened, half-empty bottle of Smirnoff's spilled over the countertop.

They struggled against the workbench, both fighting for the upper hand. Ram bit Demir on the shoulder, his serrated teeth reopening the wound. Pain bloomed on Demir's back, but his relentless focus remained on his enemy. He swiped his claws across Ram's face. The evil creature howled in pain.

"Demir!" Aramie's voice was loud, purposeful.

He glanced at her. Her eyes glowed with resolve. She raised her arm, a throwing star gripped between her fingers.

Demir dug his claws into Ram's back and threw him to the ground, pinning him there. Ram transformed back into his Gossum form and struggled to gain leverage.

Bending his hind legs, Demir stabbed his sharp claws into his prey's soft belly. The smell of blood and bile filled the air. Demir ached to finish him, but Aramie needed revenge for her sister's and Kitani's deaths. A low growl erupted from his chest, but he held back, waiting for his mate to finish the evil creature.

Ram scraped Demir's back with his claws, adding insult to injury. He gripped a handful of fur at the base of Demir's neck, holding him in place. The end of one of his fingernails extended toward Demir's eye.

A throwing star whistled through the air. Ram turned to look, and the weapon imbedded into his eye. Only the tip glinted from within the dark orb. Ram's grip on Demir tightened for a moment then relaxed.

"Sheriiiiii…" The name escaped Ram's lips on his last exhale. His body started the quick process of decomposition.

Aramie sat on the ground, her hand resting on her belt, clutching another weapon. Demir met her gaze. She was the most beautiful, brave female he'd ever known. *And she's mine. My mated female.* His chest expanded, his heart filling with love for her. He transformed into his human form. Still naked, he grabbed his pants off the dirt floor. Pulling them on, he looked at her.

"Aramie…" He choked on her name and couldn't say another word, couldn't tell her what was in his heart. Instead, he helped her to her feet and wrapped her in a gentle embrace.

"You could've destroyed him, but you waited for me." Her soft words made his chest clench. "He almost killed you, just like Sidea."

"Revenge was yours."

She assessed him, her eyes moist with unshed tears.

A heavy weight descended on his shoulders. "I attacked you…in the cave. I broke my promise to you."

She blinked and then her features softened. "That wasn't you. I knew something was wrong. You would never hurt me."

Her words eased into him, taming his anger, and stroking his sense of self-worth. Tracing his finger down her cheek to her chin, he ran his thumb along her bottom lip. With a tiny gasp, her mouth opened, and he couldn't resist the invitation. He pulled her close, their lips meeting, heated breaths escaping between the kisses. A peace and sense of rightness he'd never known eased into him. He could stay in her arms forever.

Footsteps running across the floor filtered through the dilapidated ceiling.

Aramie tensed. Gossum still lived in the house above them. The only way in or out of the root cellar was the stairs. They were trapped.

Chapter Forty-Seven

Mauree paced in her cell, driving her frustration. A headache pounded behind her eyes. From somewhere above, water filtered through the rocks, and a small rivulet ran along the edge of her cage. The fresh scent reminded her of the communal baths. After dipping her finger in the water, she wiped the cool liquid along her arm. A clean spot formed, and she continued her mini-bath.

A small rock bounced past her cell, ricocheting off the smooth stone floor. Mauree stopped her washing, and a drop of water dripped from her finger onto the dirt floor. Adrenaline coursed through her veins. She raced to the bars and pressed her face against the cool surface. Only able to see a few feet in either direction, the empty hallway seemed eerie. Goosebumps formed, tingling her arms.

"Who's there?" She inhaled, and the faint scent of pineapples infiltrated her senses. Her shoulders relaxed, and a smile pulled at the corner of her mouth. "Ginnia, dear, is that you?"

Soft footsteps shuffled down the hall, stalled, then resumed, increasing in speed and intensity. The individual stopped a few feet away, out of eyesight.

"Ginniaaaaa." Mauree drew out her name, putting on her best behavior to entice the simpleminded female to cooperate. "What can I do for you?"

Ginnia peeked around the corner, and retreated, but not before Mauree caught a glimpse of her wispy hair and her pale gray eyes. "You smell."

Mauree pursed her lips. *Of course I do, you fool, I haven't had a decent bath in days.* She exhaled to calm her irritated nerves. When she spoke, she did her best to keep her voice low and controlled. "I'm sorry. I can't help it."

Ginnia took a few tentative steps. Her gaze roamed from Mauree's matted hair to her scuffed shoes, stopping for a moment at the rip in her skirt. She covered her mouth with her hand, and her attention flicked back to Mauree's eyes. "You look bad."

Mauree curled her lip and crossed her arms. "Thanks for stating the obvious. What brings you here to see me, besides my wardrobe?"

Ginnia glanced down the hallway, first to the left, then the right. She bit her lip and peered at the ceiling. The sunstones lining the hallway brightened and pulsed for a moment. The hair on Mauree's arms stood on end.

Ginnia put her hands on her hips. Her bottom lip stuck out in a pout. "I don't like you, but you can't die."

Mauree's heart skipped a beat. "What do you mean—*can't die?*"

"You have more to do, you can't die."

Ginnia was well known for her visions. Mauree had been sentenced to death. *Craya.* "What do I need to do?"

"Live." Ginnia pulled a small sunstone out of the pocket of her dress. She moved the gem over the padlock, and the crystal glinted in the light, casting an eerie glow into the corridor.

With a soft click, the lock fell against the bar—the shank open, unlocked. A tremor rippled through the Keep, and a rock tumbled from the ceiling.

Mauree's breath caught in her chest. *Freedom.*

An odd smile graced Ginnia's innocent face. "Bye, bye, meanie Maureenie." She waved and ran down the hallway, returning the way she'd come.

Not one to overlook an opportunity, Mauree reached through the bars and wrestled with the lock. Her fingers fumbled between the bars and the pad, her frantic attempts intensified by the surge of adrenaline racing through her body. She leaned her forehead against the cool bars. *Calm down.*

Closing her eyes, she counted. *One. Two. Three. Four. Five.* Her beating heart still pounded in her ears, but the pace slowed. Gently, she cradled the padlock in her hand. With trembling fingers, she lifted the shank out of the door's loop.

The old lock landed on the stone floor, useless.

She pushed open the cell door and stood in the hallway. Something in her stomach fluttered, as if moths had found their way in. She was free, at least from the cage.

Her mouth went dry. She'd escaped the cell but had nowhere to go. Returning to the inhabited portions of the Keep was not an option. She'd only be captured and returned to her cell...until her execution.

A trace of anger built inside. The sensation grew, forming into a knot of determination. This was not her chosen path. She was supposed to be queen. Her muscles quivered, and she fisted her hand. *This isn't over, Noeh.*

Darkness called from the far end of the tunnel. Deep in the bowels of the Keep, winding, hidden corridors led to the surface. She didn't know where the manual exits were, but she'd find one, or die in the process. Once she got out, she'd figure out what to do. She ran along the passageway, eager to escape the confines of the Keep and plot her revenge.

Chapter Forty-Eight

"We'll have to fight our way out." Demir's grip on Aramie's arm tightened.

Still in his embrace, Aramie savored how his skin rubbed against hers, sending little electrical shock waves everywhere they connected. His kiss had told her everything she'd needed to know. He loved her, without reservation.

She didn't want to leave the peace and sense of belonging that his embrace evoked in her, but they weren't safe. Gossum roamed the rooms of the farmhouse above them. They either didn't hear the scuffle with Ram or they feared interrupting him. In either case, they didn't know their leader was dead.

Aramie looked around the room. "Maybe there's another way out."

"There isn't. One of Ram's minions said they made the room larger, but Ram didn't want another door." He glanced at the stairs. "We don't have a choice."

He broke their embrace, but his fingers trailed down her arm and clasped her hand in his. Their hands entwined, her sensitive pads lighting up at the contact. He brought her fingers to his lips. With a gentle kiss, his whiskers tickled her skin. "Tough stuff, when we get out of here..."

Shhh. She placed her fingertip against his lips to quiet him. "We'll have time to discuss us later."

His smile was all masculine pride. "Indeed."

He headed for the door, pulling her along, but he stopped at the edge of the workbench. Scattered among the broken beakers and old tools was Demir's knife and throwing stars. He palmed his weapons, reattaching them to his belt. As much as she loved him, a tendril of regret balled in her gut. She didn't need his protection and didn't want him to control her.

He turned to look at her. His brow scrunched. "What's wrong?"

This wasn't the time or place for that conversation, so she shook her head. "I'm ready. Let's do this."

Breaking glass and a Panthera's muffled scream seeped through the slats in the ceiling.

Aramie recognized that cat's cry—Jonue. Bits of dust and dirt rained down on Aramie's head.

"Seems we're late to the party." Demir headed for the stairs, taking two at a time.

She paused on a stair mid-step. A slight movement caught her attention. A giant house-spider sat in the middle of a web, between two railings. The arachnid spun a fine silk cord, wrapping it around her victim.

Aramie's vision narrowed. Her heart rate increased. Sweat seeped from her pores, her scent clogging the air.

Demir's warm hand wrapped around her waist. "It's okay. Breathe."

She inhaled and her body shook from her fear.

"Aramie, focus." His voice seemed distant, far away. He gripped her arm, turning her to face him. "Kill the spider or let it live, but don't let fear of this small creature rule you."

Her gaze roamed his face, the trust and faith reflected in his eyes steeled her resolve. She glanced at the spider with its eight legs and numerous eyes. Before she could think better of it, she swiped at the web, forcing the creature to flee over the banister.

Tension drained from her muscles. A small nervous laugh escaped her lips. She'd handled the spider on her own. Demir winked at her.

Something crashed to the floor in the kitchen. The door splintered and shook in its frame, but didn't break. Black goo seeped onto the top step.

"You ready?" Demir raised an eyebrow, his eyes turning yellow.

"Absolutely." She palmed a throwing star, ready for battle.

He yanked on the door. Dark sludge dribbled down the stairs. The empty kitchen bore the ravages of the fight. Three of the overturned table's four legs stood straight up as if reaching for the ceiling. The fourth leg—missing. A splatter of red blood coated the white fridge. Aramie prayed it wasn't from a Panthera.

As they walked into the room, Demir peered over his shoulder. His jaw clenched. He appeared torn.

"Don't say it. I'm going to fight. You can't stop me." She ground her teeth together, her hands clenched at her sides.

"As if I thought I could." He motioned for her to precede him. "After you."

Affection spread warmth through her chest. He'd guard her back. She nodded and headed into the melee.

*****

Aramie launched herself at a nearby Gossum. Demir's chest clenched, and fear snaked its way under his skin. His need to protect warred with his desire to respect her as a warrior. Deep inside, she was a fighter, always had been, but she was also his mated female. How could he take her need to be a warrior away from her?

A Gossum slithered toward him in it's Panthera form. The creature was even more grotesque than usual. It snapped its long tongue in his face. He dodged the spiked tip, and pulled his dagger from his belt. The edge of the knife glinted in the soft light.

The Gossum lunged, scraping a pointy claw over Demir's leg. Pain radiated up his thigh. Anger built in his chest. The energy fueled his rage. With a firm uppercut, he drove the tip of his knife into the creature's throat, severing its head from its spine. The Gossum stiffened then slumped to the floor.

Several of his Pride fought in the enclosed space. Jonue dispatched a beast with her claw, severing its jugular. Leon bit a Gossum on the back of the neck. By all appearances, his Pride had the advantage. The battle was almost over.

Nearby, a Gossum in its altered Panthera state grunted, blood oozing from a scratch on its arm. The beast focused on Aramie, and a loud shriek burst from the injured creature's throat.

Demir's vision pinpointed. His heart pounded. One thought echoed in his mind—protect. He launched himself at the wounded beast.

Aramie beat him there. She gripped the creature's injured arm and spun him to face Demir. Her eyes glinted with her conviction. "Take him, he's yours."

Demir plunged his dagger into the Gossum's chest. The beast stilled, its black orbs staring at the ceiling. With its final breath, the creature morphed into a pile of sludge.

Not a single Gossum remained. Soft moans from the wounded filled the air.

Down the hallway, a door clicked shut. Demir raced into the hall and burst through the door, shoulder first. At the open window, a pair of curtains blew in the breeze.

In the distance, Jakar loped along the road leading into the mountains. Demir ached to pursue him, but wouldn't leave his Pride, not while some had injuries which needed medical attention. He clenched his fist and returned to the living room.

A quick scan revealed the devastation from the fight. The couch sagged in the middle, its back broken in two. Wood from the busted coffee table and shattered glass from the hutch littered the paisley carpet. A DVD of *The Shining* lay on the floor, evil Jack's grin fitting right into the scene.

Members of his Pride congregated, attending the wounded. There were as many females as males—some mated.

"Did we lose anyone?" Demir held his breath.

"No, thanks to the mated females." Hallan peered at Demir, then placed his arm around Jonue and gave her shoulder a gentle squeeze. "My mate and I had a long talk. We convinced Leon to come as an entire Pride—including mated females—to fight the Gossum. Forgive us for breaking old traditions."

"I'm glad we found you, Pride leader." Leon bent his head in submission.

Demir studied the males then glanced at Jonue. The battle would've had a different outcome if not for the mated females. Had he been wrong all these years to prevent mated females from fighting? A knot formed in his throat. Apparently so.

"Everyone fought well tonight, *everyone*." He made eye contact with each of the mated females in the group, giving his praise and acceptance.

A tense quiet filled the room.

Demir took a step forward, into the middle of the group. "I always boasted myself on my judgment, for doing what I thought best for the entire Pride." He wiped his hand over his face, and exhaled. "I've made mistakes, plenty of them. The biggest one—believing mated females shouldn't fight. I'm going to rectify that, right now."

He held out his hand to Aramie.

She straightened her back and met his gaze. Pride filled him. He felt bigger, taller, stronger than he'd ever been in his life. Strength wasn't about control or physical toughness. True strength came from within and was about self-confidence, faith and trust in others.

Realization dawned on him. His father had made mistakes as well, trying to do what he believed was best for his son, teaching him how to fight and defend his Pride. No one was perfect, everyone made mistakes, and everybody deserved a chance at forgiveness. Although he'd been viciously abused by his father, a wave of understanding for the male bubbled up inside.

Aramie placed her hand in his, her warm skin sending spikes of desire through his body. He brought her hand to his lips and gently kissed her fingers. "Aramie, my mated female, I've wronged *you* most of all. I should've trusted your judgment, but instead, my disdain and need for control clouded my decisions."

Her gaze darted back and forth as she studied him. Love for her welled up inside and Demir's throat tightened. "Aramie, would you forgive my arrogant, chauvinistic attitude and return as my second in command?"

Her eyes widened, and her grip in his hands tightened. A slight smirk crossed her face. "Demir, my mated male, of course I forgive you. How could I be anything but your second in command?"

He blinked. Laughing, he pulled her into his embrace, her strawberry scent filling his senses. Shouts and claps erupted from the Pride.

As the joyful cheers quieted and he released her, a sense of wholeness enveloped his heart.

Through the gingham curtains, the night sky carried a slight tint of dawn. They needed to return to the Keep. Demir looked at his family, his Pride. "Let's go home. Who wants to celebrate?"

Chapter Forty-Nine

Tanen walked down the hallway, the weight in his pocket messing with his mind. He passed a Jixie with a nearly empty tray. Only a few crumbs of the garlic bread remained. She glanced at him and nodded a greeting. He grunted a reply. Words were so not an option right now.

He'd have to come around soon though. He needed to tell Mauree about her fate. The long corridor went on for miles, passageways branching off in all directions, but he stayed focused on his task. Others passed by, but he didn't pay attention to them other than a casual "hi" or "hello."

The old thrill of getting away with the theft made him feel in control once again. He hadn't felt this good about himself in a very long time. His inner beast savored the theft, vying to break free.

While his mind fed on visions of the stone, his feet kept up their pace. He turned at all the appropriate intersections. The number of others roaming the corridors diminished. As he moved deeper into the Keep, a cool dampness permeated his skin.

He rounded the corner into the stronghold sector and stopped. With tentative care, he pulled the decree out of his coat. A need to touch the crystal raced over his fingers, and before he could stop himself, he thrust his hand deep into his pocket. The rough edges of the stone were a sweet potion, and a shiver of delight ran up his arm. Pulling on his strength of will, he returned his focus to his task and let go of his treasure. Unfolding the paper, he reread the summons written in Noeh's cuneiform handwriting.

For treason against the Stiyaha, Mauree, daughter of Wrinton and Sade, you shall be beheaded on the morrow at nightfall.

King Noeh

Short and to the point, how like His Majesty.

Tanen folded the paper and put it back in his pocket. A coil of dread formed inside, sending a wave of nausea up his throat. *Damn heartburn.*

In the distance, an object lay on the ground—something right outside Mauree's cell. Unease rippled over his shoulders. Water trickled over stones, the sound loud in the quiet corridor.

He bolted down the hall. The tail of his shirt lifted from his pants. Wisps of hair tickled his forehead, his perfect strands falling around his ears.

As he approached her cell, the object on the ground became discernible. A padlock. His heartbeat increased, pounding in his ears.

"Mauree!" His yell went unanswered.

He slowed as he approached. The bars on her door were slightly ajar. He didn't need to look inside to know she was gone, but he couldn't stop himself. The empty space was a mockery to him. As council leader, he was responsible for her escape.

A shudder ran over his back. Sweat broke out on his skin. His collar bit into his neck. He wrestled with the button, breaking it off in his attempt to free himself from its confinement.

A moan escaped his lips. The sound echoed along the corridor, amplified again and again, beating on his psyche. His cheeks burned from his shame. She'd escaped on his watch. He'd never live this down.

He wiped his hand over his face. A loud exhale left his lungs. Now what? And wasn't that the question of the hour.

Once Noeh heard Mauree had escaped, he'd be angry. Tanen gripped his collar, scrunching the material tight around his throat. He wouldn't be able to handle the look of disappointment in the king's eyes. Tanen shook his head. *Oh, craya, no.*

A small breeze blew from the gloomy end of the corridor. The faint scent of roses filled his senses. *Mauree.* Without a second thought, he ran down the hallway in hot pursuit.

Chapter Fifty

After a good shower, Demir had stopped off at the party. The meat sandwiches and spiced ale had been exceptional, but he'd been too preoccupied with Aramie to imbibe much. She'd smelled of her own recent shower and fidgeting with frustration, he'd encouraged her to leave with him. That wasn't hard to do. She'd been eyeing him as well.

As they approached his quarters, he couldn't wait to get Aramie alone. Her strawberry scent made him wild, frenzied. The doorknob shook in his hand, putting up a fight, stalling him. He gripped the metal, twisting harder than was necessary. The door opened with a squeak, and he rushed her across the entrance.

Slamming the door with his heel, he pushed her against the wood. Caged between his arms, her warm breath tickled his cheek. She growled, and the sound reverberated from her chest to his, inflaming his desire.

"Demir…" Her lips parted, her canines extending from her mouth.

Her blatant display of need made his heart race. He answered her, his own growl low and demanding.

Grasping her head in his palms, he captured her lips in a lingering kiss. Her sweet taste wove into his senses and was now forever engrained in his mind. Their frantic kisses ignited the passion between them, escalating their combined need.

Trailing kisses down her throat, his teeth grazed over the tiny scar he'd given her on her neck. His lungs swelled as a sense of contentment filled him, making him smile. He licked the tender skin. The slight taste of her sweat tickled his tongue. A slow groan eased from her throat, and she relaxed under his gentle assault.

She threaded her hands in his hair and freed the strands from his short queue. Her nails scratched his scalp, her fingers raking along his sensitive nerves. She pressed her firm breasts against his chest, but their clothing prevented the skin on skin contact he craved. He gazed into her eyes. "Aramie...you are so beautiful..."

She bit her bottom lip, and his shaft jumped in response.

My female. His heart swelled. He loved her deeply.

She pushed against him, forcing him back. He released her, and the insurmountable distance seemed like a giant crevasse between them.

A sexy smile pulled at her lips. The skin around her eyes creased, and the yellow slits of her irises gave away her own need. She gripped the bottom of his T-shirt and gently tugged. The back of her fingers grazed his abdomen and tickled the fine hairs that led to his genitals. Her touch woke up more than his nerves, further hardening his already enlarged member.

He raised his arms, eager to shed the confining cloth. The shirt flew over his head and landed on the floor. *Good riddance.* Now—her turn.

He ran his hands along her arms to her shoulder. Her chest rose and fell with each hurried breath. Using his index finger, he traced the edge of her shirt along her collarbone and circled the spot near the dip in her neck. With a sly smile, she pulled off her own shirt in a slow tease.

His gaze followed the pink strap of her bra to the bright yellow cups. Despite her slender frame, her firm breasts filled the brassiere to capacity. He glanced at her eyes. She watched him, waiting for his reaction.

He smiled, and he raised his eyebrow, giving her an appreciative stare. He placed his finger under one of the straps and lifted it off her shoulder. The loose material dangled on her arm, revealing the rounded edge of her breast. His erection jerked in response.

"Release me," she whispered.

Warmth spread throughout his body, and his skin prickled along his arms. He couldn't deny her request. Placing his palms on her waist, her warm, smooth skin was soft to his touch. He trailed his fingers up her back and unhooked the clasp. The bra slid to the floor.

He leaned back to admire her breasts. Dark areolas circled taut nipples that begged for his mouth. She shivered and goosebumps formed on her skin.

Before he could act on his thoughts, she placed her hands on his pecs. A slow smile broke across her pretty face, and she shook her head.

Her hands slid down his chest to his abs, lighting up his skin everywhere she touched. She stopped at his belt and tugged.

Oh, gods, yes. He helped her with the buckle and the buttons of his fly. His pants—they couldn't come off fast enough.

She stared at him, her eyes wide. His cock, strained tight, reached for her as if the appendage could get to her without him. He swallowed, and his shaft bobbed at the movement.

"Oh, my…" Her grin was all feminine appreciation.

His heart and his shaft swelled with pride.

She kneeled in front of him, trailing her fingers down his thighs. With the tips of her fingers, she played with the fine hairs around his balls. She purposefully didn't touch his shaft, teasing him, making him ache for contact.

"Aramie," he groaned, "you torment me."

She giggled, and her mouth was so close to the tip of his shaft, he felt the vibration. The sensation drove him mad. Considering all the torture he'd been through, this was the only kind he craved.

She blew a soft breath across his erection. His skin tingled and he tightened his grip on her shoulders. A low moan eased from his chest.

Starting at the base of his shaft, she licked him, her tongue lapping him all the way to the tip. A bead of arousal glistened on the end. He shuddered. "Aramie…"

She took him into her mouth, easing him in and out in a slow rhythm. With a quick flick, she swirled her tongue around the tip and he couldn't take anymore.

He pulled her to a standing position and kissed her. His salty taste mixed with her strawberry essence. His cat howled inside, eager for more. When he released her, their combined pants echoed in the room. He kissed the tip of her nose, and she smiled, determination forming in the lines around her eyes.

He pointed at her pants and raised an eyebrow.

She giggled. Kicking off her shoes, she wiggled out of her black pants, swirling her hips, teasing him in a sensuous dance. Naked, she about brought him to his knees.

"Aramie…" His words stuck in his throat.

With feline grace all bottled up in her body, she sauntered toward him. Placing her hands on his pecs, she encouraged him to back up, angling him toward the bed.

Understanding her direction, he gripped her arms and pulled her along. They landed on the bed in a heap.

The bed broke beneath them. Small splinters of wood from the split headboard rained down upon them, prickling the skin on his thighs and arms. He inhaled, and the scent of oak permeated his sensitive nose.

Aramie's laughter reverberated in her chest, the gentle rhythm pulsing against him, making him smile.

"Well, good. I hated this bed anyway." He rolled on top of her, caging her between his arms. His arousal pressed against the soft hairs at her entrance. The fine mane tickled him, stroking his desire.

She ran her fingers up his arms, the contact lighting his skin on fire. As her hands passed over his shoulder, he stiffened, his reflexes honed from years of practice.

Wide-eyed, she stared at him.

His need to control every aspect of their lovemaking burned in his gut. He'd never willingly allowed anyone to touch the scars on his back. But she wasn't anyone. She was his mated female. He swallowed. A part of him wanted to give in, let her touch him, but the centuries of hiding the emotional damage still weighed on his soul, like a bad memory.

Her eyes filled with unshed tears, but her smile was all pride. She trailed a finger over his cheek and caressed his goatee. The sensation calmed him, reminded him how much he'd enjoyed her touch when he'd been in his coma.

"You are the strongest male I know, in here." She placed her hand over his heart. "I'm so proud of you."

His chest swelled. Her love for him almost broke him apart. He'd do anything for her...anything.

"Can I touch them?"

In the past, her question would've angered him, and he would've refused her request. But somehow, she'd tamed him. He let go of his fear, and a great weight lifted from him. The scars on his back would never heal, but the emotional wounds on his soul would be mended by Aramie's love.

He couldn't speak, so he nodded.

Her fingers trailed over his shoulders and down his back. When she reached the tip of the first scar, she traced the raised skin over his hip and buttocks. Goosebumps rose along the path in her wake, but not from distaste. On the contrary, her touch lit a fire inside him.

She purred as she explored him, touching everywhere on his back and buttocks. When her hands finally stilled at the base of his neck, she pulled him to her and gave him a powerful, possessive kiss. He responded in kind, matching her intensity, stride for stride.

She accepted him for who he was, flaws and all. He'd never known a love like this. It humbled him.

"Aramie—"

She nipped his bottom lip. *Shhhh.*

Taking over, she pushed him, forcing him to roll over. She straddled his hips, taking him deep inside and rode him like she owned him. A high like this he'd never experienced before. He pushed into her, letting her scent and her touch drown him. Her soft breaths turned into shallow pants, and her sheath contracted around his cock, squeezing him with her release. A soft cry escaped her lips. He couldn't hold on any longer and joined her with his own surrender.

When they were both spent, she lay on top of him, her sweaty skin mixing with his own. Their combined scent was heaven to him. He petted her hair, twirling the short ends between his fingers.

For the first time in his life, he felt whole, healed. There wasn't a better feeling in the world than holding his female in his arms. She relaxed and her breathing slowed. The last thing he remembered before drifting off was her barrette, the bright red spot peeking out between the sheets.

*****

"Good evening, tough stuff." Demir's baritone voice stroked Aramie's nerves, awakening her from the best sleep she'd had in years. Must be the ramifications of their day together. They'd flipped between great sex and cat-napping over the past several hours. A warmth heated her insides at the memory.

His strong arm wrapped around her waist, cuddling her body next to his, the sheets tangled around their entwined legs. The obvious press of his erection against her bottom let her know how awake he was. A rush of excitement pooled in the warm spot between her legs.

She rolled onto her back so she could gaze into his chocolate brown eyes. What she expected to see, she wasn't sure, but his eyes twinkled with amusement. His lip curled into a mischievous grin, revealing a pointed fang.

She purred and rubbed her face against his chin, marking him with her scent. His answering growl was all she needed to hear to set her heart racing. "Demir, my mate, my love."

"Aramie." He trailed kisses over her cheek to her throat. His breath tickled her ear, sending a shiver along her nerves all the way to her buttocks.

She never felt so loved, so cherished in her life. Trusting him with her life, he'd proven himself to her. She loved him more than words could say. As his kisses continued down her body, she arched into him. He was as much a part of her as she was of him. Mating to a male was the last thing she'd ever wanted, but he was everything she'd ever needed.

He glanced at her, his lips tenderly pressing against the soft spot between her breasts. Love and passion radiated from his eyes.

She held her breath as a sense of completion and well-being filled her. "I love you," she whispered.

Her favorite smirk played along his mouth. "Tough stuff, I love you, too."

As he captured her lips with his own, she drifted along with him, forever in his embrace.

Chapter Fifty-One

Aramie leaned against a tree trunk and stared at the moon. The giant orb seemed larger tonight, brighter, clearer. She inhaled, and the ever-present smell of pine and dampness that permeated the forest made her smile. With deliberate care, she traced the scar at the base of her throat. The two round puncture wounds were rough against the tips of her fingers. *I'm a mated female...* Her heart swelled with a newfound sense of peace and contentment.

Demir had agreed to meet her after his check-up with Gaetan. He'd be along soon and they'd go for a run. She kicked at a small rock with the tip of her shoe, overturning the stone. Worms squiggled in the fresh loam, and a spider ran for cover under a nearby fern. Aramie tensed, but then relaxed, a soft giggle easing from her throat. "Little creature, to think I once feared you."

The crack of a breaking twig echoed in the forest. Aramie's senses went on high alert. She glanced around and inhaled, reading the scents of the forest. The whiff of an unknown Panthera caught her attention. "Show yourself. I know you're there."

A male Panthera, one she didn't recognize, appeared from behind a large boulder. He was bigger than most, his broad shoulders bulging with firm muscles.

Yellow eyes peered from beneath his furrowed brow. The cat took several steps forward and stopped.

Aramie swallowed, her hackles rising along the base of her neck. "Who are you?"

The panther transformed into a man. He wore ragged blue jeans and a torn, white T-shirt. Thick, dark hair covered his head and the shadow of a beard coated his strong jaw. Deep brown eyes reflected the moon's rays. "My name is Aramond."

She stared at the male and couldn't ignore their shared resemblance. With tentative steps, she approached him.

"You must be Aramie." He had a deep, soothing voice, one that called to her. A smile of pure adoration crossed his face, and his eyes moistened.

"How do you know who I am?" She could barely speak the words through her tight throat, and they came out a whisper.

"Chantre…your mother. I ran into her a few months ago. I never knew I had…a daughter." He clenched his teeth and visibly swallowed. "I'm sorry. Had I known, I would've raised you, protected you."

Aramie's chest constricted and tears blurred her vision. An urge to race into this male's arms overwhelmed her, but her past got in the way, preventing her from seeking what she so desperately wanted. Her fingers trembled, and she balled her hand into a fist. "How did you find me?"

"You weren't easy to locate, believe me. Your mother said she'd heard from a few other strays your Pride had headed this way. I searched for months before I stumbled across your scent. Strawberries, your mother said it was always her favorite."

Her stomach twisted, adrenaline pumping through her veins. Light-headed, she wasn't sure how to respond. "This is happening so fast. I don't know what to say…"

He raised his hand. "I don't want to interfere in your life, but I had to…" he visibly swallowed, "come meet my daughter."

At his words, the walls around her heart tumbled, and she took a step forward, then another until she was close enough to smell his unique scent—earth and fresh rain. He enveloped her in his arms, and the floodgate of tears broke, spilling over her lashes. Her chest ached from bittersweet happiness, and her throat constricted. She fell into his embrace, soaking up the attention she'd craved for so many years.

"Aramie, my little Aramie." He stroked her hair, caressing her. "From the looks of you, you've turned into a fine female—a warrior…and a mated one at that. I couldn't be prouder."

She pulled back and stared into his eyes. "Father…" The unfamiliar word lodged in her throat. A tear crested over her lash, and he wiped it away, his own escaping from the corner of his eye.

"Tell me of your sister. She wasn't mine, but from what your mother says, she's your best friend."

Her chest clenched at the painful memory, and a new round of tears flowed from her eyes. "Sidea, she's gone. I miss her so much."

"I'm so sorry, Aramie." He pressed his forehead against hers. His unique scent infiltrated her senses, relaxing her. They stayed that way for several long seconds. Then, he pulled away and cradled her face in his palms. "I wish there was some way I could make it up to you…all the years I wasn't around."

"I have so many questions." She stared into his eyes, searching for what, she wasn't sure.

He took her hand and gave it a gentle squeeze. "Come, let's sit for a few minutes, get to know one another."

She nodded. They sat on the edge of one of the larger rocks in the area, and she told him about her past and about her new mate Demir. As he told his tale, the timbre of his deep voice soothed her and she listened…

*****

Demir was late and he clenched his jaw as he raced through the forest. Gaetan had detained him longer than expected, insisting on one more test. Demir's shoulder was fine, mended, but he couldn't say no to the old haelen. Even Gaetan had somehow weaseled his way into the friend category. *My, how I've changed.* He shook his head. Hopefully, Aramie was still at their meeting place. His chest tightened, and a sense of urgency raced through his mind.

As Demir approached, an unfamiliar Panthera scent brought him to a halt. His hackles rose. A deep voice rumbled between the trees, distant enough Demir couldn't make out the words. Aramie's scent blended in with the stranger's and the fact they were so close sent a spike of adrenaline into his bloodstream. He fisted his hand and changed into his panther.

He closed the distance, racing over the ground, leaping downed tree branches, and pummeling the soil with his claws. His recklessness announced his approach to the couple, but he didn't care. Aramie was with another male…

He skidded to a stop, mere feet away from the male and Aramie sitting on the log. He knew without a doubt they were kin. Not sure what he'd expected, but a family resemblance wasn't it.

Aramie stood at his arrival and held out her hands, "Demir, it's okay. He's my father."

Father? She'd told him about her mother, how she and Sidea had been abandoned by the female, but she'd never talked about either of their fathers. He changed into his human form.

The male stood. Tall and muscular, he was an alpha, one that wouldn't bow down to another. He glanced at Demir and took a step forward.

Demir growled, the threat clear.

Aramie placed her hand on Demir's arm, calming him. "Please, Demir. I don't think he means any harm."

Demir locked gazes with her, studying her, assessing her state of mind. Was she in danger? Was she worried? She seemed relaxed, in control. The tension in his shoulders eased.

"Don't be too hard on him, daughter. He's an alpha male protecting what's his. I can't blame him." Aramie's father peered at Demir. "I'm Aramond, and I'm not here to challenge you."

But you won't submit either, will you? Aramond was a rogue alpha, one that fought the war on his own terms. Demir respected his decision, he'd have done the same under other circumstances. He nodded in a sign of mutual respect.

Aramie wrapped her hand in the crook of Aramond's elbow. "Father, will you stay with us, join our Pride?" With a quick move, she pulled away from her father's grasp and looked at Demir. "That is, if my mate and Pride leader agrees."

Aramond spoke before Demir could answer. "Daughter, I'm an alpha male, a Pride of one. Things wouldn't…work out for me here. I'm sorry." The tension in his voice left no room for discussion.

Her lip quivered, but when she spoke, her words were firm, determined. "Will I ever see you again?"

"I'll be around. We'll cross paths again, I'm sure." In a quick move, he pulled Aramie into an embrace and kissed her on the forehead. Before she could say anything further, he transformed into his panther and disappeared into the forest.

Aramie's soft hitches made Demir's chest ache. He wrapped his arms around her waist, pulling her against him. He stroked her soft hair, comforting her as best he could. Leaning down, he murmured into her ear. "I'm glad you got to meet him."

"Me, too. He's different from what I imagined, but he's my *father*. You have no idea what that means to me to be able to say that." She pulled back and lifted her chin. Though there were tears in her eyes, a soft smile curved her lip. "You know, you still owe me a run. Bet you can't catch me this time."

Endorphins rushed to his head, his love for his mate filling him with joy. Tough and resilient, she challenged him at every turn—and was perfect for him. "You're on. You better get moving…"

Chapter Fifty-Two

"Jax, please give us some privacy." Noeh twirled his ring on his finger. The familiar movement helped ease the tension in his shoulders, but only for a moment.

"Of course, of course. As you wish, Your Majesty." Jax bowed as he backed toward the large double doors. His bottom rammed into one of the wooden sentinels that guarded the entrance to Noeh's Throne room.

Jax glanced up, his face turning a scarlet shade of red. "I'm so sorry, Your Majesty." He continued to bow profusely as he closed the doors behind him.

Gaetan is laughing. Melissa's thoughts invaded his mind. Her soft words were like a gentle caress. His chest clenched at his beautiful female. He was thankful she was here. Yesterday, his one weakness had finally beaten him, won the war as he knew it would. The deafening silence was eerily peaceful.

The last sound he'd heard—Anlon's laughter.

Noeh turned to face his haelen. The old male wiped his eyes, as if he hadn't seen anything so funny in a long time. Maybe he hadn't.

"Well, well, so Ram is finally dead. Hard to believe." Gaetan shook his head.

Melissa interpreted the words for Noeh. She filtered out some of the trivial stuff, but he'd been working on reading lips. That got easier every night.

"That's what Demir said." Noeh ran his hand through his hair. "But Jakar still lives."

"As you well know, there's always another one to fill the shoes." Gaetan sat down on one of the cushioned chairs. He winced and rubbed his knee. "That's not what worries you though, is it?"

Noeh exhaled. "This war has gone on for thousands of years, neither side gaining much of an advantage. Time is running short."

"I'm all for ending this war." The lines around Gaetan's eyes made him appear old.

"Not," Noeh caught Gaetan's gaze, "unless we win."

"We have to win. I won't consider the alternative." Melissa cradled Anlon in her arms.

The babe had grown considerably over the past few weeks. No longer an infant, he was on the verge of crawling. His fast metabolism even had Gaetan baffled. Noeh shook his head. Melissa was right. The Lemurians must win this war.

What would happen to them if they lost? The humans would be enslaved and forced to ship water back to Lemuria. As for Noeh and their kind? Their souls would return to the character board on Lemuria and remain there in a state of hibernation until the next war on another planet. A chill ran over Noeh's arms.

Gaetan and Melissa both looked at the door.

Someone knocked. Melissa's smooth voice clued him in. So far, they'd been able to keep his deafness a secret. Outside of the two of them, Gaetan and Saar were the only others that knew.

"Enter!" he shouted.

Speaking of Saar, his Commander of Arms rushed into the room. His shoulders moved up and down in synch with his ragged breaths. "Noeh, Mauree…she's missing. I wanted to tell you in person, so as not to raise an alarm."

Gaetan lowered his head.

Noeh glanced at his queen. *What did he say?*

As her shock wore off, she interpreted for him.

A rock formed in his gut. He narrowed his gaze on Saar. "How can she be missing?"

"Someone let her out. I found her lock on the ground, the door open." Saar raised his shoulders, palms outstretched.

"Who would do such a thing?" Noeh paced the room. Thoughts of Mauree roaming the Keep sent a sharp jolt of fear into him. He turned and looked at Melissa and Anlon. *She'll come for you.*

No you don't. You're not locking me up, again. Melissa placed her free hand, the one not holding Anlon, on her hip.

His chest clenched, but the determination in Melissa's eyes eased some of the tension. *Don't worry, I learned my lesson.*

Gaetan rose from his chair. "Does Tanen know about this? She's his responsibility."

"That's the other piece of news. No one can find him either. I have to assume he's the one that let her out." Saar shook his head. "Two of my warriors, Revin and Quoron followed their scent down the hallway into the bowels of the Keep. We'll find them."

"I trust you will." Noeh nodded at his friend. If anyone could find them, Saar would be the one.

Reviews...

Enjoyed *Untamable Lover*? Word of mouth is critical for any author's success. The best gift you can give an author is an honest review. Please consider putting a review on Amazon, Goodreads, or another platform of your choice to help spread the word and support an author.

Newsletter...

Want access to free reads, special offers, and giveaways? Sign up for my newsletter on my website at www.rosalieredd.com and you'll receive a **free ebook!** Don't worry, your information won't be shared with anyone but my muse. You can also contact me at Rosalie@rosalieredd.com. I love to receive email from readers!

Books in the *Warriors of Lemuria* series:

- Untouchable Lover - book 1 - *Available now*
- Untamable Lover - book 2 - *Available now*
- Unimaginable Lover – book 3 - *Available now*
- Undeniable Lover – coming 2017

- Unforgettable Lover – novella - *Available now*
- Warriors of Lemuria short story collection – coming 2017

Turn the page for a sneak peek at *Unimaginable Lover,* book 3 in the *Warriors of Lemuria* novels...

Unimaginable Lover
A *Warriors of Lemuria* novel - book #3

A shifter and a human together? Unimaginable…

One careless decision. The colony betrayed. Tanen's only course is a desperate hunt for justice, but his solo mission is cut short when he's mortally wounded during a fight. Rescued by a sweet, innocent female who nurses him back to health, he can't deny the passion that burns between them. Now he must choose between his duty and honor or his desire for the precious, but forbidden, human female.

Broken promises and ruined love hardened Sheri's heart. When she finds an injured and extraordinarily sexy man on her property, she's pulled into a world she never imagined. As she nurses him back to health and they bond over their love of books, she's torn between the lessons she learned from her rough past and the need to seek solace in Tanen's arms, but she must learn to trust him, and herself, in order to survive.

Glossary

Arotaars: People from the planet Arotin. Held as slaves on Lemuria. They have blue hair that sparks with electricity when they are emotional.

Chilopods: Multi-legged centipede-like insects that live on Lemuria.

Craya: An expletive.

Dren: Short for "chil*dren*." Originally human adults, but were transformed into Dren through a Panthera's bite. During the "turning," all Dren receive a unique, special power. Dren must drink blood at least once a week from the opposite sex or they become weak and lose their powers.

Gossum: Human converts turned by another Gossum through their bite. They have black eyes, and are hairless, with rough, scalelike skin down their neck and back. Gossum have a spur at the end of their long tongue which they use to paralyze their prey.

Haelen: Healer

Jixies: Small, dwarf-like characters that voluntarily serve the Stiyaha. Jixies tend to be quick, resourceful, and are great planners. Despite their short stature, they can go amongst the humans to obtain special items not made within the Keep.

Kasard: Bastard

Keep: The underground home of the Stiyaha and Jixies, located in the mountains of the Pacific Northwest. The Keep is sentient and reacts to her inhabitants with minor tremors and/or by warming or cooling the environment through the sunstones embedded in the walls.

Lemuria: A planet in the Orion constellation. Lemuria is slowly dying and its people must rely on natural resources from other planets to survive.

Lemurians: Refers to both the people on Lemuria, as well as, the characters on Earth. The people of Lemuria appear as gods to the characters in the war on Earth.

Newbs: Young children

Panthera: Sleek and muscular, these highly skilled fighters are known for their speed and agility. They transform into black panthers and are highly arrogant and confident. They respect strength and cunning and will only follow a leader who can command them.

Porte stanen: The massive stone structure in the Portal Navigation Center used to transport characters in and out of the Keep through the portal gateway.

Rhondo beasts: Fearsome creatures that terrorize the surface of Lemuria. They have black, oily skin with disproportionately long arms and short legs. A small amount of hair runs down its spine. They have a long tongue and sharp teeth, including tusk-like fangs.

Stiyaha: Stoic and just, Stiyaha are noble warriors. Tall and strong, they transform into large beasts, between eight and nine feet tall, covered in fur with large, protruding tusks.

Sunstones: Magical stones that line the ceilings and walls of the Keep, providing heat and light to its inhabitants. Sunstones are used in trade and have some healing abilities.

Tratee flies: Small flying insects on Lemuria that have translucent wings.

Ursus: A tough, burly species that shape-shifts into large bears. Tenacious and vicious, they are fierce warriors.

Visus bacin: Scrying bowl

About the Author

After finishing a rewarding career in finance and accounting, it was time for award-winning author Rosalie Redd to put away the spreadsheets and take out the word processor. She pens paranormal, science fiction, and fantasy romance in her office cave located in Oregon, where rain is just another excuse to keep writing.